CHARLES R. MARLOW

THE HELIOS DECEPTION

A Novel

ISBN 979-8-35091-571-6

eBook ISBN 979-8-35091-572-3

CONTENTS

BIG ISLAND, HAWAII

September - in the late 2030s

I t was 6 a.m. and dawn was just breaking over the Pacific Ocean. Nikhil Shrimati stood on the deck of his beach house, cradling a cup of coffee in his hands and looking out to the eastern horizon. He loved this part of his daily routine. He was the Chief Scientist at the Mauna Kea Summit Observatories. He believed it was the best job in the world for an astronomer. The great discoveries were now being made by robots and computers in the unmanned observatories on the far side of the Moon, free from light and radio pollution from Earth. But Mauna Kea was the greatest optical observatory complex on Earth. It had an important role to play, though mainly these days in education and science tourism.

For Nikhil, the Mauna Kea Observatories were truly special. There was still a mysterious connection between the individual and the universe. He experienced that magical bond every time he looked directly through the great Mauna Kea telescopes into the heavens. No radio telescope in space or observatory on the Moon could match that special feeling. No robot, even with sentient Artificial Intelligence, could sense that palpable, mystic chord.

Every day, for the entire history of mankind, humans had watched the sun rise. Nikhil's ancestors in India had worshipped Surya, the Sun God in Hinduism. As he watched the glorious dawn break over the Pacific, he could understand why – the light, the warmth, the beauty of the Sun made life on Earth possible and worth living. And every day, no matter what the troubles of the previous day, the dawn brought new hope.

He finished his coffee and walked over to the autonomous vehicle (AV) which served as his mobile office. The door opened. He stepped into the vehicle and sat at his desk.

"Where to this morning, Sir?" the vehicle asked.

"The Observatories, Curzon, please."

Nikhil had named his AV 'Curzon' after Viscount Curzon, Viceroy of India over a hundred years ago. Nikhil's great grandfather had been a servant at the Viceroy's Residence. His job had been to chase the monkeys away and keep them from disturbing the Viceroy and his guests. Being able to order 'Curzon' around pleased Nikhil's post-imperial sensibilities.

The Shrimati family had come a long way over the last 100 years. He owed it all to America. His father had arrived as an immigrant forty years ago, to work on computer programming in Silicon Valley. There were no human programmers any more in the Valley. AI bots had taken all those jobs. In fact, most of the tech industry had moved out over the last decade. Rising sea levels, flooding and extreme weather had driven out most of the firms that hadn't already fled the high Californian taxes.

'Curzon' pulled out of Nikhil's driveway and set off for the Observatories. It would take just over an hour. Only autonomous vehicles were allowed up the narrow mountain track to the Observatories complex. Restricting access solely to AVs had eliminated the risks of accidents and increased capacity on the single lane road. It took a while to get used to over-taking on blind corners, but with AVs that was not a risk. The interconnected guidance systems knew what was coming in the other direction.

Nikhil sat at his desk in his AV and began the day's work as Curzon drove efficiently through the early morning traffic in Hilo and then up into the back country.

"So, Turing, what are the big stories overnight?"

Turing, a popular Personal Assistant, came as standard with this vehicle. It wasn't the most powerful AI Bot, but it did the job.

"Good morning, Sir. The main news stories over-night concern the risk of a solar flare strike within the next 12-14 hours. The foreign media are predicting a strike between 5 and 6 p.m. tonight, local time."

"What about the American press?" asked Nikhil.

"They are still covering the President's address to the nation."

"I missed that. I can't watch that nutcase. Those politicians are going to have a lot to answer for, if this flare does hit Earth. What did the President have to say?"

"The President said there was nothing to worry about and encouraged Americans to pray. God would protect us, the President said."

"Well, that's not going to help. Why can't the great American public elect someone sensible to be President for once? This one is in total denial. Anyway, Turing, what do you think the chances are of a solar flare strike later today?"

"Sir, I am afraid I can't answer political questions."

"That's not political, Turing. That's a science question."

"No, Sir. Congress has determined that the science of solar flares is politically contested, and therefore, under the *Truth in AI Act*, chatbots are not allowed to speculate on contested science. I am afraid I can't answer that question."

'Curzon' continued on the journey up to the Observatories. It passed through the varied microclimates of Big Island. At sea level, the vegetation was tropical. Then the landscape turned into ranch country; it looked just like Texas. Then, a few thousand feet higher, the fields resembled Alpine pastures. Above the pastures, there were dense conifer forests. And then above the tree line, it looked like Mars. This is why NASA had based their Mars training camp on these volcanic uplands, over 10,000 feet above sea level.

The NASA camp was long since abandoned following the Mars mission disaster. Alongside the historic site, NASA Commercial Enterprises had built *The Mars Experience*. It was the most popular tourist destination in the State of Hawaii. The central attraction was the Mars Mission Memorial. On the pedestal the inscription read: *God has ordained that the men and women who went to Mars to explore in peace will stay on Mars to rest in peace.*

Nikhil had known a couple of those astronauts. They had become friends during their training missions on Hawaii. As he passed the memorial, he thought of their frozen remains on the crash site on Mars. On some days, he could even see the scattered fragments of their landing craft through his most powerful telescope. At least the end had been quick for the Mars astronauts. Would the same be true for those left behind on Earth? If the solar flare didn't destroy civilization in the next few days and weeks, he thought, then climate change certainly would over the next few decades.

As he passed the entrance to the Mars Memorial site, he saw that the parking lot was already full. The *Sunrise on Mars Experience* was almost as popular as the *Sunset on Mars Experience*. Over a thousand tourists would be there at sunset tonight. It was sold out months in advance. People who couldn't get tickets came to the Mauna Kea Observatories for the sunset and star gazing tour. Mauna Kea was expecting over five hundred visitors tonight.

Nikhil and some of his colleagues had suggested closing the Observatories as a precaution, given the threat from the solar flare. The director, a political appointee, had shouted them down. It was all a big hoax, the director said. And anyway, no federal facilities were to be closed. America was not at any risk from this solar strike. The President had made that very clear.

His ride had another half hour to go up the narrow winding road to the peak on which the Observatories perched. Nikhil worked through his overnight messages from colleagues around the world. Most of his international fellow scientists were offering their sympathies for America's lack of preparation ahead of the strike. European and Chinese scientists were now sure that there would be a strike later that night, Pacific time. Their nations were prepared. America was gripped in collective denial. The space weather deniers said it was all a great big hoax. Others disagreed. Several End of the World sects in Idaho and Montana were ready and prepared. They had seen this coming for years. Among the scientific community, optimists believed that the solar flare might miss or just graze the Earth. That was the only hope, thought Nikhil. There had been a near miss twenty-five years ago. Politicians had ignored the threat then. Perhaps the Earth would luck out again. Pessimists, or rationalists, as Nikhil liked to describe himself, feared that the flare was now on a direct course to hit Earth. He was appalled that America could have left itself so unprepared. Hundreds of thousands, possibly millions, of Americans, might die as essential computer and communication systems failed across the country. All the President had to offer was the power of prayer.

'Curzon' pulled into entrance and stopped outside the front door of the main office building where Nikhil worked. There were thirteen telescopes in twelve separate facilities in the Mauna Kea complex. Each building was ringed with flag poles. The American flags looked beautiful in the bright morning sunlight. For all the failures of its politicians, Nikhil thought, America was still a great nation. He was proud to be an American citizen. He stood and repeated the oath of allegiance in front of the flags. As a federal employee, he was now required to do so every day.

Nikhil spent the day backing up all his data files. The politicians couldn't stop him doing that. He stored the backups on optical files which should be immune to the solar flare strike, he thought. Any electronic or magnetic storage would be wiped out. There was nothing he could do about the computer systems. He'd just have to hope the flare wasn't too strong. They could survive a medium level strike. If his optical back-ups worked, at least he could salvage most of his records and reload the data onto new computers when they arrived. The Observatories would be out of action for months, possibly years, given the time it would take to produce enough new computer systems to replace those wiped out in the strike.

The backing up took longer than he had hoped. By 4 p.m. he was finally done. It was time to head back. He should just be able to able to make it home before the flare strike.

The autonomous shuttle buses were dropping off the last of the evening's visitors. It would be a full house tonight. They would be busy with this large crowd, Nikhil thought. He was heading home as fast as he could. The director could deal with the chaos when it happened. He was the one who'd been so keen to keep the Observatories open.

Nikhil walked back to the parking lot and looked up overhead. The Sun was already low in the Western sky. Venus was shining brightly, and Mars was faintly visible too. To the North, he could just make out Jupiter. There were no clouds in the sky. It was a perfect evening for stargazing.

He approached Curzon. The vehicle remained still; its automatic doors were shut tight.

"Curzon, open the doors," he said firmly and clearly.

Nothing.

He pulled the door open and looked inside. Curzon's control screen displayed an error message: 'All communication links lost'. The vehicle was completely unresponsive.

He looked across the parking lot. All the other vehicles were stopped in their tracks. An immobilized shuttle blocked the main entrance. The driver had opened the doors manually. The tourists were exiting the vehicle and walking to the visitor center.

The public address system explained that the Observatories had experience a temporary loss of communications, which had disabled all autonomous vehicles and all phones. They were working to restore the links as soon as possible.

He went back into his office. He tried to turn on a computer. It still had power, but it had lost all access to the cloud. He checked his phone. The screen was black. The emergency lighting flickered into life. The back-up batteries would last no more than two or three hours. He tried the emergency communications system. It was their most secure system and separate from the main phone networks. It was dead too. He realized that the heating system was controlled from the cloud. He ran his hands over the vents. There was no warm air. At 14,000 feet above sea level in September, the temperature would fall below freezing within an hour or two.

Every system had failed. All the autonomous vehicles were paralyzed, cut off from their computing power. All communications links were down. Hundreds of visitors, including young children, would be stranded here at 14,000 feet without power, heat, light or communications. The emergency services would be overwhelmed in the cities and towns across the state. It could take days, possibly weeks, to get a rescue mission up to the top of Mauna Kea. He couldn't bear to think how many would die.

He went outside and watched the Sun set. He joined the crowd on the terrace looking out to the west. The tourists were not panicking yet. A few complained that their phones weren't working. This would all change soon, thought Nikhil. Give it a couple of hours, and then the crowd would get angry and restless. By the morning, there would be the first medical emergencies. They'd run out of food and water within twenty-four hours. By the second or third night, the cold would start killing the oldest and the youngest. Each day, the death toll would rise. It would be even worse down at the Mars Memorial. They had twice as many tourists and many more elderly visitors and children. That site would soon descend into chaos as the first deaths occurred. How could the politicians have let this happen?

As the sky darkened, a strange new phenomenon appeared. It was the aurora borealis – the Northern Lights. He'd seen these in the Artic, but never had he see anything like this in Hawaii. The lights became stronger. They formed row upon row of shimmering curtains in the night sky – dancing cascades of green, orange, pink and red. The lights had a strange beauty. The watching tourists gasped in wonder at the sight.

Nikhil wished he could have enjoyed the display. But he feared that for millions of Americans, it was a dance of death.

DEPARTMENT OF PHYSICS, CAMBRIDGE, ENGLAND

October - Five years earlier

R uth Wright chained her bicycle to the rusting rack outside the Stephen Hawking Memorial Lecture Theatre. Bikes were the only way to get around the city these days. The City of Cambridge had banned the internal combustion engine a few years ago. And then last year, in response to student protests over the environmental damage caused by lithium mining, the City had banned all electric vehicles and electric bikes. Ruth, always keen to support liberal causes, gave up using her e-bike well in advance of the formal City ban.

Ruth had cycled down from her house two miles north of Cambridge, which she shared with her husband, Steve, and their twin teenage daughters, Jo and Mary. Ruth loved that journey, and not just because it was downhill most of the way. The trip home was a lot harder, especially now that she no longer had her e-bike. She loved the route mainly because she loved Cambridge. Riding her bike past the great old colleges reminded her of being an undergraduate. Those were some of the happiest days of her life. She could remember many 'perfect moments'—those times when everything seems just right.

It was a misty morning, as mornings often were in the Fenlands at this time of the year. Autumn was closing in around Cambridge. The outline of King's College Chapel was just visible through the fog as she rode down King's Parade. She remembered bicycling along these roads as a student when she was studying astrophysics. The great Stephen Hawking was still teaching. Ruth was one of his favorite and best students.

Those were simpler days for Ruth. She loved studying physics. She loved the purity of the subject and the ability to prove things right and wrong, which she did brilliantly. She met and fell in love with her future husband. She went on to win a fellowship at Trinity College and then was rapidly promoted. At the time, she was the youngest full professor – and one of the few women – in the Physics Department. She was a natural on television and became a popular presenter of science programs on TV and a regular media commentator. The British Government spotted her winning combination of scientific credibility and media appeal. She was appointed as a member of the Prime Minister's Council on Science and Technology.

Ruth was a distant descendant of a famous scientist. He had been a pioneer researcher into the structure of the atom in the early 20th century. Her grandparents and parents had followed different career paths. Her mother and father, both now dead, had been respectable but undistinguished professionals in law and accountancy. Ruth was an only child and, as far as she knew, she was the only living descendant of her great ancestor. Ruth was proud of her surname and wanted to live up to her scientific heritage. Despite her ambitions, at school her teachers had advised her to drop math and physics and concentrate on English literature. She was equally good at both science and humanities. Her school told her she wouldn't get into the best Cambridge college to study physics but would be a sure bet for English.

As so often in her life, Ruth ignored the advice she was given. It worked out well. She graduated with the top degree in the Cambridge physics department and was set on a stellar academic career. She worked under her maiden name, which caused endless confusion over her passport and her bank account. Somehow, over one hundred years after female emancipation, British officialdom couldn't cope with a married woman working under her maiden name. It made Ruth cross. As ever, she just ignored the petty frustrations that life threw at her.

Five years ago, the Prime Minister had appointed her as his Chief Scientific Advisor—a role created by Winston Churchill in the Second World War and maintained subsequently by all Prime Ministers since. She became part of the inner core of top officials in Whitehall. She was a peer with the Permanent Secretaries, who ran the great Departments of State, and with the top military and intelligence chiefs.

She turned into the courtyard outside the lecture hall and dismounted from her bike. She was short, just over five foot tall in flat shoes – and she only wore flats. She was slim, with short wavy hair. A few specks of gray were now visible. She was wearing her usual outfit of a plain black dress with a brightly colored jacket. She liked to stand out in a crowd of men in gray suits. Today's jacket was bright yellow.

"Good morning, Ruth!" It was her old friend Sir Laurence Fergusson, the Master of St Mary's College, who was taking a short-cut through the Physics campus to reach the department of Medieval History.

"Or rather, I should call you Dame Ruth." he continued. "I was delighted to see that the King had made you a Dame! That is great news."

"Well, thank you Larry. It was a big surprise—but a delightful one."

"Hugely well deserved. Though in my view, Ruth, being the Chief Scientific Advisor to this Prime Minister should earn you a sainthood, not just a damehood."

"It's really tough at the moment," Ruth complained. "Since the Covid-29 pandemic, all our politicians have viewed 'following the science' as a term of abuse. Most days, it's the scientific evidence versus the results of last night's focus groups, and the science loses every time. These politicians are driving me mad."

"Tell me about it," agreed Sir Larry. "That's why I quit public service and retired to academia."

"Very wise, Larry," agreed Ruth. "But at least our Ministers aren't all religious zealots like American politicians. Did you see the US Presidential debate last night? That Governor Wallace is scary. She's supposed to be a smart woman. She has a PhD from Georgia Tech, for Christ's sake. I just can't understand how she believes all that stuff about God creating the Earth in six days. And she's a deacon in some religious sect. Our political bosses may be difficult, but I'd rather work for them than those American crazies."

"Well, the nation is certainly lucky to have you in this important role—and good to see you back in Cambridge."

"I get 'day release' once a month to come back and lecture at the university. Today's lecture is on solar magnetic storms. There'll be plenty of room. You should come along. You might learn something."

"It's too complicated for me," Sir Laurence said. "I'm sticking to medieval history. Violence, intrigue, betrayal, sex."

Ruth couldn't help but say, "Sounds like life in Number 10 at the moment."

Ruth headed into the university lecture hall. She was hoping for a decent turnout today. She wasn't a world class lecturer, but she was the world authority on solar geo-magnetic radiation. She had developed a quantum computing model that accurately predicted storms on the surface of the Sun. In today's lecture, she would be sharing some of the history of this field and her latest research. If that didn't get today's students out of bed for a 9 a.m. lecture, then nothing would.

At 8.55 a.m., the lecture hall was still largely empty, but it filled up rapidly. By 9 a.m., it was nearly full. Ruth surveyed the room. She was pleased to see so many young women in headscarves. Fifteen years ago, she had pioneered the 'Math for Muslim Girls' program taught in primary schools. It was good to see the impact of that work. There weren't many students from the privileged private schools in the audience. She could always spot them by their clothes and accents. They were not her favorite students. At 9 a.m., most were probably nursing hangovers; they never made it to her early morning lectures. The rest of the audience was highly diverse, with a good mix of international students from India, China, Africa, and the Middle East. Ruth felt good about the global impact of her teaching.

She started her lecture. The lights dimmed and her first slide was projected on the screen above her. It was a photograph of the Sun rising over the African Serengeti.

"Think back to dawn of civilization," she began. "For our ancestors, the sun was the one thing in their lives that they could rely on. It was the source of all their light, heat, and energy. It's why our ancestors worshipped the Sun God. He, and it's always a male god, has many names: Apollo, Ra, Mithras, Surya, Helios. But he's always the most powerful God in any pantheon.

"The Sun is a source of wonder, not only to our ancestors, but also to us. We rely on it for nearly twenty percent of our power through solar panels, and we will soon have our first space solar array beaming energy down to earth with near-100 percent reliability and complete predictability. The Sun seems so stable and reliable compared to the weather on this planet.

"But up close, if you could get up close, you'd see that its surface is far from stable."

She flipped to the next slide. This was a close-up photograph of the Sun, with storms over its surface and large arcs of flame around its edge.

"See how violent the Sun looks close up. That's not surprising. After all, it is a seething mass of gigantic nuclear fusion explosions. Every second, those reactions on the Sun generate power equivalent to one hundred billion megaton nuclear bombs. It's almost impossible to understand how much power that is, but please try.

"I want you to imagine the bomb that destroyed Hiroshima. You've seen the images of the mushroom cloud and the destruction of an entire city. Now think of a bomb sixty-six times bigger—that's a megaton. Now imagine one hundred billion of those megaton bombs exploding every second, continuously, day in, day out, for billions of years.

"With all that energy surging around, it should be no surprise that the surface of the Sun is covered in a mass of storms—huge geo-magnetic electrical storms of a scale that we can hardly imagine.

"These storms rage all the time but fall and rise in intensity. They follow a fairly regular cycle of approximately eleven years. We see an increased level of 'sunspots' as these eleven-year cycles peak.

"The storms throw off huge flares of geo-magnetic energy. At the peak of the solar cycle, the Sun may throw off three of these flares every day. Most of the time, these flares just fade out a few million miles or so from the surface of the Sun. We can see the residual energy of these bursts of energy in the Northern Lights.

"We measure the intensity of this activity using a scale—the Planetary K-index. Normally, we see levels of around Kp-1 to Kp-5, which hardly affects our upper atmosphere. The scale stops at Kp-9. We don't believe the Earth has ever experienced anything higher than a Kp-9 storm. And that's just as well. It's a log scale, so a Kp-10 storm would be ten times worse than a Kp-9. But it's possible we could one day face a Kp-10 or higher storm. Just hope it's not in your lifetimes.

"Occasionally, the Sun can eject such a huge flare that the massive surge of geo-magnetic energy can travel one hundred million miles or more from its surface. That's fine for us living here on Earth, as long as it doesn't cross the Earth's path. And the good news is that these flares don't seem to cross our path very often. Perhaps one of these flares hits the Earth every few hundred years.

"In all recorded history before the 19th century, humans had never noticed that a solar flare had hit. These flares are completely harmless to humans. It's not like when the Earth was hit by an asteroid, wiping out the dinosaurs. We now know that solar flares have hit Earth quite regularly over the past millennia. But no-one noticed. Animals and plants were unaffected.

"But animal and plant life aren't our only concern now. What would happen if a massive solar flare hit modern computers and communications equipment? Would that electronic infrastructure survive the surge in geo-magnetic energy in the flare?

"Well, we have a clue. There was one recorded event in the modern era. In 1859, a huge solar flare did hit the Earth. Fortunately, in those days, there wasn't a lot of electro-magnetic equipment around. No computers, no mobile phones, no communications satellites, no electric powered airliners at thirty-five thousand feet, no autonomous vehicles.

"But in the United States, they had just started to build a telegraph network. There were a few telegraph stations. And when the geo-magnetic flare hit, they burst into flames. Some of the telegraph operators got a nasty shock—both literally and figuratively.

"A British astronomer called Richard Carrington worked out what had happened, and this event is named after him. The Carrington Event of 1859. We think the Carrington Event was probably a Kp-9. We just don't know as there wasn't the equipment then to record disturbances in the Earth's magnetic field.

"We had a near miss in July 2012, when another huge flare passed near the Earth. Had the Sun ejected this flare just a few days later, it would have been a direct hit and would have taken out any system dependent on electrical circuity. This solar flare strike could have caused trillions of dollars of economic damage.

"Scientists used to think that these events were very rare. My research, though, suggests that they are not nearly as infrequent as we'd like to think. In fact, my modelling predicts that Carrington level events occur on a long cycle of about 70–90 years. And that when one of these long 'Carrington cycles' coincides with one of the eleven-year solar cycles, then the Sun is likely to eject multiple mega-flares, big and strong enough to carry a hundred million miles. The only uncertainty is whether one of them will hit the Earth."

Ruth then took the students through the underlying physics behind her modelling of these Carrington Event level flares. She put up a lot of complicated equations on the whiteboard. Only the best students would be able to follow this part of her lecture, she thought.

At the end of the lecture, Ruth asked if there were any questions. There was an awkward pause. Then one of the students in the front-row asked:

"Professor Wright, when is the next time that one of these long Carrington cycles coincides with an eleven-year solar cycle?"

"In about 4–5 years' time. And then we can expect the Sun to expel multiple mega flares with the potential to reach the Earth," Ruth responded.

She paused to see if any of her students could work out the implications of this.

"And what do you think might happen this time if there was a direct hit on Earth?" another student asked.

Ruth paused before replying. There was no point, she thought, in protecting these students from the truth. She told them straight:

"It would be the end of civilization as we know it today."

CHAPTER 2

70 WHITEHALL, LONDON

January

I t's Wednesday. It's 8.30 a.m. It's time for this week's National Security Council (Officials) meeting. Grab your cup of HM Government's finest coffee and take your seats please. We have a hard stop at ten for the Permanent Secretaries' meeting downstairs, so we need to get started now."

Sir Stuart Matthews opened the meeting. As the PM's National Security Adviser, he was the lead official for the Prime Minister on all issues relating to defense and national security. Every Wednesday morning, he chaired National Security Council (Officials) committee—or NSC(O), as it was known by the civil servants. The committee's members were the most senior officials working on national security in the British government.

NSC(O) was one of the most important committees run by Cabinet Office, the corporate HQ and nerve center of the British Government. NSC(O)'s job was to finalize the advice on national security to the Prime Minister and the other senior politicians on the National Security Council.

The meeting was held in the heart of the Cabinet Office in Number 70, Whitehall. From the outside, this was the most beautiful building on Whitehall, the street which ran through the center of the government district, from Big Ben to Trafalgar Square. 70 Whitehall was a masterpiece by the great architect Inigo Jones. The exterior was perfectly preserved from the 17th Century. Inside it was a maze that mixed the ancient and the modern. Some rooms and corridors dated back to the Palace of Whitehall, home of Tudor and Stuart Monarchs. Other rooms were modern, functional, dull offices dating from the 1990s. Room 2/17 was one of those. It was one of the few meeting rooms where top-secret issues could be discussed. The floor, ceiling and walls had additional protections to block any sound or vibration being picked up by agents from hostile states. Just last year, a tourist had been arrested while loitering outside in the streets of Whitehall with a wall-penetrating listening device concealed in his telephoto lens. The wall coverings in Room 2/17 were made of a material so secret that not even Ruth was cleared to know how it was constructed.

"This is an important meeting," Sir Stuart began. "After our usual round-up of hot topics and our quick world tour of trouble spots, wars, and strife, we'll be stepping back to review the National Threats Register.

"We need to work out what are the most dangerous risks facing the nation now and what we need to be preparing for. It's an important discussion. That's why I asked that only four-star officials attend this meeting. I'll want only 'four-star comments' from all of you."

Ruth attended NSC(O) as the PM's Chief Scientific Adviser. Today she was wearing a fuchsia-colored jacket. She whispered to her neighbor, "What's a four-star comment? Is that something pompous, like we normally hear from the four-star generals at the other end of the table?"

"Only one conversation at a time please, Ruth. Would you like to share your comment with the rest of the table?"

"No. Thank you, Stuart. I'll wait my turn to intervene on the Threats Register."

The meeting began with the military chiefs providing an update on current operations out in the field. The Chief of the Defense Staff, known as CDS, wore his military uniform today. The polished brass, medals and crisply ironed shirt did look great on him. The senior military officers believed that wearing their uniforms to meetings with politicians increased their chances of getting their own way. It often worked with politicians, but not with their civilian peers in the Civil Service. And, thought Ruth, his smart uniform didn't make his comments any smarter.

Finally, the group got to the main event. Every year, NSC(O) worked through the National Threats Register to identify everything that might go wrong and damage the UK's security or prosperity. All the risks were identified, quantified, and then prioritized to produce the top five threats of greatest national importance.

A bright, enthusiastic young official from the National Security Secretariat presented this year's conclusions.

"First, we are concerned about another pandemic originating in Asia. This is most likely to arise in the wet markets in China. Despite repeated requests from the international community, China has refused to take action to shut down these wet markets, which have been the breeding ground for the two Covid pandemics and the devastating H2N5 bird flu outbreak last year. In this scenario, a virus spreads rapidly to the UK and evades existing multi-variant vaccines. We predict two hundred thousand to five hundred thousand deaths in the UK within the first twelve months.

"Second, we highlight the risk of extreme flooding in the South-East and East of England. Such an event would result in far fewer deaths than a pandemic, perhaps only a few hundred, but serious flooding could cause potentially billions in economic damage.

"Third, as a contrast to the flood threat, we have identified the risk of extreme heat and an extended drought. The impact of climate change is accelerating. Each summer, for the last five years, has seen record temperatures. We're in the third year now of a severe drought, and water levels in reservoirs are already dangerously low. Another dry winter would lead to water rationing, likely 'water wars' as citizens fight for limited supplies of bottled water, and failure of multiple small businesses.

"Fourth, we continue to be very concerned about the risk of a successful cyber-attack on the UK's critical national infrastructure. State-sponsored cyber-attacks have been few and far between recently, since NATO declared that a cyber-attack would count as an 'Article 5' attack, opening up the possibility of equally devastating retaliation in kind against the aggressor. This application of the 'mutually assured destruction' doctrine to cyber warfare has slowed state-sponsored activity. But there is always the risk of a rogue lone wolf or a non-state actor.

"Finally – and we are including this as we need to present the top five threats to national security – we have added 'extreme space weather'. In this scenario, we assume that the Earth may be hit by another Carrington Event at Kp-9 intensity, causing the UK and many other nations to lose all their electronic systems for weeks, possibly months. Given Dame Ruth's world-renowned research on solar activity, there is now more scientific consensus on the level of risk. We do need to recognize that the science is politically contested, both here and in the US. We put the probability of such an event within 5-7 years as about one in five."

Sir Stuart thanked the official for his presentation and opened the meeting for discussion. "Now remember," he said, "I only want four-star comments. First, though, we need to hear from His Majesty's Treasury (HMT)."

Every other department sent their top official to this meeting. In keeping with its disdain for cross-Whitehall meetings, HMT sent a relatively junior official, but it didn't matter as everyone knew what the Treasury's position was.

"The Chancellor is very supportive of this process and looks forward to the debate at NSC. She would, though, like to stress the importance of prioritization. We must focus on just one of these risks, as we cannot realistically prepare for all of them. In addition, the Chancellor is clear that there is no new money for any of this work. If further work is required to prepare for these risks, it will have to be funded out of existing departmental budgets."

"Thank you, HM Treasury," Sir Stuart sighed as he spoke. "Nothing if not reliably predictable. A lot more predictable than these real-world risks, I fear. But the Chancellor's position is noted. Now over to you, CDS."

The Chief of the Defense Staff sat up in his chair and began reading his prepared remarks. These were as predictable as the Treasury's had been.

"I can present the considered and unanimous view of all the Service Chiefs, with which I strongly concur. All the threats discussed today present a clear and present danger to the United Kingdom. It would be irresponsible not to prepare for *all* of them. Moreover, given so many other pressures on the Defense Budget, we will need additional funding from Treasury to conduct the essential contingency planning and investment in strengthening our resilience even for just one of these risks, let alone all five.

"I and the Service Chiefs cannot put our name to any prioritization that reduces this list down to just one or two. However, in the spirit of compromise, we would be prepared to prioritize just four of these risks and drop space weather. That one does sound a little far out. We're more down-to-earth types in the military.

"I just wanted to add," continued CDS, "that if the Treasury isn't prepared to provide the funding that we need to prepare for all four of these risks, we won't prepare for any of them. I fear that will put lives at risk. But the blood will be on the hands of those pin-striped warriors over there in HM Treasury."

"That's out of order," Sir Stuart quickly cut in. "I know your Secretary of State has strong feelings about the Treasury's spending controls, but those sorts of comments are not acceptable here."

"I stand corrected and am happy to withdraw my remarks. But don't be surprised if the Defense Secretary says something along those lines to the PM at tomorrow's NSC."

"Now I think we should hear from our Chief Scientific Adviser—over to you, Professor Wright. Or should I say, Professor Dame Ruth Wright? Many congratulations by the way, Dame Ruth. Very well deserved. The floor is yours."

Ruth realized she had to control her anger after the ignorant and pompous remarks from the Chief of the Defense Staff. But first, she had to declare a potential conflict of interest.

"Thank you, Stuart. I'll address the Threats Register in a moment, but I do need to disclose that my husband runs a start-up in Cambridge working on space weather protection materials. I have no personal involvement in or financial interest in this start-up."

"Yes. We are aware of that issue, Ruth. Thank you for raising it. Please continue."

Ruth then set out the scientific assessment of all five risks. She summed up as follows.

"These five risks are indeed all clear and present dangers to the UK. But based on the science and applying an evidence-based approach to prioritization, one risk stands out. It is the risk that has the greatest potential economic impact and could lead to the greatest loss of life, in the UK and across the globe. It is also the risk that we least understand and for which we have next to no defense. It is, of course, the risk from extreme space weather.

"Despite CDS' preference to keep his feet on the ground –and to be blunt, his head in the sand –this is not science fiction. This is a very real scientific fact," Ruth warned. "If the Carrington Event of 1859 happened today, modern economic life would come to a standstill.

"I am not belittling the other four risks. But we now know a lot about them. We have unfortunately had real-life experience of all four risks over the last five years. We weren't properly prepared for any of those disasters, but having survived those awful experiences, we do at least now know what to do. We have no idea yet what actions to take in response to extreme space weather.

"If the PM wants one threat to study in depth and develop an action plan for, the scientific advice is clear. Pick 'extreme space weather' and prepare a contingency plan for the next Carrington Event. Back to you, Stuart."

"Thank you, Ruth. I know you feel very passionate and emotional about this issue."

Ruth seethed at this patronizing comment. Matthews never accused the men in the room of being 'passionate' or 'emotional.' It was the usual male put-down. She thought about calling him out on it. Perhaps one of the other six women in the room of twenty men might have come in to support her. But they were silent. They'd sympathize later on the Women-only Chat group, but they left her on her own in the meeting.

Sir Stuart invited other comments from around the room. They were all entirely predictable. The Permanent Secretary from the Department of the Environment prioritized flood risk. The Permanent Secretary from the Department of Health prioritized pandemic risk. The Director of the Signals Intelligence Agency, GCHQ, prioritized cyber risk. The Permanent Secretary from Defense supported CDS and asked for funding to prepare for four of the risks, excluding space weather.

Finally, the heads of MI5 and MI6 spoke. Ruth was hoping for some support from these highly intelligent, well-informed, and well-briefed intelligence officers. The head of MI5 came in to support CDS's position. Then C, the head of MI6, spoke. Ruth hoped, finally, for some support.

"I agree with what others have said," he began.

Jesus, thought Ruth, he's going to support the military's position and kill my proposal.

"And there's another reason too for not prioritizing the space weather threat," C continued. "Even if we agreed that it was a threat, there's nothing we could do about it. The Pentagon spent $20 billion on a secret program to develop a space-based solar flare shield. It was a total write-off. They have concealed the spending, as they don't want Congress looking into this disaster. Apparently, there was a lot of fraud and corruption in the procurement. If the Americans can't find a solution with $20 billion, then I fear we're just kidding ourselves if we think we can go it alone. I support CDS' and MI5's position that we should prioritize the four top risks."

"OK, thank you everyone," Sir Stuart summed up. "I'll have to report to the PM that this distinguished group of Britain's top officials could not agree on whether we should prioritize all, some or none of these risks. That won't land well with the PM.

"Fortunately, though, he's pretty much made his mind up already. He wants to prioritize pandemic risk for the next big round of contingency planning," Sir Stuart acknowledged. "It's a straight political calculation. If he doesn't prepare for the next pandemic, he will look foolish. We have just had the final report of the inquiry into the Covid-29 pandemic, which excoriated that government for not applying the lessons learned from the Covid-19 pandemic.

"If another virus emerges next year before the election, and we haven't done a big contingency planning exercise in the next few months, the PM will pay a huge price at the polls. But if, just for the sake of argument, we were to be hit by freak space weather before the election, we'd be just as unprepared as every other nation. There wouldn't be much political risk in that."

"Lemmings," said Ruth, whispering to her neighbor.

"Ruth, I asked you already not to have side conversations. Would you like to share this one with the group?

"Well, this time, I would, Stuart. I was thinking of lemmings…"

"I am afraid, Dame Ruth, you with your magnificent scientific brain are running ahead of us mere mortals."

"I was thinking of the great investor Warren Buffett's quote on lemmings. It pretty much sums up the PM's approach to this national threat assessment," she said.

"Ruth, perhaps you would be so kind as to share that quote with us?"

"Warren Buffett said: '*Failing conventionally is the way to go. As a group, lemmings may have a rotten image, but no individual lemming has ever received bad press.*' And if this PM continues to ignore the threat from space weather, he'll be leading the country over the cliff-edge in the company of all the other world leaders," warned Ruth.

"That's enough, Ruth. Please calm down and accept the consensus of this meeting.

"I'll be recommending a pandemic contingency planning exercise to the PM.

"Meeting closed."

CHAPTER 3

TRINITY SCIENCE PARK, CAMBRIDGE, ENGLAND

February

István Szabó-Nagy, Ruth's husband, was both an entrepreneur and the main carer for their twin children, Jo and Mary. István and Ruth had met as students nearly twenty years ago. He was a brilliant Hungarian student from Budapest on an exchange program with Cambridge University. Back then, the UK was still part of the EU's Erasmus program that supported student exchanges. It was closed down a few years later, making István one of the last of the Hungarian Erasmus students. Given their brilliance, especially in math and science, the program's closure was a great loss to Cambridge. István was warmly welcomed into the Cambridge science community and made many good friends. His British classmates couldn't pronounce his name. He quickly became known as Steve S-N.

It was 8 a.m. and life in the S-N-Wright household was off to a frustrating start. Steve put the dirty plates in the dishwasher. The twins had left the table once again without clearing their dishes. Their bedrooms were a mess. Their beds weren't made. They'd come back from a party last night and had both tramped their muddy shoes up the stairs, leaving a trail of footprints on the new carpet. Their bicycles cluttered the hallway, pedals jammed into spokes. Dirty sneakers were scattered on the hall floor.

Steve didn't often regret his offer to Ruth five years ago to look after the kids when she moved to London to assume her role as the PM's Chief Scientific Adviser. But some days he did regret it. Today was one of those days.

Back then, the twins were bright, precocious, well-behaved twelve-year-old girls. At the time, Steve thought he could combine childcare with his work on the start-up. At first, it all worked well. Over time, his dual roles became harder and harder as the twins grew into rebellious teenagers. They had inherited their mother's strong will, without her diligence and academic commitment. They consistently underperformed at school. In addition to his job at the start-up, Steve had to put in hours of tutoring to try to get the twins' grades back on track. At this rate, they would struggle to get into any good university.

Ruth came downstairs at 8.30 a.m. She had taken the last train back from London last night. It had been delayed by 'works on the line.' She hadn't gotten home until 1 a.m. Steve had been fast asleep when she got back.

"So how was your week up in London?" asked Steve.

"Terrible. I am so fed up with the vicious backbiting, the petty bureaucratic infighting, the long pointless meetings, and the patronizing comments from generals."

"You could have stayed an academic and had all that every day here too…except not the comments from generals. But there'd be no shortage of other candidates here in Cambridge to patronize you if you started to miss life in Whitehall."

"I know it's not all sweetness and light here in Cambridge," Ruth agreed, "but I am beginning to wonder if I should chuck it all and return to academia. I am the so-called Chief Scientific Adviser to the Prime

Minister – but he's a total science denier. He's impossible to advise on scientific matters. With this PM, the job title is a joke."

"Well, you gave up your distinguished academic career for government service, and I gave up my slightly less distinguished academic career to become a billionaire when my start-up floats on the NASDAQ—and to clean up breakfast after our delightful teenagers."

"So, how's the billionaire thing going?" asked Ruth sympathetically. "Any luck with the investors? Or are they as skeptical about the risks from space weather as the bunch of idiots I am dealing with every day?"

"I know you've had a bad week, but I've had a terrible week. The University cancelled the funding that had been promised by the Quzran Sovereign Wealth Fund. They said they had concerns about the Quzrani human rights record. OK, I get it. We all care about human rights. But the University didn't offer me any other money. They just stopped me from getting Quzrani funding and left me high and dry. Today's meetings with investors will be make-or-break.

"I fear it might be about to turn into an end-of-the-road week for Solar Shield Limited and its sole director. That's me, by the way. I'm out of cash and I'm trading on fumes…"

"Good luck, then. I hope the investors come through with some new money. I'd rather you were not indicted for trading while insolvent. I don't think having a husband with a criminal conviction would look good for my public profile. But don't worry, I'd visit you in jail, and I'd still love you."

"Thanks a lot for your support." said Steve with only a hint of irony. "I'm trying my best. I am seeing the final two investors today. One is a serious Venture Capital Fund and the other is just an old friend, who called me up out of the blue. I've never heard of his fund. Wish me luck. And this weekend, we need to have a 'stern parental discussion' with the teenagers. They are out of control now. I need your help with that. We need to present a united front."

Steve retrieved his bicycle from behind the twins' bikes in the hallway. He scraped his shin as he tried to pull his own bike free. His bad day was getting worse.

He cycled down Milton Road and into the Science Park. Solar Shield Ltd had taken space five years ago in the Science Park's latest extension. His was one of ten start-ups in the new space. Six of the businesses had already gone bust. Four were still trading, including Solar Shield Ltd. The other three were enjoying a lot more success than Solar Shield Ltd, which had yet to earn a cent of revenues. Steve cycled past the expanding headquarters of the other three start-ups. All were now 'unicorns,' each one valued at over a billion dollars. One was still independent and two had been bought out by US tech giants. When Steve met the founders socially at the government-sponsored Cambridge *Innovation Nation* events, they said that they were now 'concentrating on their philanthropic interests,' which was the polite way of saying 'I am now fabulously wealthy, and you are not.' Steve was struggling to stay one step ahead of insolvency.

Solar Shield Ltd had started out with such high hopes. Steve may not have had the academic success of Ruth, but he had been the more promising researcher. He and Ruth had met as PhD students in Cambridge, both working on solar research. Ruth was following the path of building predictive models. Steve was working on developing a material to protect against the impact of a solar flare. On their first date, he had said, "So you'll be able to tell us with greater precision when civilization is about to end, but I'll be able to save the world." It was very nearly their last date. Ruth was so annoyed she declined his invitations to a second date for six months.

Steve finished his PhD and then followed the traditional research-driven path as an academic. As Ruth progressed rapidly through the brutal snakes and ladders (mainly ladders for Ruth) game of securing a full professorship, Steve's academic career slowly ran out of speed. His research into solar flare countermeasures was hugely promising. But academic funding in the UK prioritized 'pure science' over 'applied science,' which is what Steve was pursuing. Unlike Ruth, he wasn't viewed as a star academic. The University passed him over for promotion.

Five years ago, he had resigned his academic position and decided to turn his ideas into a marketable product, hoping to make his fortune as an entrepreneur. His first patent on Solar Shield coincided with Ruth's breakthrough research paper on predicting the next Carrington Event. Her paper generated media excitement and a flurry of interest from venture capitalists.

The first round of funding for Solar Shield Ltd was easy. The second was OK. But now, he had burned through all that cash. The Solar Shield material, while promising, was still nowhere near ready for commercialization. Today's investor meetings really were the last chance for Solar Shield Ltd's survival.

Steve entered the small office building at the back of the Science Park extension. It was all he could afford now. The building, though small, was still too big for his team. He'd started with about thirty staff, but now he was down to less than half that. If he couldn't secure funding, he'd have to lay the rest of them off within days. He'd already let go of all his research assistants - with one exception.

"Hi there, Chen. Thanks for your help on the slides. We're in great shape for the pitch meetings today."

Chen Yung was one of Ruth's students. He was one of the most enthusiastic attendees at her lectures. Chen had offered to help out with Steve's start-up too. Under the terms of his scholarship, funded by the *Anglo-Chinese New Golden Era Foundation*, half of Chen's salary was subsidized. The Foundation had been set up three years earlier as part of a rapprochement between the UK and Chinese governments, after nearly two decades of cool relations. The Foundation supported greater commercialization of British scientific research and encouraged Chinese students to take on apprenticeships in Cambridge's vibrant tech sector. Steve had kept Chen Yung on at Solar Shield long after he had let go his other research assistants.

"We've got 22nd Century Tech Futures Fund first. That's our best bet. They're one of the best firms in America. They have more money than God's VC arm. Then we have an old friend of mine, who works for a fund I've never heard of—Venture Exports. I think he's just being kind to an old friend who's down on his luck. 22nd Century Tech Futures are first up. In ten minutes, it's show time!" exclaimed Steve with slightly forced enthusiasm.

The team from 22C (as they styled themselves) entered and sat at the small conference table. There were three of them, all Americans. The more senior one could not have been older than twenty-five, and the two juniors looked as though they were straight out of university. Steve assumed this was their first investor pitch meeting. Steve's heart sank. Perhaps 22C were using this as a training session for their new employees. There were rumors that some VCs used unsuspecting start-ups as the real-world case study for their graduate trainee programs, which they held at one of the Cambridge colleges. If so, Solar Shield wouldn't be a live experiment for much longer. Steve would be hosting the graduate trainees from the local insolvency practitioner by early next week. He'd know that this was a training exercise if the juniors did all the questioning under the watchful eye of the older one, who was probably grading their performance.

"In today's presentation," Steve began "I'd like to show you the incredible progress we have made with Solar Shield and the almost unlimited commercial potential of this material once industrial strength has been reached."

"The idea of Solar Shield is to create a material – ideally a flexible, fabric-like material – that we can use to protect electronic equipment from the blast of geo-magnetic radiation that Earth would experience in another Carrington Event.

"If Solar Shield works – and if governments take the risk from extreme space weather seriously – they will need to buy enough material to protect every home, office, factory, hospital, data center, and military installation. It would make the Western government multi-billion-dollar spending on Chinese PPE during the Covid pandemics look like small change," Steve explained. "The basic concept of the science is very easy to describe. The underlying physics are a lot harder, and our research assistant, Chen Yung, can take your technical team through the details later, if you would like to return for a technical briefing.

"The simple version is that we have combined the best of Einstein with the best of Newton.

"Einstein, amongst his many amazing insights, discovered the photoelectric effect. It's one of the most practical and valuable real-world applications of quantum mechanics. If you shine a beam of electro-magnetic particles, such as light photons, onto the surface of the right sort of metal, the energy from those particles can be transferred to the electrons in the metal. These electrons pick up the energy from the incoming photons, vibrate vigorously, and then, once they get enough energy, the electrons escape from the surface of the metal. If you knock out enough electrons, you have created an electric current. You've converted a beam of sunlight into an electric current. That's how all the solar panels on your homes in California generate electricity.

"So that's the Einstein bit. The bit of magic here, and I think it's a genius bit of magic – if I say so myself – was to combine some classical Newtonian mechanics with that bit of Einsteinian quantum mechanics.

"You will, of course, remember Newton's third law. The great Sir Isaac Newton, a fellow of Trinity College Cambridge by the way, pronounced that 'for every action there is an equal and opposite reaction.'

"Now, instead of sunlight falling on your solar panels and producing electricity, think about a geo-magnetic solar flare falling on a piece of our Solar Shield. We have created a material that will radiate out geo-magnetic particles with an equal and like charge as the particles in the solar flare. You'll remember from your basic high school science that particles with like charges repel each other. This creates a 'force field' that repels the incoming particles and protects everything in the surrounding area. Once we get it to full strength, a single piece of fabric the size of a large beach towel will create a powerful force field, strong enough to repel the flare away from an area of several hundred square yards. Hey presto, we've protected all electro-magnetic equipment in that area from the next Carrington Event. We no longer have the risk of massive economic disruption and civil unrest. Life just goes on as if nothing had happened.

"But life will only go on, if the US, UK and other Western governments have been smart enough to buy tens of billions of dollars' worth of Solar Shield to protect their economies from hundreds of billions of, perhaps trillions of, dollars' worth of damage.

"At the moment, Solar Shield is the only known solution to this threat, and my firm holds all the relevant patents. As you Americans say, this is 'the only show in town'. Once we get to industrial scale, the company will be able to charge what we like for the product. It will make the profits on Covid-29 and bird flu vaccines look modest. This is a sure-fire bet for 22C. Any questions?"

The youngest looking member of the 22C team spoke up.

"So that's the theory. How is it working in practice?"

"Not bad, and about where we had hoped to be at this stage," Steve bluffed. "We now have a Beta version of the material that works reasonably well. I explained the theory to you, and now we have translated that into reality.

"With the current version of Solar Shield," Steve continued, "one square yard of material produces enough counter-radiation to repel the incoming flare over an area of ten square yards. At this point, we can't fully neutralize the impact. We need to increase the strength of the repulsion by a factor of ten.

"We have now worked out how to do that. We can create the full repulsion effect in our computer models. We can't yet translate that into a manufactured piece of material that you can touch and feel. That's where your funding would come in. Next question?"

The other young team member asked: "How many other investors are interested in participating in this round?"

Steve's heart sank. This kid had probably just passed his graduate training program. That was unfortunately the killer question. Other than this unknown fund, Venture Exports, the honest answer was none.

Steve thought he'd just go for it.

"We have a lot of interest. I'd encourage you to make your decision quickly."

It was true. Misleading, yes, but true. There was a lot of interest in Solar Shield, Steve thought to himself as he justified his answer. Lots of interest, just no funding.

"Thank you very much, Mr. Szabó-Nagy, for your time today. We will reflect on your proposal and get back to you shortly."

The team from 22C left. Steve went back to his desk and held his head in his hands.

"No luck this morning with the VCs," he texted Ruth. "They'll be turning me down, I'm sure."

After lunch, his old friend Mike Withers showed up, accompanied by a tall and impressively well-built American.

Mike had been at Trinity with Steve as an undergraduate. He was charming, witty and a brilliant sportsman. He had rowed for Cambridge and also represented the University at cricket. He and Steve had been close at Trinity. They had remained friends, but as is typical of so many English men who think of themselves as friends, they hardly ever saw each other anymore.

"It must be three or four years since we last met at the reunion," said Steve, trying to start the meeting on a positive note.

"It was actually eight years ago," Mike replied.

"No! Amazing. I've lost track of time these days. I thought you were still with the Foreign Office. But I guess you must have left if you're now a VC investor."

"Steve, I should have introduced my friend Dan McCraig. He works for our US partner, Q-Tech. He was interested in coming along."

"Great to meet you, Dan. It's nice to meet a grown-up...after the kids I just had in from 22C."

"We have a different model at Venture Exports, as do Q-Tech. We tend to have more veterans on our staff," Mike explained.

"Veteran VC investors—that's a change."

"No, Steve. I meant military veterans. Dan here served three tours in the Middle East and then one in the Caucasus."

Steve looked at Dan. He certainly looked the part. About six foot three, wide shoulders, powerful chest, close-cropped dark hair. There was not a hint of fat anywhere. Steve sat up in his chair and pulled in his less-than-perfectly-toned stomach.

"Were you in the Army then, Dan?"

"No, Sir. I served three tours with the Navy Seals."

"Impressive! So, how did you go from operations behind enemy lines in the Caucasus Mountains to the exciting world of VC?"

"The Navy put me through Harvard Business School once I finished my final tour, Sir. I joined Q-Tech straight out of HBS."

"That's a great deal!"

"Well, Sir, it certainly is. Assuming you make it through the program. Not all of my comrades made it as far as HBS. It was a very tough tour in the Caucasus. Too many brave men and women did not return, Sir."

"I'm sorry," replied Steve. He wondered if that was the right response. It was all he could think to say.

Mike tried to lift the mood.

"Steve, when we last met, you were still a struggling academic and now you are a thriving entrepreneur. Very exciting"

"I wouldn't say thriving, I'm afraid," Steve stopped himself. He couldn't be too honest about the challenges facing him. He needed money off these investors. It was time to move back into sales mode. "No, no. The business is great. It's just really hard work, so I don't yet feel particularly 'thriving.' But we have a great product here. It really has the potential to be a multi-billion-dollar business. We're just one round of financing from breakthrough. Let's get to the presentation. I'll call in my research assistant, Chen Yung."

"No, Steve. Let's just keep it to us for the moment please.

"Steve, my firm, Venture Exports and our friends over in the US at Q-Tech are very interested in Solar Shield. You don't need to do a presentation. We've done our research. Our two organizations have very strong in-house research capabilities.

"As we see it, you have the world's best technology for space weather protection, but you are hopelessly under-funded and sub-scale. You don't have even the beginnings of a credible management team. There's no way you can develop the technology you have to the next stage. In fact, without a major cash injection within the next week, we think you will become insolvent. Sorry to be so direct, Steve. But that's the reality, isn't it?"

Steve just nodded.

"That's where we come in. We are excited by your product, and we have significant financial and non-financial resources that we can deploy to bring your product to full-scale production. We'd like you to come and visit us in our London offices, tomorrow morning. You must come alone.

Please bring an overnight bag as our meetings may run over a few days. First, though, you need to sign this."

Mike pushed a piece of paper across the table and gave Steve a pen. Steve looked at the dense text and signed it at the bottom. He had signed plenty of non-disclosure documents in his time.

But these were the first investors who asked him to sign the Official Secrets Act.

CHAPTER 4

VAUXHALL CROSS, LONDON

February

The train was delayed. Works on the line outside Cambridge had slowed it down. Twenty years after the Oxford to Cambridge railway line had first been announced, the works were finally almost complete. Regular travelers had endured years of delays as they connected the East-West line to the North-South London to Cambridge line. The terrible commute was one of the many reasons why Ruth was considering resigning from her role in the government. That, and the anti-science attitude of this Prime Minister. Steve was a less regular traveler but still found the delay intensely irritating. He had a 10.30 a.m. meeting with Venture Exports. Showing up late wouldn't make a good impression.

Steve's train finally pulled into Kings Cross at 10.15 a.m. He'd never make it in time. He had called ahead to warn Mike, who didn't seem too bothered.

"We're picking you up anyway. See you when you get here."

"Where's 'here'?" Steve asked.

"Our offices. Don't worry. The driver knows where to go."

The driver was waiting just outside the ticket barriers. He looked ex-military. In his late thirties, clearly very fit, he visibly straightened up, almost as if he was saluting, when he greeted Steve.

"Mr. Szabó-Nagy?"

The driver pronounced his name perfectly. He would have passed as a native Hungarian speaker. Steve was impressed.

"Yes. How did you know?"

"The office briefed me well, Sir. Follow me, we have a car waiting."

"I'm running late. Will we get there in time?"

"No problem about the time, Sir. Mike said not to worry. Yours is the only meeting they have today."

That news rather deflated Steve. Normally VC firms were – or at least pretended to be – very busy. The idea of the top team at a VC firm having only one meeting didn't fill him with confidence that Venture Exports were a serious outfit.

The car pulled out from King's Cross and headed to central London. They pulled off the Embankment and drove down Whitehall. Steve recognized 70 Whitehall, where Ruth spent her Wednesday mornings at NSC(O). The car drove past Downing Street, past HM Treasury, and then past the Houses of Parliament. Steve wondered where they were going, as they had now passed most of the main government office buildings. Perhaps Venture Exports was off in some dingy annex south of the river.

And indeed, it was. The car crossed Vauxhall Bridge, past the iconic MI6 HQ, famous from the James Bond movies. The building, known as Vauxhall Cross, sat like a squat ziggurat, with green windows and metalwork. For some reason known only to its famous architect, the design reflected Mayan and Aztec influences. Steve looked up at the building as they passed and wondered what went on inside it. What did spies do at their desks all day? Then the car went round the Vauxhall Bridge Roundabout, looped back, and pulled up outside MI6. Two young officials met him on the pavement.

"Hello Mr. Szabó-Nagy. I'm Mary, and this is my colleague, Tom. We work with Mike at Venture Exports. We'll just take you through security and then up to our meeting rooms."

"You guys rent space from MI6, do you? Times must be hard if even the spooks have to sub-let office space."

"This way, Sir."

Steve was depressed by how unglamorous the inside of MI6 was. The outside was impressive, if strangely exotic. Inside MI6's HQ looked and smelled just like any other government department. Did they all buy the same cheap carpets with plastic backing that gave off the universal aroma of British government offices? The elevators were small and slow. Clearly the architect hadn't planned on this being a busy working office as there were not enough elevator banks. They joined a long line. All the staff looked so young. He was used to the police looking young, but spies? He felt old standing in this line.

Mary and Tom escorted him into the meeting room on the ninth floor.

"At least we managed to book a room," explained Mary. "In the last renovation, they forgot to put in enough meeting rooms. It's a nightmare booking one. Mike had to pull rank to get this one."

Steve never imagined James Bond have trouble getting a meeting room. But apparently, that was the reality of life in the MI6 HQ.

Mike Withers and Dan McCraig were already in the room, and there was one older man—balding, overweight, scruffily dressed. He was definitely not ex-military, more the academic type.

"Sorry, I'm late," Steve apologized.

"No trouble, Steve. Not a problem at all. We've got plenty of time. I'd like you to meet our Chief Scientific Advisor for Venture Exports."

"Hi, I'm Antony."

"I'm Steve Szabó-Nagy. I'm sorry I didn't catch your surname."

Mike interrupted.

"We don't really use surnames here, Steve. 'Need to know only' and all that.

"OK, let's get started. Steve, I'll start with an introduction to Venture Exports. Then Antony will share some of his scientific perspectives, and Dan can talk about our collaboration with his Q-Tech colleagues in the US. There won't be any slides. We don't write a lot down here.

"Steve, as you have probably realized by now, Venture Exports is not your typical venture capital firm. To cut to the chase, we are the Venture Capital arm of MI6.

"We were set up about fifteen years ago. I'd like to say that the idea came from a well-planned piece of strategic thinking by MI6. In fact, the idea came up in a late-night drinking session at our secret training center. We were entertaining some senior officials from the Treasury. We got them drunk and managed to secure funding for a VC fund. The CIA has long had a successful VC arm. That's what Q-Tech really is. We wanted one too. The Treasury back then was keen to put government money into venture capital. Not anymore! But we caught the right officials at the right time.

"We got a few hundred million pounds of funding in a Budget. It was wrapped up as part of some Trade and Exports drive. We needed to find somewhere to hide the fund in the government accounts. We hid ourselves in the dark recesses of the Department of Business balance sheet. If you were to read their Annual Report and Accounts – I wouldn't advise it, they are very dull – you'd see a footnote referencing Venture Exports. No one reads that far, and we never get asked questions about what we do. We had a quiet word with the Parliamentary Scrutiny Committee, and they agreed not to ask difficult questions about that footnote. To the outside world, we are just another boring government body with a mission to support exports—just one of many such bodies."

"And does that explain your name?" Steve asked.

"Nearly. The Treasury liked the 'Exports' bit, as that provided cover for funding. We liked it too as James Bond's cover organization was Universal Exports. I thought 'Venture Exports' might be too obvious, but so far no one has noticed.

"When we launched, it was all quite low-key and small scale. We had a few hundred million pounds to invest and managed to hide ourselves away in some obscure corner of the government accounting system. Our problems began once we started to hit the jackpot with some of our investments.

"We were early investors in the UK quantum computing industry. We managed to back three of the UK's now world-leading quantum computing companies. Our few hundred-million-pound fund became a multi-billion-pound fund, and success led to more success. We are, in fact, the most profitable, and probably now the largest, VC fund in the UK."

"That's great!" Steve interjected, trying to sound enthusiastic. Half of him was excited by the prospect of a well-funded VC finally showing some interest in Solar Shield. The other half was nervous, confused and bit scared. There would be strings attached to this investment. Would they let him walk away now that he knew all these secrets? He decided to play along and see what happened.

"It's an impressive track record you've built," Steve continued. "Things must be going well at Venture Exports."

"Up to a point," replied Mike. "All those profits gave us a big problem. If the Treasury had found out, we'd have had to give the money back. Our solution was to just rig the numbers. Our MI6 accountants are pretty good at that. They pride themselves on producing accounts that are 'true, fair and totally misleading.' If our accountants can't fool the National Audit Office, then we have the wrong accountants—and believe me, they hide a lot worse things than our financial results.

"Venture Exports shows a small modest profit every year, just enough to stay out of trouble and not enough to attract HM Treasury's rapacious claws.

"But that still leaves us with billions of pounds worth of profits to hide away. And that's where Dan and his colleagues come in. Dan works for the CIA, and oversees their relationship with Q-Tech. With a bit of accounting subterfuge and some off-the-books money transfers, all of Venture Exports' profits disappear from the books here.

"We transfer our surplus profits to our American friends. They can lose them in one of their huge 'black programs', which they don't have to report to Congress, at least not in public.

"We now have over ten billion dollars in an account with Dan's business in the States."

"Who knows about this?" Steve asked.

"Just the top team here at Venture Exports and the boss of MI6. We call him C, but you probably think of him as M. Also in the know are a few of our American friends."

"Isn't it unethical to hide all this money?" Steve asked, thinking he'd rather not get too involved in a scheme to misappropriate government money.

"C went to the PM, and he signed off on everything. He thought it was all fine as long as we used the money to support the UK's interests, which we do. We just do so without the unhelpful interference of government ministers or Parliament."

Steve felt pretty uneasy. In Hungary, he had seen what happened once politicians and officials decided to work around democratic checks and balances. It didn't end well.

"You mean you are doing all this without the proper oversight of the elected government and our democratic representatives in Parliament."

"Steve when you work in our world, you sometimes need to work outside that system. We're all on the same side. It's just that we need the flexibility to play by different rules when it's important and when the national interest is at stake.

"And I wouldn't be too squeamish, Steve. What this means is that we have all the money you need to turn Solar Shield into a successful product and make you rich along the way. Our money comes with a few more strings than you may be used to. But we'll come back to that later in the day.

"I'll hand over now to Antony, who can share our scientific perspective."

Antony stood up. He really was the model of a slightly mad scientist. He talked very fast and with incredible enthusiasm.

"Steve, I'm a huge admirer of your wife's work on solar geo-magnetic radiation. Her work has been brilliant. I hope one day it gets the recognition it deserves. It is Nobel Prize territory, definitely.

"Clearly though, Ruth did not have much luck in persuading the rest of the government that this is a clear and present danger to the UK. I know she was very frustrated at the NSC(O) meeting last week. We briefed C to intervene in support of the military's position. She must have been furious."

"She certainly was," Steve said. "She's used to ignorant comments from the top military types, but she had hoped C would be supportive."

"Well, he was, but he couldn't reveal his hand at NSC(O). The last thing we want is a cross-government program on contingency planning to prepare for an extreme space weather event. That would completely blow our cover on Operation APOLLO PROTECT."

"What's that?" Steve asked.

"All in good time, Steve. We'll get there. Antony, please continue."

"Well, unlike the rest of the government, we here at MI6 are taking the risk from extreme space weather very seriously, as are our American friends. Unfortunately, so are the Chinese. They too are admirers of your wife's work—and they admire your work, too. And when I say 'admire,' I should say 'admire and steal', I'm afraid."

Mike came in at this point.

"Steve. Your excellent, clever, hard-working research assistant Chen Yung is a Captain in the People's Liberation Army (PLA) on secondment to the Ministry of State Security (MSS). He is just one of many high-flyers from the MSS that China sends out on the New Golden Era Scholarship program to our best universities every year.

"I'm afraid China has completely replicated your Beta version of Solar Shield. The MSS and PLA have a fully funded program to turn it into an industrial-strength product. Fortunately, like you, their scientists are finding it hard to increase the strength sufficiently to make it strong enough to provide full protection against a Kp-8 or Kp-9 flare. Back to you, Antony."

"We love the idea behind Solar Shield. It's really clever," Antony continued. "Combining Einstein and Newton really appeals to us physics aficionados. But we think you're heading toward a dead-end. We've been following your work closely. Much as we love the idea, we don't think you're going to be able to make it work."

"Oh, thanks," Steve said. "How have you been following my work? Is one of the other members of staff a junior official from MI6?"

"No, Steve. We're more subtle than that. We've mirrored your entire computer system on our system. We know exactly what you are doing every day. It's a lot cheaper and safer than putting someone on your staff."

"Great. That makes me feel much better. What about my personal emails and messages to Ruth. Do you read those too?"

"Only if they are relevant to the mission. We delete the rest. Trust us. But before we break for lunch, I'll hand over to Dan."

Dan's training at Annapolis and in the US Navy gave him a very sharp delivery style. Steve could imagine him briefing his commander on some successful raid behind enemy lines in the Caucasus. "Target destroyed, Sir. All enemy combatants dead, Sir. No civilian casualties. Three wounded. All returned safely, Sir. Mission accomplished. Sir!"

"Well, Sir," he began, "my colleagues in the States also really like Solar Shield. It may not be perfect yet, but it's better than anything we've been able to produce. The Pentagon spent twenty billion dollars on a very large secret program. Nothing came out of it. It was a total write-off. Solar Shield is the only show in town. We're all in."

"Is that it?" asked Steve.

"Steve, once you start working with the Americans, you'll learn that they get to the point quickly. They are a lot more direct than us Brits."

"So, what's the deal?"

"Steve, we want you to come out with us to America. We have a joint facility with our American friends in New Mexico. We'll introduce you to the team from Q-Tech, who'll be co-investors with us. Antony's counterpart in the CIA would also like to share some of their thinking about how to redirect your work on Solar Shield. They have some ideas on how to increase the protection factor."

"You mentioned some 'strings attached' to your investment. What are they?"

"We'll talk about those when we get to New Mexico."

"OK. I'll need to head home to pack and pick up my passport. And I probably couldn't get to Heathrow until tomorrow evening. What time's the flight? Where do you fly into for New Mexico?"

"We won't be flying from Heathrow, and you won't need a passport. Steve, we're flying into an airport that doesn't officially exist."

CHAPTER 5

SECURE UNDISCLOSED LOCATION, NEW MEXICO

February

The Gulfstream H10 banked over the desert.

"Sir, we're right over the airstrip and our facility now," Dan explained to Steve. "Take a look out of the right-hand side."

"I can't see anything."

"That's the point, Sir. You're not supposed to see anything from the air. Not you. Not the passengers on scheduled airlines flying to LA. And definitely not the Chinese satellites overhead."

It had been a long journey. Things had not started well when he called Ruth to explain he'd be away for a couple of days. She was furious that he was heading off on an overseas trip, leaving her to sort out the childcare arrangements. That call had turned into a row. Steve felt guilty. Ruth had a point. But Steve was desperate to save his business.

The ride to the airport was not great either. It had taken nearly two hours to cover the fifteen miles from Vauxhall Cross to Northolt on the outskirts of London. An accident had turned the M40 motorway into a parking lot. The next five thousand miles were a lot faster and more comfortable. The Gulfstream H10 was an impressive plane—the first supersonic hydrogen-powered executive jet. It certainly beat Economy Class in commercial airlines, Steve's normal mode of transatlantic travel. It wasn't clear who owned the Gulfstream. As the crew were ex-US military, Steve assumed it belonged to MI6's "American friends."

The Gulfstream flew on for another ten minutes, turned, and then descended sharply. When they touched down, Steve looked out of the window. It was still hard to make out the runway. The white, unmarked concrete blended seamlessly into the white sands of the desert.

As they walked down the steps from the aircraft, he felt blinded by the brilliant sunlight. In addition to his passport, he had forgotten to pack his sunglasses. Dan gave him a pair of Ray-Ban Aviators.

"These are extra strength, Sir. You need that here."

Ten hours ago, he had been stuck in traffic in North London. It was rainy, overcast and forty degrees, with a dampness that penetrated your clothes. Classic London weather in February. Now he was in the middle of the desert. As it was still winter here in New Mexico, the temperature was a bearable seventy-five degrees. The air was dry and crisp. The sunlight was brighter than anything he had ever seen before. The sands were brilliant white, which just made the landscape feel more alien.

He could just make out some low-level buildings in the distance. They were set into the side of a low outcrop of sandstone. Other than that, it looked to be desert for miles all around. Right in the far distance, there was a range of mountains. They must have been 20–30 miles away.

Steve remembered a line from his favorite poem. If he was honest with himself, it was the only English poem he knew—Shelley's *Ozymandias*. 'The lone and level sands stretch far away.' And so they did. In every direction.

Steve wondered what he had let himself in for. The excitement of the trip had quickly faded. This all felt threatening. He began to feel nervous.

"Where the hell are we?" he asked.

"We are at what we call a 'secure undisclosed location,'" Mike replied. "Our American friends have several of these around the country, and some overseas too. This one is in the New Mexico desert. It's near where the first atomic bomb was tested. Had we driven here – which is not to be recommended – you'd have seen a lot of signs warning you about the residual radiation. You don't need to worry. It's all fine now. Those signs are just to ward off environmental protestors and adventurous tourists."

A large autonomous e-SUV pulled up by the side of the plane. It drove them towards the low sandstone outcrop. Glass doors slid open, and they walked inside. Steve couldn't believe the scale of the reception area. How was something this big set into what had looked like a small outcrop of rock?

"This is one of our newer facilities, Sir," Dan explained. "The residential quarters are to the left and our research labs are down that passage to the right. The residential corridors are blue and the working area corridors are red. It's easy to get lost and disoriented in this building, especially on the lower levels. Color coding is meant to help, but I guarantee you'll get lost a few times.

"You'll want to get freshened up and then we can meet for dinner, and I'll explain the program we have planned for tomorrow."

An enlisted Marine escorted Steve to his quarters. They took an elevator three levels down. His room was down the corridor from a central hallway. Once they were in the room, the Marine explained how the room worked, much as the bellman might at a hotel.

"As you'll see, Sir, there are no windows. But there are three LED screens. You can set them to the time of day, and location that you would like, and they will give you a pretty good view. Where would you like?"

"Certainly not North London at 10 a.m. this morning. How about the Cote D'Azur in the early evening?"

Sure enough, his room now looked out on the Mediterranean. He rotated the view through 30 degrees, so he got a better view of the Corniche. It was a live view. He could make out open-topped sports cars weaving along the road on the side of the cliffs. Perfect.

"Dinner will be in thirty minutes, Sir. Just time for a shower."

"What do you do for water out here. Is it rationed?"

"No, Sir, we are sitting on a huge aquifer. The facility has plenty of water. Power's no problem either. The only challenge was making the solar panels invisible from the air. Once we cracked that, we were good to go with the expansion of this facility."

Steve showered quickly. There was a new set of clothes in the wardrobe for him. All the right size. It was standard issue Chinos, blue shirt, blue blazer, and Docksider shoes. Why did all American spooks dress the same way, he wondered?

He had enough time to sit and enjoy watching the Sun set over the Mediterranean before taking the lift back up to ground level to join Dan and Mike for dinner.

"Here's the plan for tomorrow," explained Mike. "Given the jet lag, we'll all be awake pretty early. I think the best thing to do to bring you up to speed is if we give you some papers to read first. After that, there's someone else I'd like you to meet. We can go over our investment proposition after lunch."

Steve turned in early but hardly slept. If the MI6 HQ had been disappointingly dingy, this facility was the 'real deal.' It all seemed a long way from cleaning away the twins' breakfast. They were on their own for a couple of days. God knows what the house would look like on his return.

He awoke at 4 a.m. local time and met Dan in the main reception.

"Good morning, Sir."

"Dan, can you drop the 'sir' bit. My name's Steve."

"I'm sorry, Sir. Military habits die hard. I'll try."

They walked down one of the red corridors into a windowless meeting room. This one didn't have any LED screens and no option of the view of your choice. There was a small pile of yellow folders on the table.

"Coffee should be coming soon, and some bagels, if we are lucky. Why don't you just get started on this reading, and I'll be back in an hour or so."

Steve looked at the yellow folders. They were all marked TOP SECRET—POTUS DAILY BRIEFING.

"Can I read these?" asked Steve. "I've not got any security clearance."

"You have now," explained Mike. "MI6 has run full clearance checks on you over the past month."

"OK. I might have appreciated your telling me that you were doing that, but I'll let it pass. Anyway, what's a 'potus'?" Steve asked.

"Really? You've a lot to learn about America," Dan explained. "POTUS is the President of the United States. That would be President Marian Wallace now, in case you weren't paying attention to our politics."

"I know that! We watched the debates. I rather liked Wallace, but my wife really didn't."

"Well, she's the President now, Steve. She's fully briefed on all this. Happy reading."

Steve opened the first one and started to read.

POTUS INTELLIGENCE BRIEFING—TOP SECRET. NSC CLEARED 12 DECEMBER

Subject: Summary of Chinese Extreme Space Weather Research Program

1. President Han Guan has instructed the PLA and MSS to accelerate their research program into countermeasures to protect Chinese facilities from the impact of the geo-magnetic radiation that would strike Earth in another 'Carrington Event.'

2. Han believes that Western powers are underestimating the threat from space weather. If China can secure a technological lead in this field, they would have a strategic advantage over the West.

3. They could use that advantage either to sell their protection material back to the West or keep it for use solely by China, which could allow them to exploit the West's loss of capability in the aftermath of a solar flare strike. Han is undecided at this stage about which path to take.

4. He is attracted by the huge commercial potential of a successful solar flare protection product. He built his reputation in the Communist Party through his successful Covid PPE-protection strategy, which earned the Chinese state billions. Most of these profits went to entities controlled by senior party members and their families. This underpinned Han's rise in the party over recent years.

5. However, he is also tempted by the opportunities to exploit a two- to three- month degradation in Western military capability that might follow from a direct solar flare impact on an unprotected West.

6. The Chinese research program began five years ago and made little progress initially. The MSS and PLA then launched an Intellectual Property Acquisition Strategy (IP-A-271) to acquire – legally or illegally – Western IP on solar flare countermeasures.

7. The security breaches at Fort Meade and the Pentagon under the previous Administration confirmed what the Chinese already suspected about the failure of the US program. They then prioritized their efforts in the UK, and quickly secured full access, through theft, to the intellectual property developed by a small Cambridge start-up called Solar Shield Ltd.

8. After a year's intensive development, Chinese scientists still have not improved the performance of the Solar Shield Beta product. The Chinese version of Solar Shield, like the Cambridge version, is still only ten percent effective. In frustration at the lack of progress, Han dismissed the head of the program. He has not been seen since, and there is no trace of him on social media. We assume he was terminated.

9. The new Program Director is one of the Chinese state's most highly regarded scientists. Professor Ma Jing has led several successful IP acquisition strategies for the Chinese state. He built his reputation on China's synthetic lithium program. Initially, this IP was developed in the UK. China acquired the IP largely through legitimate academic collaboration and investment in the UK-based start-ups. China now has a ninety percent share of synthetic lithium production, which underpins their control of large-scale battery manufacturing. Given the consumer boycott of mined lithium (supported by Chinese disinformation), China now controls this critical component of all electric vehicles. Ma Jing's star rose very high on the back of that work.

10. There is a real risk that Ma Jing and his team are good enough to make the necessary breakthroughs in Solar Shield effectiveness on their own. Given this concern, the CIA launched a deception program to mislead Jing and his team. Our cyber-agents successfully penetrated the German-built calibration machines Jing uses to test the materials. As they test incremental improvements on their version of Solar Shield, we adjust the calibration of the testing machines. Ma Jing is reporting to his superiors that they have now reached fifty percent effectiveness. In reality, they have only improved the material's effectiveness to twenty percent.

11. It is in our interests that Ma Jing remains in charge of China's program. He is a known quantity, and he is arrogant enough

to believe that his research is driving all the improvements. He appears not to have any suspicion that his testing machines are increasingly mis-calibrated. As long as he continues to make progress, we believe Han will keep him in position. However, if he doesn't achieve 100 percent protection within two years, we expect Han will terminate him.

Steve put down the paper. However much he and Ruth complained about the challenges of academic life in the UK, at least you didn't face 'termination' if your research proved a dead-end.

He opened the second yellow folder.

POTUS INTELLIGENCE BRIEFING—TOP SECRET. NSC CLEARED JANUARY 24

Subject: Summary of US Extreme Space Weather Research Program.

Madam President, in briefings during the transition, we updated you on the failure of the Pentagon's program to develop a space-based protective 'shield' against a solar flare strike. To date, the Joint Chiefs have concealed the existence of this program and its failure from Congress.

Our adversaries, unlike Congress, are aware of this failure following the cyber penetration of the Department of Defense and the defection of an NSA Defense Intelligence analyst to Moscow just over two years ago.

Given the rising risk of a solar flare strike in the next five years, you authorized the CIA to work with our UK Intelligence Partners to develop a contingency plan.

We have identified a promising technology being developed by a UK-based start-up in Cambridge, England. This start-up is sub-scale and badly managed by its founder/CEO, István "Steve" Szabó-Nagy. He is married to Dame Ruth Wright, the Chief Scientific Adviser to the British Prime Minister. Szabó-Nagy is a capable scientist but a poor businessman. He is also distracted by domestic problems, as the primary carer for two teenagers. The company is on the edge of bankruptcy and is likely to fail within the next few weeks. [A technical appendix provides more detail on the science behind Solar Shield].

The Chinese attempted to purchase Solar Shield through their collaboration with the Quzrani Sovereign Wealth Fund, but MI6 intervened to block that. As China have already stolen the IP, we wondered why they also wanted to acquire the company. This may be part of their wider strategy to legitimize IP theft after the event.

With your approval, we will work with our colleagues in MI6 to secure access to this technology for further development in the US.

At the bottom of the page, someone—presumably POTUS—had scrawled 'Approved.'

The rest of the papers were more technical. Steve was impressed. MI6 and their 'American Friends' had done their homework. They really understood the science behind Solar Shield. Some of the papers explored options for improving its effectiveness. The ideas were actually very good. Steve kicked himself for not having thought of them himself. He'd lost some confidence over the last year and had gotten into a downward intellectual spiral. These fresh American eyes had spotted some things that he shouldn't have missed.

Mike and Dan returned after an hour.

"Did you enjoy the reading?" asked Dan.

"Not really. I'm depressed to think that the Chinese have stolen all my IP and might beat us to the punch in commercializing it. I'm reassured that you're trying to stop that. I was impressed with your ideas for improving Solar Shield.

"On the other hand, I could have done without the personal feedback on my business skills. And did you really need to tell the President of the United States about my difficult teenage children?"

"POTUS was a lot more interested in the technical appendix, which she studied closely. She said it was 'pretty neat science.' But she also loves personal color in these reports. We put it in there to make her more sympathetic to your situation. And let me tell you, some of the personal details we put in these briefings are a lot more interesting – and salacious – than the revelation that your seventeen-year-old twins are going through a rebellious phase. She also went through a period of dealing with teenagers when she was Governor. At least yours didn't get arrested on drunk and disorderly charges, causing a minor political scandal."

"OK," said Steve, "putting that aside, I was impressed with the technical work your team has done. Who did that?"

"We recruited the best researchers out of the Pentagon's failed program," Dan explained.

"Can I see any of that work?" asked Steve.

"No, Sir. I am afraid that is at an even higher level of classification. The Pentagon chiefs are terrified Congress will find out about all the corruption and fraud. $20 billion with nothing to show for it. That will make for some tough hearings if it ever comes out.

"That program may have crashed and burned, but we do have some brilliant scientists and they are now on the case here at this facility. They have reverse engineered your Solar Shield product and they were very impressed. They think it's the right basis for a very effective product. They are all here now, working in the labs on Level minus 5. If you sign up for our proposition, you'll get to be the Director of this program."

"And if I don't sign up for your proposition?" asked Dan.

Mike intervened. He wanted to avoid any discussion of the 'proposition' just yet.

"Time for lunch, I think. After lunch, Steve, there's someone else we'd like you to meet."

They returned to the central hallway and went down a purple corridor to the canteen. Steve felt he was putting on weight just looking at the amount of food on offer. He went for the healthy option. It was the biggest portion of salad he'd ever had. And the dressing must have been a thousand calories on its own.

When they returned to the windowless meeting room after lunch, there was already someone waiting for them. Steve was taken aback. Was it really Leslie Fayne? It certainly looked like Fayne. He was tall, slim, white-haired, and dressed in a well-cut, light gray suit. He was the only person in this facility wearing a tie. Naturally, it was Hermès. He had high cheek bones, sharp features, and an elegant pair of horn-rimmed glasses. Steve was no judge of male beauty, but he could see that this man had never lacked for female attention.

"Hello. My name is Leslie Fayne. I am a big admirer of your work and your wife's research."

Steve was impressed. Sir Leslie Fayne was the most successful British venture capitalist of his generation. He had made his first billion in the UK and then moved to the States where he made his second, third and fourth billions. He had never married but was always seen with a beautiful woman on his arm at society events. What was he doing here?

Mike entered with four coffees in a cardboard holder. Whatever advance in technology the CIA's VC arm had funded, they still hadn't improved this lo-tech coffee holder.

"I see you've met Sir Leslie. We work together a lot. We often collaborate on investment opportunities. Sir Leslie is a very good friend of Venture Exports and Q-Tech as well."

"Thanks, Dan," replied Sir Leslie. "I'm always keen to help. Steve, if I were able to speak publicly about our collaboration, which I can't, I would have to admit that many of Fayne Capital's most successful investments were actually handed to me on a plate by Venture Exports. It's been a very good collaboration for all of us."

"I can see that's good for you, Sir Leslie, but what do Venture Exports and Q-Tech get out of it?" Steve asked.

"We both get a lot," Dan answered. "Sir Leslie is a brilliant front man when we need a public face for one of our initiatives. He has a key part to play in our proposition to you."

"OK. Time's up. You've been floating this 'proposition' in front of me ever since we met in my office back up in Cambridge. It was just two days ago, but it seems like a life-time and from a different world. This facility is all very impressive. However, back in the real world, my business is still about to go bankrupt. My teenagers are home alone without adult supervision. My wife is frustrated in her job. I am ten thousand miles from home and I'm getting tired of the cloak-and-dagger stuff. What exactly are you offering?"

Mike pushed another folder across the table. This, too, was marked 'Top Secret'.

"Read this," he said.

HEADS OF AGREEMENT BETWEEN VENTURE EXPORTS, FAYNE CAPITAL, AND SOLAR SHIELD LTD

Corporate Finance package

1. Fayne Capital to acquire 100 percent of share capital of Solar Shield Ltd, Cambridge, for $100 million.

2. Payment to be made, in two tranches, to a joint account at Citibank New York in the name of Mr. István "Steve" Szabó-Nagy and Professor Dame Ruth Wright.

3. Fayne Capital to refinance Solar Shield Ltd. with $50 million of working capital.

4. Fayne Capital to appoint a Venture Exports 'Operating Partner' as the new CEO.

5. All existing staff to be retained.

6. R&D to continue in Cambridge under the direction of a new research director, also to be appointed by Venture Exports.

7. IP rights to be transferred to Solar Shield Inc, a Joint Venture between Venture Exports and Q-Tech, incorporated in New Mexico.

Relocation package

1. István "Steve" Szabó-Nagy to relocate with immediate effect to Solar Shield's research facilities in New Mexico, hosted by Q-Tech in the CIA's Secure Facility.

2. Professor Dame Ruth Wright to be offered the Sir Leslie Fayne Chair of Solar Research at a new research institute at the University of New Mexico in Albuquerque.

3. Two fully funded scholarships to the University of New Mexico available for the Szabó-Nagy Wright children.

4. Accommodation to be provided for the Szabó-Nagy Wright family in Albuquerque.

5. Weekly transportation for Mr. Szabó-Nagy from the Solar Shield Inc research facility to family home in Albuquerque.

Steve was stunned. He couldn't believe what he was reading.

"This is for real, right?"

"Absolutely. It has been approved by POTUS and fully funded by Q-Tech and Venture Exports. We're using all those dollars in our secret US account that we hold with Q-Tech. I told you that money came in useful from time to time."

"You said there were strings attached. What are they?"

"We'd like you to call Ruth on her secure Cabinet Office phone line and ask her to come and join you out here with the children, ideally as soon as possible. She can fly anytime. We'll cover the tickets and sort out moving your possessions out here. We'll buy your house at market price. And, Steve, we want you to stay here. The deal depends on your staying here. You cannot return to your home or your office in Cambridge. Your house is being monitored by the Chinese. If you return to the UK, the risk of a leak is just too high."

"You're mad," protested Steve. "I can't just leave my family and home."

"That's the deal, Steve. We can't risk you returning to Cambridge right now—at least not until we've got you fully bought into this program. You have to stay here. We'll organize the move. We'll sort it all out."

"Ruth and the kids will never agree."

"Steve, you're not the first husband to have to tell their wife and children that the family is relocating. Most husbands can't say that the move comes with a $100 million windfall. We're sure you can persuade Ruth."

"You haven't met Ruth," lamented Steve. "And anyway, won't the Chinese suspect something if we just up and move to the States?"

"Not really. They know that Ruth is very unhappy in her current role. She told you the other night that she was thinking of resigning."

"But that was a private conversation in our bedroom."

"Exactly. A private conversation. Just you, Ruth, our friends in GCHQ, and a voice-recognition computer system in the MSS offices in Beijing."

Steve felt awkward. This collection of spies had been listening in on his and Ruth's private conversations – and everything else – in their bedroom. What had they said? What had they done?

"Don't worry, Steve" said Mike. "Our AI systems delete all the personal stuff before any of our staff get to see it. I'm afraid I can't say the same for the Chinese. But that's life these days for people married to senior officials and politicians. You never know who's listening in on your most intimate moments. But let's get back to our proposition.

"Sir Leslie will be the public face of this deal. Who better to rescue a plucky British start-up from imminent bankruptcy? He'll commit to the Department of Business that he will keep on all existing staff and increase the R&D spending at Solar Shield in Cambridge. He'll position this as a merger with a US business that he owns that has been spun out of the University of New Mexico. The Secretary of State for Business and his officials will approve the takeover without looking at the detail. They'll be relieved to avoid the negative publicity of another promising UK start-up going bust or getting bought by the Chinese. A US merger led by Sir Leslie is a dream outcome for the Department of Business. Sir Leslie is an icon of propriety and held in the highest regard by the government (and a major donor to the party and most of the members of the Cabinet).

"We'll retain your research assistant, Chen Yung. The new Operating Partner and Research Director will both be MI6 employees. We will feed them misleading research results from our work here. These will go straight to China via our reliable dupe, Chen Yung. This should slow down the Chinese program. And all the time we'll keep recalibrating their test results so they will think they are making good progress."

"OK. I get it. All very clever, and there's a lot to like. Ruth will take some persuading. She can be very stubborn. This may take some time. She's no fan of the United States, especially under this President. But you're right that she's very fed up with this Prime Minister."

"And he with her, I am afraid," replied Mike. "He's planning to fire her shortly. She'd be well-advised to take up Sir Leslie's very generous offer to return to academia here in the States."

"How do you know that? Is there anyone you aren't listening in on?"

"All in the national interest, Steve. But that's not from any illegal surveillance. That's just Whitehall gossip. Ruth will be the last to know.

Number 10 plan to brief it out to the press in the next day or so. The PM will then 'express confidence' in his Chief Scientific Adviser. There'll be another round of negative briefings and Ruth's fate will be sealed. She needs to get out before they force her out."

"And what if I don't sign?"

"We think it's a great deal. You should sign it."

"And if I don't?"

"Albuquerque Airport is two hundred miles away. It's desert most of the way. There's no public transport. And you don't have a passport."

CHAPTER 6

NUMBER 10 DOWNING STREET, LONDON

February

R uth was sitting in the waiting room outside the Prime Minister's Office. It was a small, windowless room that had once been a restroom for visiting dignitaries. Sitting in that room, any visitor felt far removed from the magic and history that infused the other rooms in Number 10. They should have left this as a bathroom, thought Ruth.

She had been summoned to brief the PM ahead of a difficult meeting on whether to bail out the last remaining UK semiconductor company. The PM wanted to understand the scientific consequences of the UK not having a sovereign capability in semiconductor manufacturing. Her mind, though, wasn't on the travails of the UK semiconductor industry. She was still upset following her very difficult call with Steve earlier that morning.

She was totally mystified by his call. It was as though he had been captured by some religious sect. He wanted her to drop everything, leave her job and her home, and move with their twins to somewhere in the middle of nowhere in New Mexico. She loved Steve, but this was so out of character and so extreme. She was worried for his mental health. The call had ended in a row. Ruth told Steve that he was being completely unreasonable and that she wasn't going to give up her career and her life to join him in New Mexico. She slammed the secure phone down on him.

The PM was running late, so that just gave her more time to sit and worry about the call. Steve seemed pretty clear that he couldn't and wouldn't return to the UK. He said that they would be rich beyond their dreams, that the twins had full scholarships at the University of New Mexico, and she had a fully funded chair at a new research center waiting for her. Why was she turning all that down to serve this science-denying Prime Minister? Steve had warned her that she might be about to be fired, but she didn't believe him. She had had outstanding annual appraisals and was held in the highest regard by the scientific community. Only last week, the PM had quoted her in the House of Commons and called her 'one of the UK's most distinguished scientists.' No right-minded government would fire her.

A Private Secretary came into the waiting room and announced that the PM was running late but didn't need a briefing. He was clear on the issues. They'd just go straight into the meeting in the Cabinet Room next door.

Ruth walked down the narrow corridor, past the famous staircase with all the pictures of former Prime Ministers. There had been a lot of them in the last ten years. Britain had been through a period of political instability, ending only with a decisive election victory by the current Prime Minister three years ago. A group of Ministers and Officials were standing outside the Cabinet Room. One of the house staff was serving coffee.

The double doors to the Cabinet Room opened and Ruth walked in with the rest of the attendees. The long, oval-shaped table was covered in a green cloth. She took a seat at the end, furthest from the door. She was struck by the musty smell in the room. It smelt like the dining room in an old stately home. In a way, that's exactly what it was. Every time she went into that Cabinet Room she felt a special thrill. That room had seen so much history—good and bad. She thought about the fateful moment in 1940 when, in this very room, Chamberlain had offered the role of Prime Minister to Lord Halifax, but he had declined; Winston Churchill stepped forward to volunteer to take on the role. How history would have been different if Halifax had said yes. Then she thought about the more recent, famously fractious Cabinet meetings in the dying days of the last government, which had been torn apart by internal feuds and leaking.

The Prime Minister's chair was in the center by the fireplace. In the two chairs opposite sat the Secretary of State for Business and the Secretary of State for Science.

"Where's the Chancellor?" asked the Secretary of State for Business.

"She couldn't make it, so she's asked me to represent the Treasury position," responded a senior Treasury official, who was sitting at the far end of the table.

The Prime Minister walked in and started the meeting.

"It's very obvious," he said, "that we need to preserve our sovereign capability in semiconductors. What do you all think?"

Ruth was appalled. The proposal was to invest two billion pounds into an uncompetitive fabrication facility in the Northeast of England—and it just so happened to be in a battleground district where this government was facing a difficult special election. The PM was just going to railroad it through without any discussion. Had Ruth been able to brief the PM, she would have advised against it. The technology was out-of-date, and the UK lacked sufficient scale to compete with the major facilities in the US, EU, and Japan. Clearly though the PM didn't want to listen to reason.

The various Ministers all agreed with the PM and then he said, "OK then. Hands up everyone if you want to save the British semiconductor industry."

Everyone around the table put their hands up except the Treasury official and Ruth.

The PM turned to the Treasury Official. "So, the Chancellor doesn't want a UK semiconductor industry then?"

"It depends on the cost," replied the Treasury Official. "The Chancellor would be delighted if we had a globally competitive semiconductor industry. But we don't. Our industry is high cost and not competitive with the world leaders. She doesn't want to throw a further two billion pounds into this facility that we bailed out just a few years ago."

"Typical Treasury. Counting the pennies as usual and not seeing the bigger picture," said the Prime Minister. "We'd be the only G7 country without a sovereign capability in semiconductors. I cannot expose our country to that risk."

The Prime Minister then turned to Ruth.

"And what does my Chief Scientific Advisor have to say? Ruth, you were sitting on your hands too. Have you been captured by the Treasury bean-counters?"

"No, Prime Minister. My position reflects the science. This facility uses an out-of-date technology. Two billion pounds isn't enough to upgrade it to a level where it can compete with the much larger, more state-of-the-art facilities in the EU, US, or Japan. We had the chance to join one of those initiatives, but we chose to go it alone to preserve the UK's only chip manufacturing facility. As a result, we do have a sovereign capability—but it's an obsolete one. If we want access to the latest, highest tech capability, we'd need to join one of the EU, US or Japanese initiatives."

"That would be politically unacceptable, I am afraid, Ruth. I do wish you'd stick to the science and avoid getting into politics. Leave that to me."

Ruth was furious but remained silent. She *had* been sticking to science. But this PM once again was ignoring the science. The PM closed the meeting with a firm commitment to provide a two-billion-pound grant to keep the semiconductor facility open, at least until after the next election.

As the meeting broke up, Ruth caught the PM as he walked back to his office.

"Prime Minister, I hope you didn't mind my speaking my mind. My job is to advise you on the science and so I feel obligated to tell you the scientific truth, even if it is uncomfortable."

"Ruth, of course," the PM said cheerily. "I do so value your advice. Please keep it up. I want you to tell me the truth. Don't sugarcoat your messages to me. You're doing a great job."

Ruth left Downing Street and walked back up Whitehall to the Department of Business, where she and her team had access to shared desks. She found an empty desk and sat down. She put her head in her hands. What was the point of it all? The PM ignored her, but then when pressed, he expressed enthusiasm for her advice. She had learned not to trust politicians, but this Prime Minister was a particularly brazen liar.

Her mind wandered to her call with Steve. It was all too good to be true. The full scholarships for the twins would be great. Their university applications had been terrible, and they'd struggle to get into a top-tier university in the UK. They weren't stupid. Far from it. But they had gone off the rails over the past two years and that was going to cost them dearly in their university entrance exams. Was that her fault? Had she prioritized her career over their education? Had she put too much of the burden on Steve?

She checked her phone to see if Steve had sent her a follow-up message. He had. Please call me, he had texted. She didn't want to call him yet. He had been horrible on the call. She'd make him suffer a bit longer. And in any case, she wasn't going to give up her career to join him on this mad venture out in New Mexico.

"Ruth," one of her team called out. "Have you seen this article in the *Times*? You need to see it."

Ruth opened the *Times* app on her phone and saw the headline: "*Government planning further spending cuts.*"

Nothing new in that she thought.

"What's the big deal?"

"Keep scrolling down, Ruth. You need to see the bit at the bottom."

She scrolled down.

"Among the savings agreed between the PM and the Chancellor, it is believed that the Government will shortly abolish the Government Office of Science, including the role of Chief Scientific Adviser, currently held by Professor Dame Ruth Wright."

The Prime Minister had lied to her. She'd been fired.

CHAPTER 7

SECURE UNDISCLOSED LOCATION, NEW MEXICO

February to May

"Steve," Dan called. "You are needed upstairs on the video call with London. It's Ruth. She seems pretty upset."

"Can you ask her to call back? We're in the middle of discussing today's test results."

"Steve, I could. But I don't think that's a good idea."

"Dan, please tell her I'll call her back tomorrow."

Dan left and Steve resumed the meeting going over the results. The team here had already made some great advances. The enhanced Solar Shield material now projected a much stronger 'forcefield'. They were already halfway to achieving the required level of protection. Steve was excited. These first few days in the facility had been among the most exciting in his professional life. He was totally absorbed in his work.

Later that evening, Dan asked Steve to join him for a drink after dinner. The facility only had one bar and it got pretty crowded in the evenings. They managed to find a quiet corner.

"I'm sorry to ask, Steve, but is everything OK between you and Ruth?"

"Of course. Why do you ask? And anyway, it's not really your business, Dan."

"It is our business. It's partly out of concern for you and Ruth, and partly self-interest. We've seen too many marriages fail when people come out to this facility. It's just too easy to get isolated and out of touch. We need to get Ruth out here working at the new Fayne Institute. We need her modelling skills to predict if and when one of these flares might strike. We can't afford to have you and her break-up. And Steve, the deal depends on your persuading Ruth to move out here. The second tranche of the money won't be paid into your account unless you persuade her to join you. Please call Ruth."

"It's all fine. And anyway, why do you think it isn't?"

"You wouldn't take her call. And you still haven't called her back."

"Look, Dan. If I want marriage counselling, I'll ask you for it. Let's just stick to the research program, shall we?"

Dan let it drop. He could see that Steve had gone into a defensive shell. He would try again in a day or two. He went back to his windowless room and turned in for the night.

In the morning, Steve had a video conference back with his team at Solar Shield Ltd in Cambridge. He explained the exciting news that the company had been acquired by a subsidiary of Fayne Capital and its funding was now secured. Some executives from Fayne Capital and Venture Exports would be arriving shortly to take over management. Steve assured the staff that all existing jobs would be protected. The call went pretty well. The staff were reassured. They had some understandable questions about pay and benefits. They asked practical questions like–what happens to our pension plan? Towards the end, Chen Yung asked a bit more about the new investors. "Steve, Fayne Capital are obviously a very well-known firm and a great investor. It's fantastic to have them backing us. But I don't know much about Venture Exports. They seem to keep a low profile. What other deals have they done?"

Steve was thrown. How was he going to answer that one? He passed it to Dan to answer.

"It's a very private firm, Chen. It operates mainly with family offices on very confidential deals. They keep out of the public eye as their investors tend to be publicity shy. But we'll get you some more information on them."

After the call finished, Dan told Steve that he'd get onto to Mike Withers who had just flown back to London. The team at MI6 needed to do a better job creating a footprint for Venture Exports. They'd need to be smart about it. Chen had obviously spotted something that didn't quite fit. They'd need to make sure the fake backstory was convincing.

Over the next week, Steve became ever more engrossed in the work. Dan didn't understand the science, but whatever the team had come up with clearly excited Steve. He was working fifteen-hour days, rushing his meals, and declining all Dan's offers for a late-night drink.

Finally, Dan succeeded in persuading Steve to call Ruth on the secure video link. She was at home in Cambridge.

"Hi Darling," Steve began. "Why are you in Cambridge? Are you working from home today?"

"I'm not working. End of story. If you had taken my calls, or called me back, I could have told you sooner. I've been fired. Steve, come back. I'm miserable here. The twins are being a nightmare. You've just disappeared. I never hear from you. What's going on?"

"We're making great progress here. I've got an amazing team and incredible facilities. We've already increased the forcefield by a factor of five."

"Steve, I don't care about your fucking forcefield. You've got a family here. You need to get back to help out. You're being really selfish."

"Oh, now I'm the selfish one, am I?" Steve protested. "I gave up my academic career to look after the children, so you could do your big fancy Government role. I supported your career for five years. I've done my bit. It's your turn now."

"Fuck you, Steve."

The screen went black.

Steve realized he had been too insensitive and tried calling back. Ruth wasn't picking up. She'd get over it, Steve told himself. He needed to get back to his team. They had another important test run today.

"How was Ruth?" Dan asked over dinner.

"She was fine. She's just a bit upset about losing her job."

Ruth called back a week later. That didn't go well either. They had an argument about American politics. Ruth had seen an unflattering profile of President Wallace on the BBC and called her a right-wing zealot. Steve had pushed back, saying that the more he learned of President Wallace, the more he thought that she was an intelligent and capable woman. She was, after all, backing his research and seemed well informed on the science. Ruth lost it and accused Steve of having a soft spot for right-wing autocrats, 'just like the rest of your fellow Hungarians.' As Steve had taken UK citizenship when they got married, he was pretty upset.

The next day, Ruth called back and gave Steve an ultimatum. He had to come back to Cambridge. She and the twins were staying put. Steve had to make a choice—his family or his work. Steve ducked the question and tried to persuade her to change her mind. She shouted at him that she was never going to move to New Mexico, which was, she said, "a cultural waste-land with no history." That call had not ended well.

The fights reduced in frequency, but only because they had fewer calls. Ruth and Steve both went into 'conflict avoidance mode.' They both sulked, waiting for the other to make the first move towards reconciliation. Neither did. Time passed. Days and then weeks.

Steve had plenty to keep him distracted with his work. They now had reached 60% of the target strength for the force field projected by Solar Shield. They realized the last 40% would be much harder, but they had made incredible progress already.

Dan threw a party for the research team to celebrate the progress over the last three months. They roped off a corner of the main canteen. It was the best they could do. Morale was so high that they could have had a great party anywhere and they did. Late in the evening, Dan sat with Steve and put his arm around Steve's shoulder.

"Steve, you've done an amazing job. We're in great shape on the project. I'm going to head back to Washington for a couple of days to see my family. I could try to persuade the boss to let you take a break back in England. You need to see Ruth and the twins. Do you want me to ask?"

Steve drained the rest of his scotch. He put his glass down.

"Dan, I don't think it would help. Ruth's asked for a trial separation."

"I'm so sorry, Steve. But that's exactly the time when you need to get on a plane and just show up. I'll ask for permission."

"No, I think it's for the best." Steve poured himself another large Scotch. Dan leaned over and took the glass away.

"Steve, let's call it a day for now. I think you need to turn in. Let's talk in the morning."

The next day, the research team met for their regular progress meeting. Dan had messaged the group pushing the start time back to 11 a.m. Even then, some of the team were late and looked pretty rough. Especially Steve.

Dan summarized the situation. They had made fantastic progress in getting Solar Shield up to two thirds of the necessary strength. Now they had to start work on designing the production processes. They would need to be able to produce the material at massive scale. His first estimates were that would need to produce billions of square yards of the material. They'd be setting up a new team to design the industrial processes and the factories needed to achieve roll-out. They would also need to prepare a procurement request for the massive scale-up. This program would cost billions, and they'd need Congressional approval for the funding. New team members would be arriving to help on the next stage of the work. They would restart in a week's time. Everyone was free to take a few days off and see their families.

As the meeting broke up, Dan approached Steve.

"I've checked with the boss. If you want to go back to England, we can arrange it for you. We can fly you back. Everyone's taking a break for the Memorial Day weekend. Take the whole week off. Just get on a plane and go see Ruth."

"Thanks, Dan. I thought about your offer. It was kind of you to suggest it. I asked Ruth. But she said no. She thinks it's better for us to spend some time apart. I've got an apartment now in Albuquerque, so I'll go up there and start planning the new house."

"By yourself? For a week? Will you be OK?"

Dan was worried and would have offered to stay. He had grown to like Steve. Yes, he was stubborn and obsessive. He disappeared into his work bubble for days on end. At those times, he was uncommunicative and remote. But underneath it all, he was a kind man. When he opened up, he was fun and engaging. He told funny stories about his children. They were at the stage of their lives when they tested their parents' patience to the limit, but he obviously loved them. He spoke with incredible pride of Ruth's achievements. It was clear he loved her too. At first, he pretended to be relaxed about the trial separation. Dan could see that it was now really beginning to hurt him.

Dan said goodbye to Steve and left the facility to fly back to Washington to join his wife, Lisa, and their young daughter.

"Look after yourself, Steve. We'll regroup after the break. We'll hatch a plan to get Ruth and the kids out here."

The next morning, Steve took a flight up to Albuquerque on the facility's jet and moved into his temporary accommodation. The first tranche of the funds for the sale of Solar Shield Ltd had now cleared. He was now worth $50 million; the rest of the money depended on his persuading Ruth to join him. He could afford any property in this city. Albuquerque wasn't exactly Santa Barbara when it came to up-market real estate. But he couldn't face house hunting. Was he looking for a family home or a bachelor apartment? He'd never been more miserable. He was alone in a town where he knew no-one. His family didn't want to join him.

He watched TV. At least they showed Premier League matches over here. Once that was over, there wasn't much else he wanted to watch. He flicked channels. A news item caught his attention.

"SOLAR FLARE DEFENCE SCANDAL – NEW ALLEGATIONS"

Oh my God, he thought. Someone's leaked the Pentagon's failed program. That won't be pretty. Sure enough, they had.

"Washington is totally absorbed in this new scandal," the news anchor reported. "The Republican Senator Jesse Landry has called a news conference claiming he has new compelling evidence of corruption and fraud at the heart of the Pentagon. Yesterday, Senator Landry broke the story of the failed Solar Flare Defense program. Now he's claiming there's even more damaging evidence. We'll join our reporters now as they wait for Senator Landry's news conference to start."

Steve watched in horror as Senator Landry made his allegations. Nearly ten years ago, Landry explained, the Pentagon had launched a covert program to build a massively expensive space-based system to protect the US from a solar flare strike. They had sunk $20 billion into this black hole with nothing to show for it. Finally, the Pentagon had closed the program down. Desperate to avoid criticism in the media and in Congress, the military chiefs tried to eliminate all trace of this program's existence. They failed. Someone had leaked the highly classified program files to Senator Landry.

"Today I will share some shocking new evidence about the corruption and fraud at the heart of the Pentagon," the Senator was beginning his statement. "Papers have been shared with me that show a disgraceful pattern of waste, mismanagement, and corruption in this madcap Space-based Solar Flare Defense program.

"It is bad enough that the Pentagon decided, without Congressional authority, to go off and blow $20 billion on this ridiculous theory that some solar flare is about to hit the Earth. We humans have been around a long time. Solar flares have never been a problem. All that stuff about telegraph stations catching fire back in the 19th Century. It's just a hoax. The Western Union Telegraph Company invented it all to cover up for their dangerous equipment. That was a long time ago. Nothing's happened since. And that near-miss in 2012. Did you read anything about it at the time? No. It's all a big hoax.

"And now worse, it turns out the Pentagon was funneling millions of dollars in illegal payments to their favorite contractors on this secret scheme. Today, I am announcing hearings into these corrupt practices. I will hold the guilty accountable.

"I yield to no-one in my commitment to keep this nation safe. I have never voted against a defense appropriation. I will always support investment in our nation's defenses. But when it comes to this solar flare scam, I will stand firm. Not a cent more of taxpayers' money on this hoax."

Steve couldn't bear watching any more. He turned off the TV. He messaged Dan.

"How bad?"

Dan replied in minutes.

"It's terrible. Landry's very powerful. He can block any funding he doesn't like. The Pentagon really screwed this one up."

"What does it mean for our program?" asked Steve.

"Not good. Our current funds will last until next Spring. Once they run out, we'll have to close it all down."

Steve stared out of the window. Was it all going to be for nothing?

CHAPTER 8

CAMBRIDGE, ENGLAND

June

"**S**top watching that rubbish on TV," Ruth yelled at the twins. "Come on, Mum. It's Love Lagoon's 25th Anniversary. It's all the highlights from last night's show. Bet you watched it when you were young."

"I didn't. I had better things to do when I was your age. Like study for my university interviews for starters. Yours are next week, remember! You're not prepared, are you? It's time to do some revision today."

Jo and Mary grudgingly switched off the TV and joined their mother at the breakfast table.

"Mum, about university. We're not so sure now."

They had both set their hearts on getting into one of the more prestigious universities at the top of the 'fun night life league' rankings. They had applied to all of the top five—Newcastle, Edinburgh, St Andrews, Exeter, and Bristol. Their grades were not good enough. They only got an offer from the University of Barchester, a worthy but dull institution with a low 'fun' index. Even that offer was dependent on the interviews next week.

"Bit late now, girls, I am afraid. If you'd worked harder, you'd have a better choice of university. You'll never get a decent job without a degree." Ruth was firm. "You can't screw up these Barchester interviews. It's the last chance. Get smart on current affairs. They're bound to ask. Watch the news for once."

They put on the BBC News. The reporter from Washington was updating on the Solar Flare Scandal. The President had sacked the Secretary of Defense and Chairman of the Joint Chiefs for withholding information from Congress and the White House.

"Look, Mum. That's what you work on, isn't it? And there's that fascist President Wallace."

"Jo, you can't just go around calling people fascists."

"Well, she is, Mum. You said you hated her."

"That doesn't make her a fascist. I dislike her policies on women's rights, social justice, inequality, the environment, you name it. But she's not actually a 'fascist' or a 'Nazi'. You'll need to be more specific in your comments on current affairs if you're going to get through your interviews."

Jesus, thought Ruth, parenting was hard work. The twins had reacted badly to Steve's move to the States. They missed him and they took it out on Ruth. When Ruth explained that she and their father were separating for a while to work things through, the twins had shouted at her not to be so selfish.

"Dad looked after us while you worked up in London. You were never around."

That really hurt Ruth. It hurt all the more, as she knew it was true. She tidied away the breakfast dishes. She couldn't face another row with the twins, so she just put their plates in the dishwasher without complaining. It was time to leave for work.

She rode her bike into town. It was a fine, sunny June morning. Cambridge was at its most beautiful at this time of year. She'd forgotten it was May Week which, for reasons no-one could ever explain, always happened in June. She crossed over Magdalene Bridge, past St John's College and then stopped in front of Trinity Great Gate. It was the morning after the Trinity May Ball. The last revelers were emerging through the small door in the huge wooden gates that dated back to Henry VIII. They were mainly happy couples making their way to bed after a memorable night dancing by the river and partying in the ancient courtyards of Trinity College. There was one young woman in a lovely ball gown sitting by herself, on the low wall beside the Gate. It was clear she had been crying. For all the happy couples at the end of a May Ball, there were always a few broken hearts. Ruth felt for that poor woman. It was no fun being alone.

She remembered the May Ball she and Steve had gone to as students. That was the night she knew she loved Steve. She remembered dancing barefoot on the grass as the dawn broke. Then they climbed up onto the edge of the Great Court Fountain. She dangled her bare feet into the fountain and made Steve do the same. She'd leaned across to kiss him and told him, for the first time, that she loved him. He replied in Hungarian and then translated it.

"Ruth, I loved you from the first time we met."

Watching the young couples, in their ball gowns and white ties, wandering back to their rooms, Ruth felt a pang of remorse. She and Steve had been happy for so many years. Sure, he could be difficult and was obsessive about his work. But he was kind to Ruth. He'd been a great father. The twins missed him a lot. Right now, though, he was being impossible. She just couldn't cope with his selfishness. She couldn't forgive him for leaving her for his job in America.

She didn't have time to worry about that today. She had to get to the University Administrative Offices by 9 a.m. for a meeting on her future research funding. She got back on her bike and rode down King's Parade.

She was expecting a tough meeting. In order to fund the Government's election commitment to abolish inheritance tax, the Chancellor had announced deep cuts into scientific research. She was furious. It was bad enough to lose the money. She thought it was egregious that the money was being used to make dead rich people's children even richer.

Science had lost 20% of its funding overall and the great universities of Oxford, Cambridge and London had been asked to take even bigger cuts to support the less well-endowed universities elsewhere in the UK.

The Funding Review Committee was chaired by her old friend, Sir Lawrence Fergusson. Lovely man, thought Ruth, but he knows nothing about science. There were three other old (male) professors and just one woman, an English literature professor.

"Ruth," Sir Lawrence began. "We are facing a very difficult situation. The Government cuts are forcing us to make some really tough choices. Our committee's unenviable task is to share the pain. I'm afraid we have bad news for you. Our average cut is nearly 30%, but some of the more established research programs have fixed costs. Your program, promising though it is, is new and you haven't yet recruited your team. I am afraid we have had to cut your budget by 50%."

"Jesus Christ," Ruth shouted. She was furious. "That's outrageous. I bet you didn't cut Andrew and Simon's budgets that much." Sir Andrew Robertson and Sir Simon Goffrey were, respectively, the Regius and Queen Elizabeth II Professors of Physics.

"As I said Ruth, the more established programs still had to take significant cuts. I can assure you that Andrew and Simon aren't pleased."

"Lawrence, you didn't answer my question. Did you cut them 50%?"

"We are not publicizing the individual program cuts Ruth. It's tough for everyone."

Ruth had had it. She decided she had nothing to lose.

"I'm done with you lot. I'm the last world-class Physics professor here at Cambridge. All the others have gone off to America where they get paid more and get decent research funding. You have some old dinosaurs like Andrew and Simon who are only still here because they're past it. They haven't published anything original in twenty years. No American university would waste good money on them."

"Ruth, I appreciate you must be very upset…"

Ruth cut him off.

"Fuck you, Larry. And fuck the whole system. I can't do my research with only 50% of the money. Keep the whole fucking lot."

She left the room, slamming the door. She was overwhelmed by the anger of being patronized by men and treated as second-class to useless older male professors. For years, she had held in her resentment. Today, she couldn't. She'd let rip. She'd also just thrown away her career at Cambridge.

She went back to her office and started to tidy her papers. She knew how it would work. She'd have to apologize for her intemperate use of language. The University would then give her the 50% funding with lots of strings attached. She'd be known as the woman who lost her temper at the Funding Research Committee. She'd always have that tag of 'being too emotional' hanging round her neck. She'd be passed over for more senior positions.

She killed time in her office. She didn't want to be back in the house with the twins, trying to make them do some revision. In the late afternoon she rode back home. A June shower drenched her as she pushed her bike up Castle Hill.

She got back home and found the twins watching more TV. She couldn't face another argument. She made them dinner and they went back up to their rooms, claiming they would do some revision. Sure, she thought. You'll just be chatting to your friends online.

She opened a bottle of red wine. She paid some household bills. It wasn't long before the bottle was empty. She resisted the temptation to open a second bottle. She started to make herself a cup of tea before taking an early bed.

Her phone rang. It was Steve. This time she answered it.

CHAPTER 9

SANTA FE, NEW MEXICO

August

R uth sat in the courtyard of the historic Inn of the Zuni Elders in Santa Fe. It was a beautiful, clear morning. At 8 a.m. it was already in the 80s. Ruth was getting to appreciate the weather in New Mexico, despite the heat. She looked at the old Spanish fountain in the center of the courtyard. The water caught the bright sun, casting flashes of light on the paving stones by her table. Bright red and pink bougainvillea cascaded over the side of old terracotta pots. It was a lovely scene.

She and Steve had driven up from Albuquerque two days earlier for their first weekend away together in several years. Steve was still upstairs in their room on a call with his team at the research facility. He just wouldn't take the complete day off and was checking in each morning. Ruth was relaxed about that. They were having a great trip and had had a wonderful dinner last evening in an open-air restaurant. After a very difficult period in their marriage, last night they had remembered and recaptured the passion of the early years of their time together. Ruth was very happy. She reflected back on the past few months.

In the end, the decision to move became inevitable. The generous funding for her position in the new University of New Mexico research center made Cambridge's revised 'last and best' offer look pitiful. One weekend visiting UNM convinced the twins that this was their dream university. With full scholarships, they'd have no student debt. For them, it was a no brainer. Steve's heartfelt apology had helped too. Ruth and the twins flew out for a holiday at the end of June—and stayed.

By late July, Ruth was settled into her role as the Director of the Sir Leslie Fayne Centre for Solar Research. Her research began to make good progress. Fayne Capital gave her access to their servers, which were secretly linked into the CIA 'cloud system'. Ruth was able to use the CIA's best quantum computers for her latest predictive models.

Steve's work at the facility was also going well. The commute was made a lot easier given his access to the Q-Tech corporate jet. With his research team, they were steadily increasing the protection factor on the new Solar Shield material and closing the gap on 100% protection. He hoped they'd be ready for production by the year end. He and Ruth had to keep up the pretense of Steve's 'working out of town' at another university campus so that the twins never knew the truth about the secret facility in the desert. The risks of that were just too great.

Finally, after six miserable months, she was back on a good path again, both personally and professionally. When Steve suggested a long weekend in Santa Fe, she was excited.

The first day was spent visiting the ancient Puebloan sites, the oldest of which date back to 7500 BC. In the afternoon, they drove to Los Alamos, the secret location of the Manhattan Project. Not much was left of the original buildings, but the location, high on a remote mesa, was very evocative. For a physicist like Ruth, it was a fascinating place to visit. She was beginning to revise her view that New Mexico had no history.

Steve had booked dinner at an outdoor restaurant. They had a table under a fine old cottonwood tree in the center of a Spanish hacienda courtyard. It was still in the 90s as they ate under the stars at 9 p.m. Given their new-found wealth, it was nice not to have to check the prices on the menu and wine list. Whatever Steve had ordered, thought Ruth, was pretty good. What was better was being back with Steve again. She loved their dinner together. She had missed the clever conversation, his humor, his interest in her research. They tried not to talk about his work but, over cognacs after dinner, Steve's resolve failed.

"Ruth, things are going great, but we're going to have to find a way to get funded past next Spring. We're personally fine from the sale proceeds on Solar Shield, but if I can't get new program funding from the US Government, we'll have to shut down and I'll be out of a job."

"Now you tell me. You said the funding outlook was tough, but you didn't say how tough. Do you have a plan?"

"We do actually, but you may not like it."

"Try me."

"It involves the President."

"Not her."

"Yes, I know you don't like her. But to be fair, she does believe in the program. She just can't say so publicly. Dan and I think that our best bet is to get you in front of her to appeal to her, scientist-to-scientist as it were."

"Just as well you didn't say, woman-to-woman, or you'd be dead. Steve, it's a lovely evening. Let's not spoil it by talking about Marian Wallace."

On the second day, they headed out to Santa Fe Opera to see Ruth's favorite opera—Mozart's *Marriage of Figaro*. She was amazed by the opera house. It was covered by a large sloping roof, but all the sides were open to the elements. The performance started late, timed to coincide with sunset. As they took their seats just before 9 p.m., Ruth realized why. There was no back to the stage. Instead, they were looking straight out at a spectacular range of mountains, about thirty miles in the distance.

As the Sun set behind one of the mountain peaks, the overture began. The familiarity of Mozart's great music did not dim Ruth's enjoyment of it. The orchestra was accompanied by a spectacular sunset behind the distant mountains. The glorious colors in the night sky faded slowly as the magical first act unfolded.

During the intermission, Steve suggested that perhaps Ruth would reconsider her opinion that New Mexico was a cultural wasteland. "Watch it, Steve. Don't push your luck, or you'll be sleeping on the sofa tonight."

They returned for the second act. By then, the sunset was long faded, and the back of the stage was pitch-black. Some lightning flashes occasionally lit up the clouds over the mountains in the far distance. The auditorium lights went down and the whole stage was in darkness. A spotlight shone on the Countess in a gleaming gold dress. She was completely still as the orchestra played the opening bars of *Porgi, Amor,* one of Mozart's greatest arias and a particular favorite of Ruth's. The Countess sings of her pain. She continues to love her husband but feels totally alone and abandoned, betrayed by his infidelity.

Ruth closed her eyes as the sublime music washed over her. She held Steve's hand. Whatever problems they had been through, they were over now. Her marriage was back on track. Her professional life was great. They were financially secure. The twins were happy. The family was together. It was a perfect moment. She wanted to hold it and treasure it. She didn't want it to end.

She felt a gust of wind on her cheek. Then the beautiful stillness of the music was interrupted by the noise of a display stand being blown over in the car park. The banners down the side of the theatre flapped noisily. There was a flash of lightning and two seconds later, a loud roll of thunder. A car alarm went off in the car park. Then the torrential rain started.

The perfect moment was over.

It would be many years before Ruth would experience another perfect moment.

CHAPTER 10

WASHINGTON D.C.

March - the following year

I t was Ruth's first visit to Washington D.C. She had been in America now for nine months. She'd finally agreed to Steve's plan. They'd have to get the President on board. Dan's boss at the CIA had offered the President a confidential briefing on the space weather threat. Wallace had immediately agreed. The program had only a few weeks funding left. Everything hinged on Dan and Ruth's presentation. It was their last chance.

Ruth was looking forward to seeing the famous cherry blossoms in Washington, which her old guidebook said peaked in mid-to late March. But Spring came earlier now in Washington. The official Cherry Blossom Festival had recently been moved to late February. By the time of Ruth's visit, the glorious cherry blossoms were long gone. Today, it was forecast to reach 85 degrees. Ruth wondered why Americans could not see the threat from climate change. The evidence was all around them. Perhaps it was just because the changes were happening so slowly that they were easy to miss. It was proving even easier to ignore the threat from solar flares. There would be nothing to experience until disaster happened. Senator Landry was on a roll with his hearings. He'd turned his whole party against this so-called hoax. Sadly, the Pentagon scandal only helped strengthen his case.

Ruth was up early and was waiting in the foyer of the Willard Hotel, just a few minutes' walk from the White House. She and Dan were due to give the President a briefing at 9.30 a.m. Ruth was wearing a new blue designer suit; no chance of Wallace wearing blue, she thought. Ruth was also wearing heels. She'd bought a new pair of Manolos as part of upgrading her wardrobe now that she finally had some money to spend on herself. She'd heard the President was tall. She didn't want to have to look up to Wallace too much.

They'd need about ten minutes to walk over to the White House's East entrance and then thirty minutes to get through security. Ruth always allowed plenty of time, especially today. There were protests all around the White House.

Dan came down from his room at 8.45 a.m.

"Good morning, Ma'am," he greeted Ruth. "Time for a quick coffee?" he asked.

"No," said Ruth. "We'll be late. We've got to get through these protestors."

"There are always protestors around the White House these days. President Wallace isn't very popular with the locals here in Washington. It's a very Democrat city—and she's definitely not their favorite politician. What are they protesting about today?"

"She's not my favorite politician either. She's a religious nutcase, a threat to women, and a danger to democracy," replied Ruth. "When it comes to President Marian Wallace, there's plenty to protest about. But I don't understand what this crowd is angry about. They've got all these signs. "D.C. Statehood Now." "No Taxation without Representation." I thought you fought that war against us Brits in the Revolution and you guys won. At least that's what they taught us in school."

"Yes, Ma'am. We certainly did beat you Brits in the Revolutionary War. We threw off your oppressive colonial yoke. And yes, we now do all have the right to vote for the representatives who set our taxes in Congress…All of us, that is, except the residents of Washington D.C. That's about one million people these days. They don't get to vote for a Senator or a Representative in Congress. For those one million American citizens, it really is taxation without representation."

"That's terrible! We'd never allow that in the UK. How can you justify that?"

"Well, Washington D.C. is a very Democrat city. If it were a State, it would return two deep blue Democrat Senators, and there's no way the Republican controlled Senate would allow that. And even if they did, this Republican President would veto it. There's no chance these protestors will win this one... but they keep on protesting!"

"We need to leave now, if we are going to make it to the White House on time."

The crowds were already large and were getting angry. The D.C. Police were trying to hold them back but had already lost control of part of the crowd gathered on 17th Street. That was the street Ruth and Dan needed to cross. There was no way they could get through.

"Ma'am, we'd better do a big loop round to the West entrance. We should still be there on time."

"Jesus, Dan. If I had known we'd be hiking half-way round Washington, I'd have worn flats and changed when we got there. These new shoes are killing me."

Ruth and Dan walked back down Pennsylvania Avenue and then worked their way around the crowds, finally making it to the West Gate of the White House by 9.15 a.m. It was already 80 degrees and humid. They were both sweaty and flustered by the time they got to the security screening facility on the West Gate.

"Dan, I told you we should have left earlier."

Finally, they got through security by 9.28 a.m., and they were met by a young official who guided them to the Oval Office.

"You'll need to wait here in the Roosevelt Room for a few minutes. The President is just finishing up a press interview in the Rose Garden. Then she'll need a bit of time to freshen up."

Ruth admired the artwork in the Roosevelt Room. There was a portrait of Franklin Delano Roosevelt and another one of Teddy Roosevelt. That's very bipartisan, she thought. FDR was the only Democrat in there, though. Portraits of Ronald Reagan and Donald Trump made it quite clear where President Wallace's loyalties lay.

President Marian Wallace had been elected nearly two years ago in a landslide victory. Her Democratic opponent had only just held his home state and won a few deep blue states, but Wallace carried the South and all the traditional swing states. It wasn't hard to see why.

She had been a very successful two-term Governor of a conservative Southern state. She had a strong pro-business record and her state had created over a million new jobs on her watch. She was pro-military, pro-guns, pro-life, and pro-God. A committed Christian, she was a deacon in the Church of Jesus Lives Today, and often gave the sermon on Sundays in small towns throughout her state. On Wednesdays, she hosted prayer evenings, open to all, at the Governor's Mansion. She was tall, nearly six feet, and striking in appearance, if not classically attractive. The press had a rich store of Homeric epithets for Marian Wallace—flame-haired, emerald-eyed, quick-witted, sharp-tongued, and strong-willed were just a few of the more polite ones. She was a formidable presence on TV, where she was able to come across as both charming and forceful at the same time.

Her political genius came in her ability to build consensus with political opponents. Her rhetoric was reassuring and calm. She quoted Lincoln and evoked his 'better angels of our nature' at every opportunity in her campaign speeches.

As Governor, she had been a pragmatic administrator working with the Democrats and community leaders in her state to address difficult social issues. She worked with black church leaders on a successful drive against homelessness in her state capital. She used tax-breaks to attract investments into wind, solar and nuclear power. Her party was against action on climate change. But she justified her energy policy as a great economic opportunity. She never talked about reducing carbon or saving the planet. She knew that would alienate her party and her own donor base. But, by the end of her second term, her state had quietly become the nation's leader in green energy. Most of the workers in the oil and gas industry had been retrained for green jobs. Overall employment in energy was up on her watch and emissions were down 50%. The climate movement still hated her.

She had a challenging family life. Her teenaged twins, one boy and one girl, had had some well-publicized problems with drugs and alcohol. She was open about these and sponsored effective rehabilitation programs across her state. She embraced the liberal wing of the Republican party on social issues, especially gay rights. Her eldest son was gay. Governor Wallace had been the first Governor to host a gay wedding at her Governor's Mansion. She held annual Pride Parties and marched with her son and his husband in the Pride Parade. Governor Wallace wore an exotic Carmen Miranda headdress. She proudly posted pictures of herself dancing with the Gay and Lesbian Marine Corps Veterans. This was more than enough to win over the independents and the economically conservative but socially liberal Democrat votes.

To top it all, she was a war widow. Her husband, a senior officer in the Marines, had been killed on active duty in the Caucasus War. President Wallace had raised her three children as a single mother.

In short, she was the Democrats' worst nightmare as a Presidential candidate, and they ran a weak candidate against her. The Democratic primaries had thrown up a radical Progressive as the nominee. In the debates, her opponent had questioned President Wallace's patriotism given her position on climate change. "How can you love America if you don't love the planet?" was meant to be a 'zinger' but it rebounded badly on the Democratic candidate as no reasonable person could question Wallace's love of America, even if they disagreed with her decision to allow some limited oil and gas exploration in her state.

In the second debate, in the section on abortion rights, Governor Wallace set out her belief in the sanctity of life, a belief deeply rooted in her Christian faith. In response, the Democratic candidate challenged her commitment as a mother. "How can any mother of a teenage girl not support abortion rights?" he asked. "You have put your ambitions as a politician over your responsibilities as a mother." Wallace had responded with quiet fury. "Don't you ever question my faith. Don't you ever try to make political points at the expense of my daughter. Don't you ever challenge my commitment as a mother. You, Sir, should be ashamed of yourself. I demand an apology—and an apology now." The Democratic candidate refused to apologize. Many swing voters disagreed with Wallace's position on abortion, but they thought it was a cheap shot against her in the debate. They also admired her success at combining a career with single parenthood following the death of her husband in the service of his country. The election wasn't even close.

As a committed liberal, Ruth knew she'd dislike President Wallace when she finally got to meet her. Ruth would, of course, be professional. Steve needed the funding. Even so, she was determined to maintain her defenses. She wasn't going to fall for the President's legendary charm.

After about fifteen minutes, the Chief of Staff came out and apologized for the delay. The President's interview in the Rose Garden was running over. He made small talk for a while. He gave a brief tour of the portraits in the Roosevelt Room. He explained the tradition that the portraits of FDR and Teddy Roosevelt were retained by all Presidents of either party. If a Republican was in office, the portrait of Teddy Roosevelt hung in the center of the main wall, right between the two doors that led to the Oval Office. Visitors could not miss the portrait in this spot. FDR hung over to the side, slightly out of line of sight. And when a Democratic President was in the Oval Office, FDR hung in that central place. The Chief of Staff also gave a brief history of the glorious Childe Hassam painting of the Stars and Stripes hanging on all the buildings down Fifth Avenue during World War One. America really loved their flag, thought Ruth. She imagined the Chief of Staff often had to entertain visitors as the President ran late.

Finally, the art tour was over, the President was 'freshened up,' and Ruth and Dan were shown into the Oval Office.

"Well, hello there everybody," President Wallace greeted them in her courteous, light Southern drawl. She was wearing a bright red suit and matching red shoes. Manolos, too, like Ruth's. Damn, thought Ruth. I hope she doesn't notice mine.

"I hope y'all are enjoying your trip to the nation's capital. You are definitely getting the premium tour of the White House today, and from the very best tour guide there is!"

"Madam President, may I introduce Professor Dame Ruth Wright, the Sir Leslie Fayne Professor of Solar Research at the University of New Mexico?"

President Wallace greeted Ruth and welcomed her to the Oval Office.

"And I believe you know Dan McCraig, the Program Director for Operation APOLLO PROTECT."

"I do indeed know Dan. The rest of you may not know this, but Dan served with my late husband in the Caucasus. The good Lord sent Dan back safely, but He chose to take my husband to His side rather than send him home to his family. Such is the will of the Lord."

There was an awkward silence. Ruth and Dan had no idea what to say. The President broke the silence.

"I am so delighted to meet you, Dame Ruth. Is that what I should call you? I do love these English titles, but they should come with an instruction book for us poor simple Southern folk."

"Ruth is fine, Madam President. It's an honor to meet you."

"And does being a Dame make your husband Sir István Szabó-Nagy?" The President pronounced Steve's name perfectly.

"No, it doesn't, Madam President. If my husband were knighted, then I would be Lady Szabó-Nagy, but if I am made a Dame – the equivalent of a knight in our Honors system – my husband remains plain Mr. Szabó-Nagy."

"Well, that doesn't sound very fair," President Wallace opined. "If we had that system in this country, I imagine the American Civil Liberties Union would be challenging it all the way to the Supreme Court. If they could find the time, given all the other cases those ACLU folks are bringing against me.

"And how are the twins? Are they settling into university life? It's a difficult age. Mine were just awful at that time. I had my hands full trying to keep their antics out of the newspapers, and on a few occasions I failed. Those were tough years. They took the loss of their Daddy badly. They're fine now. They both followed their father into the military and that certainly straightened them out. How are your and Steve's twins? It's Mary and Jo, right?"

"Ours are doing well, thank you. We're all very happy in Albuquerque. We had no idea what a beautiful state New Mexico was. Mountains, wine country—fantastic champagne, or do I need to call it sparkling wine?"

"Champagne is just fine, but don't tell the French I said that. They get very prickly on such things. I do love President Giroud, but he has a thin skin. I have to calm him down when he gets exercised by some perceived slight. Fortunately, my French is good enough to smooth his ruffled Gallic feathers."

"We're looking forward to skiing next winter if the snows come back. And of course, the amazing desert. We just love it in New Mexico."

"Dame Ruth, I am just so pleased to hear that. Of course, New Mexico is now a deep red state too, though perhaps that is not quite so much to your liking. Albuquerque's a fine city, but not great for shopping. I'm impressed you found Manolos there, Dame Ruth. Anyway, the good voters of the great state of New Mexico honored me with a ten-point margin. I'm so pleased that you and your lovely family have settled in so well in our country. We do love our British friends. It is such a special relationship. And personal friendships are so important in underpinning that relationship. Don't you think so, Dame Ruth?"

The Chief of Staff intervened. He knew that the President could use up more than half the meeting charming her guests, and there was urgent business to cover. Ruth was relieved her conversation with Wallace was over. She had felt drawn in by Wallace. The charm was certainly there. She couldn't fault Wallace for courtesy. And was that just a touch of self-deprecating humor about Wallace's problems with the ACLU? But Ruth felt uneasy that Wallace knew so much about her. How did she know all those details about her family? It was all a bit creepy.

"Madam President, Dan and Dame Ruth are here to brief you on the risks we face from extreme space weather and the current state of our readiness, or not. They'll also cover what we know about the Chinese program. Dame Ruth will start with an update based on her latest research."

Ruth took a sip of water to calm her nerves and launched into her presentation.

"Madam President, extreme space weather is a clear and present danger to the Earth. It poses a potentially existential threat to our modern way of life. I know that some Congressional leaders and media figures dismiss it as a hoax, but it is real."

"Now Dame Ruth, don't you worry about some of the more excitable members of my party and the right-wing media. I'll handle the politics.

You just stick to the science. You are world class at the science and believe me I am world class at handling the right wing of my party."

Ruth paused. She'd been told to stay out of politics before. She'd found it patronizing then as well. She thought momentarily of pushing back but decided to let the President's comment pass. She went on explaining the underlying science—the cycles in solar activity, the regular ejection of geo-magnetic plasma, the occasional mega-flares that could reach Earth with enough power to knock out the entire electronic infrastructure of an advanced economy.

The President listened attentively and asked penetrating questions. She had flipped from charming Southern politician mode to being a sophisticated science PhD. She's no fool, thought Ruth. These questions would challenge most professors in a post-graduate class.

Ruth then shared her latest research, which she was not able to publish. The Sir Leslie Fayne Chair came with strings attached, just as Steve's funding had. Ruth's research had to be cleared by a CIA agent on the faculty at University of New Mexico. He had the right to classify it and prevent its publication 'in the national interest.' Ruth was sometimes frustrated with this arrangement, but there was nothing she could do. This latest classified research underpinned today's briefing for the President. It would be wasted on Wallace, she thought.

"Since moving to New Mexico," Ruth began. "I've been able to build much more powerful models of the Sun's activity. Under my contract, I can't publish the results of this research."

"I appreciate that must be frustrating," said Wallace sympathetically, "but it is in our national interest."

"It compromises my integrity as a scientist," Ruth replied sharply. "I appreciate we may disagree on this, but I find that very difficult."

"Dame Ruth, are you implying that you scientists have more integrity than us politicians?"

"Well, with respect Madam President, that is the generally accepted view."

"Dame Ruth, I hope in time to win your respect. But one word of advice from a seasoned old hand. You are now playing in the major league of national security. You'll need to develop a much broader view of 'integrity', both mine and yours. I think you'll come to appreciate that us politicians have to operate in some pretty murky waters. Don't be too hasty to judge us. Now, do please continue with your presentation."

Ruth was pleased to have challenged Wallace head-on but wondered if she had over-played her hand in her first meeting. She wasn't bothered. They couldn't fire her, at least not yet.

She continued explaining her research.

"I have also benefitted from the information gathered by NASA's network of solar satellites, which is pretty good. It is not as good as the Chinese network. They take this threat more seriously than we do. The Chinese probably have better data to put into their models. But we think that our models are more accurate, and we do possess more quantum computing power than they do—at least for the moment."

The President pressed Ruth on the level of risk. She wanted to understand the evidence behind the assertions that a large-scale flare would knock out communications systems. She hadn't forgotten much of her advanced physics from Georgia Tech. She asked Ruth to go through the science in full theoretical detail. She challenged hard but after fifteen minutes of scientific give and take, the President said:

"OK, I'm persuaded. Well, nearly persuaded. Send me more of those scientific papers you mentioned, and I'll go over them in detail. I'll come back to you directly if I have questions. Now, assume I'm convinced that one of these flares would be devastating to our economy, what's the risk of one happening anytime soon?"

"My latest models suggest that we are now entering a critically dangerous phase in the cycles of solar activity. I have been worried about this for some time. Two years ago, I thought the Sun would reach peak activity in 5–7 years' time. Now, I am pretty confident that we will enter the most dangerous phase in 2–3 years' time," Ruth explained.

"Well as long as it comes after my re-election, that would be good. I'm not sure I'd want to run on a record of having left my nation defenseless if this threat ever actually happens."

The Chief of Staff cut in.

"Dan will cover our defenses, but Ruth needs to wrap up presenting the science and then Dan will brief you on what we can do to protect America."

Ruth continued.

"We are already picking up increased frequency of large flares. These are reaching out tens of millions of miles into space. The Earth is just over ninety million miles out. At this distance, this scale of flare poses no threat. However, the flares seem concentrated on a particular plane, which unfortunately is the very plane on the Earth's axis. Now, a mega-flare reaching out all the way to Earth would probably last about a day or two. We only have a one in 180 to one in 365 chance of our planet being in the wrong place at the wrong time. But my models suggest we are building up to an intensity of activity that could result in over hundred mega-flares being ejected in a couple of years' time. We could be looking at a one in three or one in two chance of direct impact."

"Those aren't good odds. But now Dan can reassure me that we are better prepared than the Chinese."

"Well, Madam President, let me start with the Chinese program. As Ruth said, they have been taking this threat very seriously for nearly a decade. They have some of their best scientists working on their research program. You'll have seen that they have twice as many satellites in orbit around the sun as we do. In addition to their scientific efforts, they have directed the People's Liberation Army Intelligence Corps and the

Ministry of State Security to prioritize theft of intellectual property from Western universities.

"Unfortunately, there wasn't much useful IP for them to steal from the Pentagon's program, which was unsuccessful. But they did steal the IP from a start-up in Cambridge, England run by Ruth's husband. You may remember the papers on that in your transition briefing."

"I remember it well. I felt for you and your husband, Dame Ruth. I've been there. It's not a fun time being a parent when your kids are that age."

"Madam President, you authorized a two-pronged strategy," Dan continued. "First to acquire the UK IP and transfer it to the US, which we have done successfully—that is codenamed MEXICAN GAME. And second, to launch deception programs on the Chinese to degrade and weaken their program, codenamed DOUBLE TAKE.

First, the DOUBLE TAKE program. We have successfully compromised the testing equipment being used by the Chinese. We have also fed promising (but ineffective) research ideas back to China. Our staff in the Cambridge business have 'made' these discoveries—or rather they have been fed them from our facility in New Mexico. These ideas look good on paper, but don't actually work in practice. The Chinese spy in the Cambridge facility feeds them back to Beijing without realizing that they are largely worthless. The Chinese lead scientist, Ma Jing, and his team then test them on their version of Solar Shield, using the testing machines we have mis-calibrated. Lo and behold, the test results show progress.

"Last month, the Research Director proudly reported to President Han that they had achieved 100 percent effectiveness and were ready to move into full scale production.

"Han has authorized a large-scale manufacturing effort in China, under the brand of One Shield. Han has also commissioned a global information program to be run by Chinese intelligence and a disinformation campaign, which they have sub-contracted to the Russians. President Bortsov was only too keen to accept this commission. He is still smarting from his humiliation in the Caucuses. He sees this as his chance to get retribution against America for their defeat and two decades of economic sanctions. The Russians have put their best teams on this campaign to spread disinformation minimizing the threat from a solar flare strike. Just as they did with the Covid and Bird Flu vaccines.

"The positive information campaign run out of Beijing will be targeted at Chinese allies and client states, especially in Africa and Central Asia. It will correctly flag the risks of extreme space weather and will highlight Chinese scientific leadership in the field. Han then intends to offer One Shield at cost to friendly nations as part of his expanded 'One Belt, One Road, One Shield' program."

"And what are the Russians up to?" asked the President.

"Well, the Chinese do respect Russian capabilities in disinformation," Dan replied. "Han was hugely impressed with their work in the Ukraine war and before that during the Covid-19 pandemic in undermining Western acceptance of vaccines. They also nearly scored a home run with the campaign to undermine American support for the Caucuses War. It's just as well we won that before Congress cut funding completely. Han has commissioned the Russians to run campaigns saying that space weather is a hoax. They're channeling money to politicians who speak out against spending government money on R&D into space weather. On social media, the mere mention of the risks from space weather generates aggressive trolling. Ruth has had to come off all social media as she was a prime target for the abuse. And the Russians are also funding religious groups who believe that this is all God's will and proof of the Second Coming."

"Now you be careful there, Mr. McCraig. I value the support I get from the religious right, and I will always stand up for their constitutional right to believe that the "end of the world is nigh"—as long as they believe it is coming after my next election and they still show up to vote!"

"I didn't mean any disrespect, Madam President. The Russian disinformation campaign is already well underway and building momentum. I realize that us officials need to stay out of politics, but I can't hide from you that the anti-space weather belief is particularly strong in your party."

"I know. I've had Senator Landry and his friends onto me already," Wallace explained. "Not a penny of federal money on this hoax. That's his line. And our friends at the Pentagon haven't helped. What on earth were they thinking? I had to fire the top brass for that little problem."

"Just because the Pentagon program had problems doesn't mean the threat isn't there," Ruth interceded.

"I know, Dame Ruth. I may be more conservative than you would wish, but I'm no fool."

Ruth felt embarrassed and wished she had kept quiet. She didn't want to push her luck in this first meeting.

"So, here's what you are telling me," Wallace continued. "The threat is real, it's increasing and within two to three years, we could get a devastating solar flare strike on Earth. My party and my political base all think this is a hoax and will block any federal funding on this research. The Chinese are taking it seriously, but you have undermined their program, so they are not as well protected as they think they are. They're covering themselves in sunscreen which they think is factor fifty, but is only factor five—wow, that could be painful! That's bad for them but shutting down the Chinese economy for a few months is also bad for us. Now tell me the good news."

"We do have some good news. Our MEXICAN GAME program has been an outstanding success. Our team in New Mexico, led by Ruth's husband Steve, has had a series of breakthroughs. Our material is now extremely effective."

"Factor fifty?"

"Factor 500, Madam President. A single, two square yard piece of this fabric can create a protective field with a 100-yard radius. It is extremely effective. We now need to ramp up production and work out how to deploy the material. And that's the hard bit. We need to get two square meters of

Solar Shield on every home, office, factory, hospital, military installation, courthouse, prison – you name it, every single building in the United States and in all of our overseas territories. That's not easy."

"Well, Mr. McCraig, it's not much use if your clever material is just stacked up in your secret lab down in that desert facility in New Mexico. How do you plan to manufacture it and deploy it?"

"As I said, that isn't easy. We are running low on funding. To date, the program has been funded jointly by the CIA and MI6 with various 'black' pots of money, but we've exhausted those. We need more funding urgently, or else we will need to shut the program down within weeks."

The President got up from her chair and walked over to the windows behind her desk. She looked out at the White House gardens for a moment. She needed some time to think. It was clear that she didn't welcome the news she had been given, but she was taking it very seriously. She spoke in her low, soft Southern drawl. Very controlled, very polite, and very authoritative.

"Well, Dame Ruth, I'm impressed with your science. And Dan, I am impressed with the progress you've made in undermining the Chinese program.

"But right now, you're telling me that I and the American people are completely 100 percent unprotected from this clear and present danger. To put it more bluntly, you have just told me that I'm standing stark naked in the desert with no sunscreen.

"And if this thing hits, the US economy shuts down for several months. And that sounds like the best case. It could be even worse if we lose all our electronic storage records.

"You have some neat piece of technology that you don't know how to deploy. And no funding to roll it out. That's not good enough.

"Remind me again what President Han did to the previous head of research on the Chinese program. Wasn't he sent off for re-education in Western China?"

"That's if he was lucky, Madam President. He almost certainly didn't make it to the re-education facilities."

"Well, Dan. I want you to come back here in one month's time with a plan. A plan to manufacture your product at scale and deploy it across the entire United States of America and all our overseas facilities.

"And you'll need to work out how to fund it, as I can't see Congress approving one cent to protect our fellow citizens against this so-called 'space weather hoax'.

"So that's your Mission—and you'd better deliver on it. Or I'll be sending you off to be the FBI Bureau Chief in Belfry, Montana. The last time I passed through that fine town on my campaign, I noticed it had a population of three hundred, but a surprisingly good high school football team. Mr. McCraig, in one month, you'll deliver me a good plan. Or else you'll be coaching the Belfry Bats in your spare time. Understood?"

"Yes, Madam President."

"Ruth, don't you worry though. I think you and I are going to become the best of girlfriends."

Ruth was silent. She couldn't imagine anything worse than being friends with Wallace. Ruth despised her political views. But the President was smart, and she was listening to the science. It was hard to resist that charm too. Ruth wondered perhaps if she'd been too quick to judge Wallace.

Allies, perhaps, Ruth thought.

Friends, never.

CHAPTER 11

HARVEY'S RESTAURANT, WASHINGTON D.C.

April

The *maître d'* showed Senator Landry to his table. Harvey's had recently reopened after a long refurbishment, which had restored the interior as an exact replica of the restaurant during its prime in the 1950s and 1960s. It had been the original 'power lunch' restaurant in Washington D.C.. Back in its heyday, Senators, Representatives, administration officials, and spies all hung out there for lunch.

Since reopening, Harvey's was slowly reclaiming its position as the premier power lunch spot in Washington, helped by generous discounts on the meals for self-styled power brokers such as Senator Landry. As discounts were not allowed under Senate ethics rules, the Senator was given his own menu, which just happened to have lower prices.

The walls were covered in framed black-and-white photos of frequent guests. As a concession to the passing of time, the display now included more current political figures, especially those who frequented Harvey's regularly. Senator Landry was very pleased that the *maître d'* had hung his photo right in the line of sight of the guests who sat at his regular table. The Senator was always keen that his guests knew how important he was.

Landry was a portly man. He was about 5'6" and quite seriously overweight. He looked older than his fifty-five years, with a ring of fluffy white hair on his otherwise bald head. His cheeks were slightly flushed, giving him a gentle cherubic appearance. He had the courtesy and charm of many Southerners. In the Senate, he was known for his implacable partisanship and fiscal conservatism. He was not alone in the Senate in that regard. Where he stood out was in his self-promotion as 'America's Most Patriotic Senator.' This infuriated his colleagues, on both sides of the aisle, who all considered themselves patriots. Senator Landry was unrepentant. The moniker polled well in his home state. His supporters were proud to be represented by such a committed patriot.

Like many Senators, he had a 100 percent record in voting for more spending on the military. But he alone had led the campaign over many years for the "I Believe in America" Act. This required not only schools, but also all elected officials, government employees, and military officers to pledge allegiance to the flag every morning at the start of the working day. He wasn't called the 'Senator for Old Glory' for nothing. He also secured federal funds (he didn't oppose all federal spending) for flag factories in his state, which now controlled nearly fifty percent of all flag manufacturing in America. Presidential hopefuls always stopped by one of his state's factories for the mandatory photo-op.

As a committed patriot, he was also a strong supporter of the intelligence agencies. Today's lunch was with his friend Aaron Douglass Thomson, the Director of the CIA. Landry's senior position on both the Intelligence Committee and as Chair of the Appropriations Committee positioned him well to support the CIA. He'd never turned down a request.

Director Douglass Thomson was a Washington D.C. native. He had been born in Southeast Washington, one of the most depressed parts of the city in the late 1980s. Back then, Washington had terrible crime and drug problems. It was the "nation's murder capital" with nearly five hundred murders a year. The first child of a single mother, Aaron had been born in one of the most violent neighborhoods in the city. He was one of the lucky few. His talents were spotted by an inspirational teacher who took a close interest in Aaron's education. He made it through the public school system and won a scholarship to Howard University in the Northwest quadrant of the city. Howard was one of America's leading historically Black colleges. He'd graduated top of his class and then joined the Foreign Service. In his early thirties, he became a career intelligence official and rose through the ranks. President Wallace had broken the recent run of political appointees by nominating this career official as CIA Director. Douglass Thomson was confirmed unanimously by the Senate.

The *maître d'* showed the Director to the Senator's table.

"Mr. Director, great to see you!"

"Senator, very good to see you too. And can I introduce my colleague, Dan McCraig? He's one of our technical experts. I think you'll enjoy meeting him."

"Well, Aaron, always good to meet you and your colleagues. But first, and most important, please tell me about your lovely wife. I hear she has not been well."

"Senator, thank you asking. Ailsa's much better now. The chemo has worked, and the doctors say she's in remission. It's a huge relief."

"Aaron, I am so pleased for you both."

With that pleasantry out of the way, the Senator got back to business.

"I hope you don't mind meeting here at Harvey's. I appreciate it may bring back bad memories for you Agency types."

"I'm not sure I understand, Senator."

"Well, Aaron, it was in this restaurant, at this very table, I believe, that your former colleague James Angleton used to meet up for lunch with his friend at the British Embassy. K or J or P or something, the Head of the MI6 Section here in Washington. Well, Angleton would drown three or four, or sometimes five, martinis and then reveal all the CIA's best secrets. His Brit friend held his martinis better than your former colleague. After lunch, the Brit would go back to his house on Nebraska Avenue and send a telegram to his handlers in Moscow. And all that happened right here, at this table, all those years ago."

"It was not our Agency's finest hour, Senator."

"Trust the Brits to send a Soviet spy to be their head of station here in the capital of their closest ally."

"To be fair, Senator, the Brits didn't know Kim Philby was a Soviet spy when they sent him over here."

"Well, hell! They damn well should have realized. It was obvious. Philby Senior hated the Brits. In fact, his Daddy hated the Brits so much that he persuaded the first King of Saudi to chuck out the British oil guys and bring in some good ol' American oil guys. I'm very grateful he did, to be honest. My own Daddy's fortune in oil owed quite a bit to Mr. Philby Senior.

"Anyway, the Brits really should have known. And your former colleague should have noticed something strange about Mr. Philby. His first name, for starters. We don't have any men called Kim where I come from. That's a woman's name in my part of the county. And most of his pinko friends at Cambridge were obviously security risks. But you East Coast types with your fancy Ivy League educations can sometimes miss things. Where I come from, we may not have the same classy education as you folks, but we do learn a lot in the school of hard knocks. I can tell you that I may not have a first-class degree in political science like you do, but I do have a first-class degree in bullshit detection. I can spot bullshit at one thousand yards. Some smooth-talking Brit like that Philby guy wouldn't get his treasonous bullshit past me."

"No, I am sure he would not, Senator. And these days, rest assured, when it comes to our British friends in Washington, we apply the old Russian proverb: 'trust but verify.' We double-check all their clearances nowadays. The Brits are good allies and they have helped us a lot recently. Their signals intelligence was critical to our victory in the Caucasus. And they are being very helpful on some of our current problems with the Russians in the Balkans."

The Senator called over the *maître d'* and ordered for the table.

"We'll start with a round of martinis for the table—in honor of Mr. Angleton's lunches with Mr. Philby. And then I'll have the crab to start and then the prime rib. My friends here will no doubt order some healthy salads. But then they do not have a long session in the Senate ahead of them tonight."

"What's keeping you up late tonight, Senator?"

"I'll be first up on our filibuster to kill the D.C. Statehood bill. A couple of my Republican colleagues have gone all weak-kneed. They've fallen for that nonsense about how we fought a revolution on the principle of 'no taxation without representation.' They think there's some principled case to support D.C. Statehood. If they support the bill, it will pass. Well, I say, over my dead body. I think there's a very principled case to prevent two more progressive Democratic Senators flipping control of the Senate. I'm ready to talk this one out all night and well into tomorrow afternoon if need be."

As a lifelong Washington resident, Aaron nearly spoke up in defense of D.C. Statehood. He had won his high school's debating contest with a speech in favor of the proposition "This House deplores the disenfranchisement of half a million American residents who live in Washington D.C." Now, the district had nearly one million citizens. There had been a remarkable renaissance over the last forty years and Washington D.C. had changed from the nation's murder capital to one of the fastest growing, and most livable, cities in America. Aaron thought it was shocking that one million citizens, half of them African Americans, were still denied the vote in Congressional elections. But he thought he'd better keep quiet. He didn't want to antagonize the Senator.

Aaron and Dan did indeed order salads, and they just sipped at their martinis. When Senator Landry took a bathroom break, they topped up his Martini with the remains of theirs.

Dan leaned over to Aaron and spoke quietly. With all the background noise in the restaurant, he was confident no-one could hear.

"Sir, are you sure it's a good idea to ask Landry for his help on APOLLO PROTECT? He's a noted sceptic and is on the war path against the Pentagon's failed program."

"It's a risk, Dan, I know," replied Aaron. "But we need to test him out. If we scare him on the China angle, he might be willing to give us some covert funding. But if it's a dead-end, we need to know that soon. We're either going to have to work with Landry, or work around Landry. Anyway, end of discussion. He's on the way back now. I'll lead the conversation, Dan. Stick with the plan."

When the Senator returned, he didn't seem to notice that his Martini glass was now full. He took a large draw as he settled into his chair.

"Senator, we were keen to meet today to update you on some work we are doing where we'd value your support. Dan here is the expert. Perhaps he can summarize."

"Please do. If it's good for the US and bad for China, I'm all ears."

"Well, Senator," Dan began. "It does concern China. We have been tracking their research programs very closely. They have made a very significant investment in research into the Sun. As you know they have twice as many solar satellites orbiting the Sun as we do. They control ninety percent of the world market in solar panels. And one of their scientists recently won the Nobel Prize for his research into solar cycles."

"I bet they stole that research from one of our guys."

"Not this time. This was all their research. There's plenty of other research that they have stolen. The Nobel Prize they won last year in chemistry was based on work from some poor academic here in the US. They hacked into his computer to access his research and then, before he could publish his own work, an international student made claims of sexual harassment. The university obviously didn't know she was a junior officer in the People's Liberation Army. The poor innocent academic's career was destroyed. When the Chinese won the Nobel with his research, he killed himself. It was all really sad."

"Just shows that we need to stand up to China more. That's why I have sponsored the "Time to Confront China" Bill."

"Yes, Senator, we appreciate your help. That bill has important funding for our China program. Thank you. But back to Dan."

"Senator, one of the Chinese programs that we have been tracking has been their work on space weather. You will be familiar with this. We are concerned by the very real possibility that a huge solar flare could reach Earth and knock out all of our electronic communications systems. The Chinese have invested a great deal of funding in their program, and they have achieved breakthroughs recently. They have developed a material that protects their equipment from a solar flare with 100 percent level of protection. Since the failure of the Pentagon's Space-based Solar Flare Defense program, we have a major 'solar protection gap' with the Chinese."

"Gentlemen, I fear this will be a short conversation. It's disgrace what the Pentagon got up with their secret program. I'm going to hound the culprits out of office. I'm just getting started."

"Senator," Aaron intervened to try and get the conversation back on track, "you're quite right on the Pentagon program. It was a disgrace. A classic Pentagon procurement program —over-engineered, over-ambitious and totally over-run by lobbyists. I'm not going to defend what they did. But there is a real threat here. Could we persuade you to have a confidential briefing on it? We can also share what the Chinese are up to."

"Aaron, my friend. My mind's made on this one. This solar weather nonsense is all a big hoax. I'm surprised at you guys falling for it. I watched the MTX Newshour report on it last night. They had all these scientists saying it was just a big lie. Apparently, it's a conspiracy by a group of tech billionaires trying to shake down the federal government for billions of dollars. It's shameless. They failed the first time with the Pentagon's secret program, and now they're trying again with all these scare stories in the liberal media. Aaron, I'm surprised at you for falling for this. It's the Y2K playbook again. These tech guys come up with some scare story and they persuade the rest of us to pay billions to them to protect us against a fake threat. Nothing happens. And then they have the balls to say 'Well done. It's just as well you spent billions on our services to prevent this from happening. You saved yourselves from disaster.' I say—Y2K was all a scam. We're not falling for it again. If we hadn't done anything about Y2K, it would have been just fine anyway. Now my world class bullshit detector tells me this solar flare nonsense is just one more big scam by Big Tech."

"Senator, I appreciate your skepticism. You should know that all those scientists that you saw on TV are funded by fronts for China and Russia. The scientists don't know it, and we can't reveal that publicly. But any scientist who is a sceptic about space weather will start getting anonymous donations and support from 'concerned citizens.' It's all dirty money from Russian and Chinese agents. Their Twitter accounts will get followed by thousands of Russian and Chinese bots who will like their tweets and retweet them. These scientists think they are rock stars. They get invited on TV and hit the lucrative speaker circuit."

"Well, I still think it's all bullshit," Landry replied. "As do all my good voters. Well, not quite all of them. The 'End of World' sects in my state think this is a gift from God. They pray that the Second Coming will soon be upon us. I'm not going to disabuse them of their hopes for Armageddon. They've been strong supporters of mine—and generous donors. It's a good business predicting the end of the world. It seems to be good repeat business too, as long as you don't overdo it. A gap of seven years seems to be long enough for people to forget your last prediction that the end of the world was coming soon. These good folks actually want it to happen. They certainly won't want their taxes – the few they pay as protected religious organizations – going toward preventing their dreams from coming true. And the rest of the state agrees with me. It's a conspiracy by Big Tech to shake us all down for money."

"Senator, we really think there is something to be concerned about here. There's a real risk. The Chinese have protected themselves. We have not. We need your help to secure funding for a new, CIA-led program to catch up. We'll learn the lessons from the Pentagon fiasco and do it all with proper Intelligence Committee oversight."

The Senator took another large draw on his martini. He leaned back in his chair.

"Gentlemen, it's been a pleasure. I've enjoyed our discussion. But if you were hoping for my support on funding your space weather hoax, then my message is clear: not a chance in hell."

CHAPTER 12

LANGLEY, VIRGINIA

May

Ruth and Dan had had just over a month to prepare for their second meeting with the President. They were nowhere near ready, but they were out of time and had to present a plan.

They had left their first meeting with mixed feelings. President Wallace was clearly smart. Ruth had been impressed with her knowledge of advanced physics. Despite Wallace's reputation as a hard right Republican, she was no 'space weather denier.' She respected the science and saw the risks. That said, she had little room for maneuvering politically, given Republican control of Congress and the resistance from the Republican grassroots voters. The right-wing media was stepping up its campaign against wasting taxpayers' money on this 'Big Tech Hoax.' The President was willing to help and had tasked them with developing a plan. But the conditions Wallace had set made their task all but impossible.

Ruth and Dan had taken the first weekend off. They both felt they needed a break. They knew they weren't going to get another day off again for the next month. That had probably been a mistake as they were now very pushed for time.

Ruth headed back to New Mexico to see the family for the weekend and then flew to Washington D.C. on the red-eye landing at Dulles, early on Monday morning. She was met by a CIA driver, who took her to Langley. They pulled off Route 123 and into the George Bush Centre for Intelligence. Ruth recognized it all from the movies. The great seal on the floor. The famous wall of stars honoring fallen officers. The bright white marble.

Dan greeted her in the lobby.

"Dan, this is amazing. It looks just like it does in the movies."

"That's because this is where they actually do film the movies. We have a whole department here that works with the entertainment industry. We often have film crews in at the weekend. It's a pain as all the officers have to avoid this entrance in case we get caught on film and our covers are exposed.

"We've got a few minutes. Come and see the CIA Museum."

They walked through the security gates and turned left down a long corridor. At the end, there really was a museum. Ruth found it fascinating. She was captivated by the exhibits of old spy cameras, listening devices and other elements of 'tradecraft'. She enjoyed the cabinets setting out the CIA's perspective on the Cold War, Iraq, and Afghanistan. The display on Vietnam made clear what the CIA thought of the Pentagon's intelligence capabilities.

"Yes," said Dan, "that was another Pentagon disaster."

Then Ruth's eye was caught by a dirty sneaker in one cabinet. No mother would have missed it.

"Dan, what's a dirty sneaker doing in here?"

"Those are the sneakers the Navy Seal leader wore for the raid on Bin Laden's compound. Those burn marks are from all the practice jumps abseiling out of helicopters. And the mud is the actual mud from the raid. He never washed his shoes before donating them to the CIA for this museum."

"Sounds like my twins," replied Ruth.

Further along the corridor, and not shown in the movies, was the CIA Gift Shop selling CIA merchandise. Ruth made a note to buy some of this for the twins. It would be good for their Christmas stockings. CIA branded coffee mugs, pens, and Post-it notes, and a nice line in CIA-branded hoodies.

Ruth and Dan walked along a final corridor hung with portraits of CIA Directors – almost all white men, thought Ruth – until they reached the elevators and descended to Basement level Minus 3.

Dan had organized a secure 'brainstorming space' in the bowels of the building. He had expanded the team with more CIA analysts, especially experts on China, and he brought back some former CIA officials who were now in the private sector and still had their clearances. More importantly, they worked in various Washington lobbying and consulting firms and would bring insights into the political challenges that Dan and Ruth would need to overcome.

Dan brought his full team together for a briefing on the Monday after their first meeting with the President.

"Thanks for coming in, everyone. You're probably wondering why you have all been brought here today. I'm sorry I couldn't tell you more last week. But you are now all cleared for this compartment—APOLLO PROTECT is the code name. We'll probably change the name a few more times over the course of the month. This is absolutely the highest level of security classification. You cannot discuss it with anyone who is not in this room here today.

"The President has tasked us to solve a really tough challenge. She has given us one month to solve it. Professor Wright and I have written a short problem statement. I'll give you a few minutes to read it and then we'll break into smaller groups to work out how to approach it.

APOLLO PROTECT—CLASSIFICATION TOP SECRET.

SECURE COMPARTMENT READERS ONLY

Latest US research by Professor Dame Ruth Wright at University of New Mexico predicts a one in two chance of a large-scale solar flare hitting Earth in 2–3 years' time.

Without protection of all electronic infrastructure, the US faces potentially devastating damage. Outages could last 2–3 months. Large-scale loss of life and an economic crisis are inevitable as critical national infrastructure is disabled.

There is a high level of skepticism among US Congressional leaders and the wider population about the nature of this threat. Many dismiss it as a hoax, perpetrated on the American people, these sceptics claim, by the Big Tech firms looking to make money out of Federal investment in protection programs.

Powerful Senators have made clear that there can be no funding for a US response to this alleged 'hoax.' The President does not believe she has the support in Congress or her party to override this block on funding.

While the US has no credible contingency plans, there is a potential technical solution. A fabric developed by a US/UK Joint Venture, funded by the Agency and MI6 in secret, does provide a high degree of protection. Two square yards of this material, Solar Shield, will react with incoming geo-magnetic radiation to protect an area within a radius of one hundred yards.

However, at present, we have no plans for manufacturing this material at scale. We have no credible plan for deployment and installation on the approximate five hundred million properties that need protection across the US and in our overseas territories, embassies, and military bases. And we have no funding for this critical initiative.

Meanwhile, we know that the Chinese have developed a product, largely through IP stolen from the UK. While they have confidence in its effectiveness, we have manipulated their test results. The Chinese are unaware that their product does not work.

The President wants us to present a plan to protect the US from the threat of space weather within one month. We need to demonstrate to her how we could scale up manufacturing of Solar Shield, deploy it across five hundred million locations without any federal funding within 18–24 months at the latest.

The APOLLO PROTECT team read the problem statement. As they each finished, they looked up. The room was quiet. A young Asian American woman spoke up first.

"Dan, I know you said this was a challenging project, but this looks downright impossible."

"That's why I've assembled the A team here today. If you all can't do it, no one can."

One of the China specialists put his hand up.

"For those of you who don't know me, I'm Sean Baines. I lead our China Analysis cell here at Langley. I agree that the President has given us a near-impossible task. It's really tough, but I'm sorry that I am about to make it harder. I have permission from the Director to bring all of you into our most secret compartment on China. Dan, can I have the floor?"

"Sure. I don't think I'm going to like what you are about to tell us, Sean, but go ahead."

"In recent years, we have developed better insight into President Han's strategic thinking. Han gathered his inner circle a few weeks ago and set out his strategy. We are highly confident in our assessment as we have dual sourced it via both HUMINT and SIGINT—for those of you new to this game, that's Human Intelligence, old-fashioned spies, and Signals Intelligence, electronic snooping. I have to give huge credit to our Agency colleagues for collecting this intelligence—with a bit of assistance from the Brits, who gave us some incredible SIGINT. I can't tell you any more about how we got this information but trust me we are highly confident in it.

"Last month, President Han assembled his inner team for a strategy seminar which was titled: "Space weather—a new opportunity for China." As you probably know, Han fancies himself as a master-strategist. He was the Junior Chess Champion for all of China in his youth. He really believes he can out-think and out-strategize the West.

"Chinese science on space weather is now pretty good. Fortunately, we have Professor Wright on our team. Her models are better than the Chinese models. But the Chinese have put more satellites up into solar orbit, so they have much better data than us. Their reporting to Han is more pessimistic than Ruth's analysis. The Chinese team are predicting a 50–75 percent probability of a Carrington level event within 2–3 years. Han shared all that with his team.

"Han said he viewed this not as a threat but as the biggest strategic opportunity for China since the early days of the Covid-19 crisis. After a promising start, their Covid-19 strategy went downhill for China with the failure of the Chinese vaccine roll-out and their inability to maintain a zero Covid strategy. They were surprised at the speed of the Western response, which after a few false starts, allowed the Western economies to emerge much faster than China. But Covid-19 was good for Han personally, and Covid-29 was even better. He made his fortune in PPE sales to the West. And he enriched his supporters in the Party. The embarrassing failure of China's Covid-29 strategy, where they repeated the mistakes from a decade earlier, cleared out the previous leadership making the way for Han's emergence as General Secretary.

"Han is determined not to repeat the mistakes that turned Covid from a short-term strategic success for China into a colossal long-term failure. He is convinced that space weather is his chance to achieve what he is calling a 'great geo-strategic leap forward.' Han believes it will put him into the pantheon of the Great Leaders, alongside Mao.

"He believes that the West is seriously underestimating the threat from space weather. He puts that down to Western decadence, the superiority of the Chinese Model, and the rigors of Han Thinking, the new Chinese Communist Party doctrine. We may disagree on his diagnosis, but we can't disagree on his conclusion that we are hopelessly unprepared.

"Han has been pleased with the success of the Russian disinformation campaign, which has outperformed relative to Han's expectations. He feels he has finally got some payback for his bankrolling Russia over the past two decades.

"Han's strategy is simple. Here it is.

"When the solar flare strikes, the West will be totally disabled for a period of 2–3 months. There will be economic collapse, civil unrest, widespread loss of life, and political chaos. However, China and its client states will be protected due the successful roll-out of their One Shield product.

"Han will use this window of opportunity to launch his long-planned invasion of Taiwan. He has recommitted to reunification before 2049, the centenary of the founding of the People's Republic. The Chinese military have been ready since 2027 to launch an invasion. To date, the US military commitments to Taiwan have forced China to hold back. But if the US is immobilized by a solar flare, it's just too good an opportunity to miss.

"Han has put the Chinese military on notice that they will need to be ready to mobilize and launch an invasion within seventy-two hours of a predicted solar flare strike. His scientists believe that they can predict a strike within seventy-two hours with 90 percent accuracy. Once the flare has left the surface of the Sun, it takes about 24–48 hours to reach the Earth. At that point, when a strike is certain within twenty-four hours, Han will authorize the invasion so that the troops go ashore just as Taiwan's defenses – and the entire US military – are disabled by the solar flare strike. Han's troops will land unopposed and occupy all major Taiwanese cities within twenty-four hours. They will then bring in humanitarian assistance to their 'compatriots' in Taiwan. He is confident that the Taiwanese in their desperation – and seeing the chaos unfolding in the West – will welcome the PLA with open arms. A bloodless reunification of Taiwan with the People's Republic—welcomed by the grateful people of Taiwan. That alone would put Han in the pantheon alongside Mao. But there's more.

"Han has prioritized additional funding for the Chinese 'One Belt, One Road, One Shield' program so that all China's allied states in Africa, Asia (and several Eastern European states too) get access to the One Shield product. He is confident that when the solar flare hits, all Chinese allies will be protected. The success of the Chinese model will be contrasted with the failure of the Western model. Han boasted to his politburo that this will result in a decisive tilt to the East in geo-strategic alliances.

"Our stations in all the China-aligned countries report active information campaigns highlighting the risks of space weather and celebrating the assistance being provided by President Han for implementing protective measures. On our latest count, this will give China a clear majority in the General Assembly and a majority in the Security Council. That said, as New York will be paralyzed by the strike, there won't be much voting going on at the UN in New York. Han will generously offer temporary facilities in Beijing, with a new UN headquarters to be built in Taipei. We think he would have the votes to get that through the General Assembly. He thinks, probably correctly, that the US will be so preoccupied with its own problems that the US won't veto this. Likewise, the French and the UK will let it pass. And even if the US did use its veto, it wouldn't have a credible counteroffer to make to the UN to keep them in New York. Han is confident he can relocate the UN from the US to China.

"He's also planning on a rapid expansion of the Asian Infrastructure Investment Bank in Beijing to take on, temporarily of course, the functions of the World Bank, which will be disabled along with the rest of Washington D.C. And the Chinese Ministry of Finance is preparing large-scale lending facilities to substitute for the International Monetary Fund, which would be out of action for months.

"Han's plan is mad, but it has a certain genius to it. In one leap, Han will discredit the Western economic model, reunify Taiwan with the mainland without firing a shot, switch alliances from the West to China and relocate the post-World War II supranational institutions from the US to China.

"The good news is that he has no idea that we have undermined the effectiveness of his One Shield product. The bad news is that he is 100 percent correct in his assessment that we have no plan to protect our economy and our citizens. At the moment, the best-case scenario is that we in the West go down through lack of protection and China goes down because its protection doesn't work. So, both our economies and societies are equally devastated. Even in that scenario, China looks better than us because at least they tried.

"We briefed the President on this new intel last week. She mentioned her recent meeting with Dan and Ruth and asked us to combine forces. She mentioned the challenge she had given you. She said she was confident you'd be coming back with a plan but asked me to add an additional condition."

"Thanks a lot Sean," said Dan. "Just what we need."

"It's actually two conditions. In addition to manufacturing and installing up to a billion pieces of your magic material without any federal funding, you need to do so without the Chinese finding out."

"So that's the first condition, what's the second?"

"The second one is probably more important for the President. The second condition is that you need to do all this without Congress or the American people finding out either. The election is in eighteen months' time, and she can't be seen to be wasting taxpayers' money on this so-called 'space weather hoax.' She'd never get through the Republican primaries. But it's really the same condition. You can only fool the Chinese if you also fool Congress and the American people."

The room went silent. This was truly an impossible task.

Dan finally spoke up.

"Well, folks, you signed up for a tough challenge—and I can assure you that you'll never come up against a tougher one that this. Let's get to work!"

Dan split his group into three parallel teams, working independently without any interaction.

For the first three days, they came up with as many strategies as they could and then regrouped. Each team shared their best three options. Out of these nine, they winnowed it down to four front-runners. None of them were very promising.

Dan assigned a team to each option. After three days, each team presented back to the full group, and they tore the proposed plan to pieces. They were much better at destroying each other's strategies than they were at developing new ones. But some promising ideas survived the first week.

In the second week, they worked to improve and refine the plans, and ranked them one to four. The final stretch was a 'champion/challenger run-off.' They took strategies one and two and ran full-scale war-games to test how each could unfold. One strategy emerged as the best, and then that was pitted against the third strategy. The winner of that run-off was pitted against the fourth strategy.

By the end of week three, they held the final run-off. The two strategies were given names – 'Truth' and 'Bodyguard of Lies'. The winner would be presented to the President as the recommended option for APOLLO PROTECT.

Ruth led the Team presenting 'Truth'. They proposed that the President should level with the American people and tell them the truth. She would announce that there was a real threat from solar flares and that the US had some technology that might protect America. It would require a national effort costing billions. She would send a bill to Congress seeking approval for the necessary funding. Dan went through all the details and then threw it open to challenge from the group. They tore it to shreds. The political team made a convincing case that the bill would be dead on arrival in Congress. The states would split along party lines and at least half the country would be left unprotected.

Dan got up to present 'Bodyguard of Lies'. Even hardened CIA operatives were impressed by the scale of deception this strategy required. The key was getting the President to accept it and play her part. There were a lot of sceptics. Slowly, a consensus emerged. If they could maintain that level of deception, it might just work. It was the only option that avoided getting caught in the polarization of American politics. But only by lying to everyone.

The team voted overwhelmingly for 'Bodyguard of Lies'. In the final days, they went over it again and again, finding the weak spots and building in contingencies and mitigations.

After a month of fifteen-hour days, Dan and his team were exhausted. Dan dismissed the team.

"Great work, team. You can go home now to your families for the night. Take tomorrow morning off. Ruth and I will be seeing the President first thing. We need to head into town now and get some sleep. We will regroup here afterwards at 2 p.m. and debrief. Wish us luck!"

Ruth and Dan had checked into the Willard Hotel to get a good night's rest before the meeting with the President. Neither slept well. They both ran over the APOLLO PROTECT strategy in their heads as they lay awake. It might just work, though it was a huge gamble. But it was the best plan they could come up with. How would the President react? After restless nights, they met in the foyer at 8.30 a.m. for their 9.30 a.m. meeting at the White House.

The D.C. Statehood protestors were out in force again. The issue was spiraling out of control for the President. It had started as literally an 'inside the Beltway' issue—a classic political issue that only political geeks and residents of the District cared about. But Democratic activists from across the country had latched onto and made it a national issue for Democrats. It was also beginning to divide the Republicans. After years of ignoring the issue, some more libertarian Republicans were holding it up as a symbol of tax injustice. The Republicans were normally against taxation, period. Now some of them were joining the District's cause and opposing taxation without representation.

And it wasn't just the D.C. Statehood protestors making life difficult for anyone wanting to get around central Washington. The British Prime Minister was in town. The roads were closed all around the White House. Ruth and Dan took a circuitous route down to the Mall and then back up to the Western Gate. Ruth was getting to see the sights of Washington. Today at least, they arrived on time. Ruth changed out of her sneakers into a new pair of Prada shoes.

Ruth and Dan waited in the Roosevelt Room for only a few minutes. Dan caught a glimpse of Senator Landry leaving the Oval Office. He wondered why he was there.

The Chief of Staff came out to greet Ruth and Dan. This time they didn't get the cheerful curatorial guide to the Roosevelt Room portraits. He looked pretty glum.

"I am sorry, but the President needs to take a meeting urgently. She sends her apologies. Feel free to make yourselves comfortable here. It should only take half an hour or so."

The Chief of Staff showed them to a small waiting room adjacent to the Roosevelt Room. Various staffers rushed past them into the Oval Office. It looked as though the President had called an urgent political meeting. What had Senator Landry said to her?

The time passed slowly, but eventually the political aides all trooped back out, and Dan and Ruth were summoned into the Oval Office.

"Good morning, everybody," the President said cheerfully. "I am so sorry to have kept you waiting. I hope y'all are doing just fine. I do apologize for my tardiness this morning. I just have a little political problem on my hands. I think I can trust you two with it. Well, if I can't trust you two to keep a secret, I've got bigger problems on my hands.

"It's this D.C. Statehood issue. Senator Landry was telling me that any effort to address this problem is 'DOA - Dead on Arrival' in the Senate. He was proud of his success in killing the last bill. His view is that the D.C. Police aren't being tough enough on these protestors. He says that, as they all live in the District, they have a conflict of interest, and that I should call in out-of-state National Guard and Police forces to control these protests. I pointed out that the D.C. Police hadn't exactly been soft. There have been two deaths in the most recent protests. Last weekend, they used tear gas. Two teenagers had asthma attacks and died right outside the White House. It made America look terrible.

"It's hurting me in the country too. Independents and Democrats obviously support D.C. Statehood—it's hard to justify disenfranchising one million American citizens. But worse, I am losing some Republican support from the libertarian wing, who are rediscovering their Revolutionary zeal for overthrowing oppressive regimes that tax Americans without a vote.

"I've got no good options. I could concede and lose my party's control of Congress, or I could tough it out and lose the support of voters across the spectrum. Politically, I just cannot concede D.C. Statehood. The last thing I need is two more Democratic Senators and at least one more Democrat in the House, but I need a solution. The first President created this problem and the next fifty Presidents have ignored it. Why did it land on my desk?

"Sorry to bore you with this. This is my political problem. But I always say that a problem shared is a problem solved. Don't you think?"

"Madam President," interrupted the Chief of Staff, "we need to talk about the plan for APOLLO PROTECT. And we don't have long, as you need to go and see the British PM, who is already in the Rose Garden."

"I had better go and pretend to be best friends with the British Prime Minister. It's all part of the Special Relationship. The press is constantly looking for tension between us. To be honest Ruth, I really don't like this one. And he was mad to fire you. But his loss is my gain. I had better put on my 'best friends' face and go and make nice with him."

At that point, the Marine Band outside struck up *God Save the King*.

"Oh yes. I need to get up to speed on this plan. You'd better be quick. We've got about three minutes. The Marine Band can stretch out any national anthem for that long if they think I'm running late... but after three minutes, it gets embarrassing. So, Dan and Ruth, do you have a plan?"

"Yes, Madam President," said Dan reassuringly.

"Will it work?

"Possibly. It's a real long shot, but it's the best we can come up with."

"Will I like it?"

"I doubt it, Madam President. We don't think you'll like it at all, but it's the only show in town."

"Time to go, Madam President. You are needed in the Rose Garden," pressed her Chief of Staff.

"Dan, it will have to wait till I get back from this trip with the PM. I'm back on Friday. Take me through it then."

The Marine Band struck up the *Star Bangled Banner.*

As the President left through the French doors leading on the colonnade, she started singing and picked up the final bars.

"O say does that star-spangled Banner yet wave, o'er the land of the free and the home of the brave?"

CHAPTER 13

CAFÉ AMALFI, WASHINGTON D.C.

May

irector Douglass Thomson was hosting lunch today, and he got to pick the restaurant. For his regular catch-up with Senator Landry, he had picked Café Amalfi, the other popular power lunch choice for the Washington elite. This restaurant was on the waterfront in Georgetown, further from the center of D.C. but still full of Congressional and Administration figures. Aaron had invited Sir Leslie Fayne to join the lunch with Senator Landry.

Aaron arrived early and was shown to his preferred table at the rear of the restaurant, where he was less likely to get buttonholed by passing journalists or lobbyists. He also sat with his back to the bar. His security detail was on the adjacent table looking as discreet, as CIA bodyguards always look. Short hair, smart suits, white shirts, sunglasses, perfect physiques.

Sir Leslie arrived on time and joined Aaron at the table. They had spent the morning together in Langley with Dan and his team going over the plan. As always, Sir Leslie was willing to step up and front the private sector part of the plan. And as always, he cut a very attractive deal for Fayne Capital. Sir Leslie's patriotism and support for the UK/US Special Relationship came at a price—a very high price, but one that both the CIA and MI6 were happy to pay. The results were plainly visible.

Fayne Capital's intervention in buying Solar Shield Limited in Cambridge had been critical in preserving the cover of the entire program. He had taken a healthy commission on that transaction. He had also been happy to accept MI6's money and gift it in his own name to fund Ruth's professorship at the University of New Mexico. He hadn't received any direct payment for that donation, but it helped him win *Time* Magazine's Philanthropist of the Year Award and several puff pieces in the British and US press. That award enhanced his already legendary status with the glamorous young models in the New York fashion world. Sir Leslie was now without question the most eligible and most sought-after bachelor in the city.

When the Director had called him the week before, he immediately agreed to fly down to Langley. He was happy to help, especially on such a critical program, where the national interest so clearly aligned with Sir Leslie Fayne's personal interest. This one sounded like a lot of fun too.

Dan, Ruth, and their ARTEMIS ARISE team (this was their sixth code name in as many weeks) briefed Sir Leslie on the problem that the President had set and took him through their proposed plan. Fayne had seen some bold and innovative ideas in his career as an investor, but this one was quite something. The President had set the team an impossible task. Protect five hundred million homes and buildings within two years with no federal funding and without anyone finding out what was going on. Amazingly, the team seemed to have found a way through. Even Sir Leslie was impressed, and he was looking forward to playing his part. It was an added bonus that his involvement was starting with a good lunch at his favorite Georgetown restaurant, Café Amalfi.

Senator Landry arrived late. It took him at least ten minutes to work his way to the back of the restaurant. Lobbyists greeted him at almost every table. While they waited, Sir Leslie and Aaron Douglass Thomson watched the TVs over the bar. To preserve its bi-partisan appeal, Café Amalfi always played the right-wing media on the TV at one end of the bar, and the left-wing media on the TV at the other end.

Two stories dominated the news that day.

The first item on both channels was D.C. Statehood. 'Radical left-ists infiltrate D.C. Statehood movement' was the headline on the TV showing the MTX Newshour. 'Police brutality leaves three dead in latest D.C. Statehood protests' led the story on the ANN channel at the other end of the bar.

The second item was space weather. 'Top scientist denounces space weather as a Big Tech Hoax.' Or for patrons who didn't like that version of the story, the other TV channel was reporting 'Growing concern over space weather protection. China leads world. West dangerously exposed, says top scientist.'

Finally, Senator Landry made it through the gauntlet of lobbyists and journalists to join Aaron and Sir Leslie.

"Sorry, I'm late, Mr. Director. I was delayed by the protests across town—and then by all these lobbyists and hacks in here! Can't your security detail clear a path for me next time?"

"I'm not sure our excellent CIA bodyguards provide that level of protection, Senator. But perhaps next time we'll arrange for you to get in through a side entrance."

"Next time, we'll be back at Harvey's. I know it brings back bad memories for you Agency types... Kim Philby flashbacks and all that. But it's good to keep you on your toes. You've got to keep honing your bullshit detectors. We can't have you lot falling for smooth-talking treasonous Brits again, can we?"

"Indeed not, Senator. Can I introduce my good friend, Sir Leslie Fayne? You must have heard of his incredibly successful venture capital fund. He is also a trusted friend of the Agency. And don't worry, the CIA did his clearance. He's definitely on our side. Sir Leslie and I would like to put a proposition to you over lunch."

"First things first, gentlemen. We need a round of martinis. Well, I definitely need one after that nightmare journey across town. I've had it with the D.C. Statehood protests. In fact, I'm seeing the President on this again next week. This time it is at her request. I'll be pressing her to get tough. Us Republicans need to put an end to this insurrection. We can't have violent mobs rampaging around the Capitol and the White House just because they don't like what's written in the Constitution. The Founding Fathers decided not to make the District into a state—and that's the end of it."

"Well Senator, that's certainly true. But I don't think the Founding Fathers ever imagined the District of Columbia would be a city of one million people. Back in 1790, when George Washington picked this site, it was a hundred square miles of swamps, scrubland, forests, and a couple of creeks. There were a few colonial buildings here in Georgetown, too, I suppose. At most back then, there were a thousand or two thousand citizens living in the District. There were also several thousand slaves. But, as you know, my ancestors got a pretty raw deal in the Constitution. George Washington's Federal District was nothing like the major metropolis we have now. I doubt the Founding Fathers really wanted to disenfranchise the one million American citizens living here today."

"Hold your horses, Mr. Director. You're getting political now. That's my job, not yours. You stick to the spying stuff. By the way, I sure hope you have dropped all that nonsense you were talking about with that solar flare hoax."

"Absolutely, Senator." Aaron said reassuringly. "We've dropped all that. Your advice was very timely and wise."

"That's good to hear, my friend. You made the right call. Now what's this proposition you want to put to me?"

"Senator, as you know, the Agency's remit has expanded these days from the traditional 'cloak-and-dagger' stuff of intelligence and national security. We now do a lot more on economic security, especially in relation to China. The Chinese have dedicated large parts of their security apparatus to work out how to damage the US economy. We need to fight back."

"Damn right we do. And I have always been your friend on that when it comes to appropriating the money you need to stand up to the Chinese."

"We need your help again, Senator. But we don't actually need federal money. We need your help with your state legislature and your friend, the Governor. It's not a big ask. And we think this proposition is great for America, great for your state, and I am sure Sir Leslie can make it great for you personally, too."

"I'm all ears. Fire away, Sir Leslie. While you talk, I'm getting a second martini."

Fayne took a sip of his sparkling water and began.

"Senator, I was asked a few months ago to advise a CIA team working on an industrial strategy to reclaim American leadership in the fabric industry. As you know, Chinese dumping and unfair competition wiped out most of our domestic industry. Even our flags now rely on imported cotton."

"That's a national disgrace. My state leads in flag production, but even our factories had to switch to importing the cotton. Otherwise, they'd have gone out of business. Some of our former cotton towns lost thirty, forty, fifty percent of their jobs. It was just terrible for the poor families."

"Indeed, Senator," commented Aaron. "The Chinese targeted this industry and they won. We were asleep at the wheel. That's why we've been working with some of our trusted partners in the private sector to develop a response. Back to you, Sir Leslie."

"My firm, Fayne Capital, has been backing a number of promising start-ups in the synthetic cotton industry. One of them now has a fantastic cotton substitute, which we can manufacture at scale here in America at a price that undercuts imported Chinese and Asian fabrics. It is indistinguishable from real cotton and costs half the price. And as it will be 100 percent American, we'll be branding it the 'Fabric of America.' We think that will allow for some great advertising campaigns with a strong patriotic theme.

"Fayne Capital is prepared to fund this expansion. We'll do it at scale and with the latest technology. We think we need to build two large-scale factories to supply all of the demand in America. Our aim is to completely substitute Chinese and Asian imports. We've been looking across the states for the right location for our first Fabric of America 'giga factory.' This will generate over one thousand new high-quality manufacturing jobs. We want a state that is pro-business and with low, ideally no, taxes. We need a 'Right to work' state as we can't afford Union labor. We need rapid planning approvals. And we don't want to get tied up in a bunch of environmental lawsuits by animal rights activists protecting some rare insect breeding site. We have a short list of five states, including your great state. We'd like your help."

The Senator ordered another martini and leaned forward across the table. He lowered his voice and spoke in a conspiratorial tone.

"Well, gentlemen, that does sound like a really interesting proposition. I am always keen to help bring jobs and growth to my state. There's a problem though. This sort of local economic development and state lobbying though doesn't really fit with my broader responsibilities as a Senator. I would need to think through the propriety of my using my office as a Senator to help on this."

"We quite understand, Senator. We recognize that we need to respect your status as a Senator working on national issues. We can see that lobbying your own Governor might not look good. We often work in these situations with close associates. For instance, in this case, we could work directly with your wife and her very successful lobbying firm here in D.C., or we could work with your brother's firm back in the State— or both."

"Sir Leslie, that's mighty thoughtful of you. And that might help. I personally couldn't take a lead here. But as you say, my wife runs her own independent business. We have a strict separation of our professional interests. I'd see no problem in your working with her. My brother's firm doesn't really do lobbying. They are more of a financial advisory outfit. For instance, they run my blind trust."

Aaron waved at the waiter for the check. He was keen to wrap this up quickly as the Senator seemed to be willing to help.

"We can certainly be discreet here, Senator. If you can't trust the CIA to be discreet, who can you trust? Sir Leslie, can you just wrap up, as I think the Senator needs to go soon."

"Certainly. Senator, I won't discuss this proposition with you anymore, but if it's OK with you, I will follow up with your wife's firm here in D.C. I'll be in touch with your brother's firm to explain the Fayne Capital 'Friends and Family' investment program. Of course, it will be an independent decision for the trustees of your blind trust, but we do offer very advantageous terms to 'friends and family' for some of our major investment programs. The principle is that you commit funds, but they only get drawn once the investment's success is assured. If the investment fails, we don't ask you to pay the money and Fayne Capital writes it off. We put it all down to relationship-building, which will pay off in the long term for Fayne Capital. Over time, we do fine. But our friends and family investors win every time."

"That sounds like a sure bet."

"It pretty much is—and for this investment, it's a sure bet for America, too. Rebuilding our textile industry, creating jobs, pushing back against China, and making a handsome return for patriots, who are willing to invest in America."

The Senator drained his third martini and leaned back in his chair.

"I'm all in."

CHAPTER 14

OVAL OFFICE, WHITE HOUSE, WASHINGTON D.C.

May

President Wallace got up from the Resolute desk. This was the historic, 19th century desk that most Presidents chose to work at. President Wallace found it reassuring to know that other Presidents had sat here and worked through crises even more daunting that those she faced. She stood in front of the desk when she wanted to intimidate her staff. This made it clear to them that she wasn't planning on sitting down. That put them on the defensive.

Her political team were assembling. They knew she was in a diffi-cult mood. Until she sat down, they couldn't sit down. She showed no sign of sitting down. This was going to be a standing-up meeting. They knew they were about to face the full blast of the famous Wallace temper. She rarely lost her temper, but when she did, she crushed her staff with a cold fury that they never forgot. Most of the time she managed to maintain her poise and composure even when provoked. Famously, she showed charm and conciliation throughout the Presidential debates as her Democratic opponent become more and more heated. But today, she was not at all happy with her political team. They were braced for an unpleasant dressing down in the Oval Office.

"So, this is the best plan you can come up with to neutralize the D.C. Statehood issue, is it?"

The Chief of Staff felt he had to carry the can for this one, so he spoke up.

"We recognize the political challenges posed to you by this D.C. Statehood issue. We have tested it from all angles, and we really think this is the best approach."

What was really scary about President Wallace when she got angry was that she lowered her voice and spoke in a cold, calm, quiet tone. All the charm was stripped out. She conveyed anger and disdain in equal measure. The political team stood uncomfortably. No one wanted to look the President in the eye in case she called on them to justify their plan. They didn't want to look at the carpet or the paintings on the wall as then they would look evasive. They didn't know where to look. They all hoped this meeting would be over soon. Perhaps she would just throw them out. No such luck.

"OK, then let's go through it. Your plan has three parts. First, tough out the civil unrest in Washington D.C. by calling in more police from outside the District. Second, rely on the Republican majority to block the bill in Congress and if they fail, I have to veto the bill. Third, defend no votes for D.C. on the grounds that that was the intent of the Founding Fathers. Have I got your plan right?

"Yes. Exactly."

"That's what I feared. OK let take them one by one. Point One. Get tough on the protestors. Violence on both sides has escalated. We've had ten deaths this month. Two police have been wounded. Last Sunday the police shot a fourteen-year-old in the back as he ran away. He wasn't armed. He was just a kid attending a political demonstration because he wanted to vote for Congress when he grew up. It was the first political event he'd ever attended. He got scared and wanted to run home to his mother. And now he's dead. Your plan is that we get more police in from out of state to shoot more kids, is that right?"

"That incident was very unfortunate, Ma'am. It is being investigated. We do think the D.C. Police have a conflict of interest here. They are being tough but not tough enough. A more robust approach would restore order faster."

"And as part of your 'get tough' approach, you are also recommending more prosecutions of our fellow citizens for exercising their First Amendment rights of free speech and free assembly."

"Madam President, we think the violence gives us grounds to prosecute the protestors despite their First Amendment rights."

"And which jury of their peers made up of D.C. Residents is going to convict these protestors—especially when their defense attorneys introduce compelling evidence of police overreaction? I just don't think the US Attorney's Office for DC is going to bring these cases, either as Federal or District crimes. And if we ever did get a case to court, no District jury would convict. You guys just aren't thinking.

"So that's Point one rejected. Now Point two. Block it and then I veto the bill if it ever emerges from Congress. Now you may remember my election. People who liked my politics voted for me and that got me two hundred and fifty electoral college votes. But what got me the majority – in fact, what got me the landslide – was that a lot of people who didn't like my politics still voted for me. They liked my principles and my values. Old-fashioned, I know. But it worked. Now please, you political experts, give me the principled reason why I should veto a bill that gives one million Americans the right to vote in Congressional elections. Just try. I'm keen to hear."

The Oval Office fell silent. The President let the silence run for at least two minutes. The longer the silence ran, the harder it was for anyone to speak up.

"That's Point two dispatched with. Point three... Argue the Constitution. Well, well, well. Are any of you lot lawyers? Most of you are, I know, so don't be shy. Didn't they teach you anything in law school about how to argue a case in court? When you can argue the facts, argue the facts. When you can't argue the facts, argue the law. When you can't argue the law, argue the Constitution.

"Arguing the Constitution is the refuge of advocates with weak cases. Do you also suggest that I also propose that Native Americans should have no votes as they are not recognized as citizens in the Constitution? Or that slavery should be allowed to continue, with African Americans having no votes but being counted as three fifths of a free person to increase the representation of slave states in Congress? Believe me, I love the Constitution almost as much as I love the flag. But it's not perfect. It needs to evolve with the times and that's why we have all those amendments. Remember them?

"To sum up. Your advice is that I run next year on the promise that although we have changed the Constitution and enfranchised the African Americans and Native Americans, one million good, law-abiding citizens of D.C. will still be denied the right to be represented in Congress. And why? Just because it's politically inconvenient to my party. It's just not good enough. You're meant to be the political A team. I am very disappointed.

"Meeting over. You are all dismissed."

The Chief of Staff stayed on. He felt he needed to apologize and take the sting off her anger.

The President was having none of it.

"You are dismissed, too. I'll need to solve this on my own."

She called her diary secretary. "Cancel my next meeting. I need time to think. Then what do I have? JUPITER SPEAR? What's that? OK, one of those secret things that keeps changing its name. OK, I'll do that. Then what's after that? Oh Christ, not Senator Landry. Fine. But please leave me in peace for the next thirty minutes."

The President walked along the colonnade outside the Oval Office and paused to reflect on the challenges she faced. She remembered the iconic photos of President Kennedy walking here locked in conversation with his brother. At least he had someone he trusted right by his side. Every other President had had a close aide, or failing that, a wife they could turn to at times like this. She had never felt so alone. Her mind wandered off to a remote valley in the Caucasus. What had he been doing? He was a senior officer. Why had he gone on that mission? It wasn't his job to go and kill the enemy up close—and get killed. Why had he been so selfish?

She would always regret their last evening together. He had been back on home leave. She had heard the rumors, but she didn't want to spoil their week together. But on the last night, she could no longer bear the thought of his going back to that Pentagon lawyer attached to his Command HQ. She had challenged him. He had confessed and put it all down to the stress of combat. He begged her forgiveness. She was so devastated and hurt, she could not forgive him. Not that night. They slept in separate rooms, and he left the next morning without saying goodbye. She was anguished. She prayed for guidance and sought help from her priest, Father David Douglas. Finally, one night she drafted an email setting out how much she loved him and how she forgave him. She saved it in drafts so that she could take a fresh look in the morning and then hit send. At 5 a.m., the doorbell rang. It was the Marine Chaplain and Father Douglas. The email remained, unsent, in her draft folder to this day.

He'd been honored and posthumously decorated, but that didn't help. She had been left to bring up their three children. All through their teenage years, they worshipped their dead father. He could do nothing wrong, and she could do nothing right. At the beginning of her political career, he had been her most trusted adviser. And where was he now when she needed someone she trusted to help her get out of this political nightmare? And that was just the domestic politics. She still had this space weather strike on the horizon. That though, was at least a couple of years away.

"Madam President. The JUPITER SPEAR team are here," the Chief of Staff called out to her.

The President walked back into the Oval Office to find Aaron, Dan, and Ruth already in the room. She asked her Chief of Staff to leave.

"Well, hello there, my friends. Do sit down please. Can I get any of you a cup of coffee? Or some tea, perhaps for our English friend? Look, I read your paper. You warned me I wouldn't like it. I don't. I thought you were all as crazy as dogs chasing the jailhouse cat."

Ruth was still struggling to follow some of the President's more colorful Southern figures of speech. She assumed this wasn't good news.

"It requires me to deceive Congress and the American people. It is totally dependent on the most untrustworthy Senator in my party—and there's quite a lot of competition for that title. I need total confidence that you guys in the CIA and our British friends can keep a secret, and that the Chinese don't have a mole in Langley or Vauxhall Cross. And I need to pretend to be a space weather denier for the next two to three years. That's fine with my base but might cost me a few swing states next year. And even you guys put the chances of success at less than fifty percent.

"You were right. I really didn't like your plan. I thought it was mad.

"But as I read it and read it again, I came to think that actually it might just be brilliant. The more I worked it through in my head, I saw the logic and began to believe it could work. You've thought through all the contingencies. Then it began to dawn on me that this crazy, mad, brilliant plan might just work. And it solves my two biggest problems at once. So, Aaron and Ruth, please be good enough to take me through it again, line by line. We've got an hour or so until Senator Landry shows up.

"Before that, Dan can you recut the political section of your plan into a memo in White House format. Draft it as though it's a memo from my Chief of Staff to me. I want something I can share with the Senator in confidence. Strangely I can trust him on this as, if he buys into playing his part in the plan—as our 'useful idiot'—then he stands to get very rich. Dan, I assume you brought your laptop, and your drafting skills are up to a short memo to the President? Good.

"Now Ruth, while Dan is preparing that memo, I assume you know the joke about my distinguished Republican colleague?"

"I'm not sure I do, Madam President."

"How can you tell when Senator Jesse Landry is lying? When his lips move."

CHAPTER 15

OVAL OFFICE, WHITE HOUSE, WASHINGTON D.C.

May

"Jesse, how wonderfu! to see you! Come on in. So good of you to come over. And how is my favorite Senator?"

"I'm very well, thank you, Madam President. I bet you say that to all the Senators."

"Oh no Jesse. I can give you a very long list of my not-favorite Senators. And that's just from the Republicans. All the Democrats are on my dirt list. But enough of politics. It's such a lovely day, let's go and sit out in the Rose Garden."

They walked through the French doors onto the colonnade and then into the Rose Garden. President Wallace had recently overseen a renovation, which restored it to its original design under Jackie Kennedy. The only difference this time was that President of the United States couldn't delegate garden design to a spouse. She had to do that herself, too. Senator Landry had not been in the Rose Garden since its renovation. The President gave him a detailed guide to the layout, her choice of flowers and her decision to reintroduce the crabapple trees, which had been controversially removed under a previous administration.

"Can you believe, Jesse, that one of my predecessors had all those lovely crabapple trees removed because they blocked the camera angles on some political event he was hosting? Those trees had been planted by Jackie Kennedy! Now I am no fan of the Kennedy administration, but Jackie did wonders for the White House. I think we should show some respect to her legacy in this garden. That's why I have restored it in a way that I think Mrs. Kennedy would approve."

They sat at a table, close to the Oval Office and well shielded from the public eye or even wandering members of the Press Corps. It was one of the gorgeous late Spring days in Washington when the residents convince themselves it has the best climate in all the US. The humidity and mosquitoes of summer are still a few weeks away. The azaleas and dogwood trees are out in full bloom. On most days, there is crystal-clear sunlight—a beautiful, bright, clean light with a rich, dry warmth.

"On days like this, Jesse, I think Washington is the most beautiful city in the world."

"Well, Madam President, fifteen years ago I ran against Washington. I told the good voters of my great state that Washington was a swamp full of corrupt politicians, liberal journalists, overpaid lobbyists, and too many mosquitoes. Even on a day like today, it's hard for me to accept that it is also a beautiful city."

"I won't blow your cover, Jesse. You can admit it to me."

"OK, Madam President. I confess. I do actually like it here in Washington. It's a great city. But please never reveal that I said that to you."

"Jesse. Your secret is safe with me. Now it is actually about Washington that I wanted to talk with you. More specifically about D.C. Statehood."

"Madam President, you know my position on that. The Constitution is clear. The District is not a state. I am afraid it is just bad luck that the residents of the District aren't represented in the Congress. That's the will of the Founding Fathers. I, for one, respect the sanctity of our great Constitution. And of course, it's helpful that the will of the Founding Fathers keeps two Democratic Senators out of the Senate, which as you know is the last thing we need right now."

"Jesse, I agree. We can't hand control of the Senate to the Democrats. But I have a real political problem with the D.C. Statehood issue. The police have overreacted. I have more than a dozen dead citizens here on my doorstep, including kids. More protests are planned for the coming weeks, and at this rate, the D.C. police will be clocking up more domestic casualties on my watch than LBJ had over Vietnam. And look how that played in 1968. I need a solution, Jesse, and I need your help."

"Well, Madam President, you have no bigger supporter in the Senate than me, but I won't change my position on D.C. Statehood. My mind is set."

"Jesse, I'm not asking you to vote for D.C. Statehood. That's the last thing we need. But I do want you to read this memo from my Chief of Staff. I am so lucky. I have just the best political team in the business. They really are the A team. I challenged them to come up with a plan, and I think they have really cracked it. It just needs the leadership of one patriotic Senator. And that's why I need you. Read this . . ."

She handed over the memo that Dan had crafted earlier.

Memo to the President

From: Chief of Staff

Subject: D.C. Statehood

Date: May 6

Madam President,

You have asked for a political strategy to address the continuing civil unrest over D.C. Statehood. You have made clear that you want an outcome that gives D.C. residents the opportunity to vote in Congressional elections so that they are represented in the US Senate and House of Representatives, which set their federal taxes. You have also made clear that you do not want to create a new state with two new Senators and one new Representative representing the District of Columbia in Congress.

The political team has come up with a strategy to deliver this outcome.

First, we will need legislation to give the citizens of the District the right to vote in Maryland elections. This will increase the Maryland Congressional delegation by one Representative. It will increase the majorities by which the two Democratic Senators from Maryland are elected, but that will not change the balance of power in the Senate. It might even win over two Democratic votes for this bill, as the two Maryland Senators would realize that their reelection chances would be more secure. This change decisively addresses the central issue. Citizens in the District would get to vote for elected representatives in Congress. There would be no more taxation without representation. We can point to the historical precedent of 1846 when Congress returned to Virginia the land within the original District west of the Potomac River. This, however, is a better deal for the District as we are not proposing carving up the District and returning the land to Maryland. The District as currently configured would remain intact. We believe we can enact this change through legislation and without a Constitutional amendment. That may be challenged in the courts, but that process would take 2–3 years, so it would solve our problem until after your reelection.

Second, we need a package of federal funding for the District of Columbia. The Mayor is facing a challenging reelection campaign next year from the Progressive left of his party. He has staked his reputation on ending taxation without representation. So far, he has nothing to show for it. Our political team believe that a $10 billion package of federal assistance, to be distributed by the Mayor, should be sufficient to win his support. He is a sophisticated operator from the 'all-politics-is-local' school. With $10 billion of 'no-strings-attached' federal funding, he should be able to secure his reelection. We are confident this is sufficient to win his support.

Finally, the Mayor and the people of the District need some symbolic victory. They need recognition if not as a state but as a more integral part of the Union than was initially envisaged by the Founding Fathers. As you know, the Mayor has revived the fifty-one star version of the US flag. He flies this at the D.C. City Hall, in clear contravention of the 'I Stand Up For America' Act. To date, the DOJ has chosen not to provoke the Mayor and Citizens of D.C. by prosecuting them for this act of defiance. In any case, it is not clear that the 'I Stand Up For America Act' is constitutional, in that it limits the freedom of expression of those who choose to fly an alternative version of the national flag. Even so, we believe that you should offer the Mayor and the people of the District the inclusion of a new star on the national flag. It could be slightly smaller than the fifty stars representing states, but you could position it in the center of the 'star field' symbolizing the importance of the District in the Union of Fifty States.

We believe this plan will address the legitimate concerns of the citizens of Washington D.C. for representation in Congress while still preserving the current balance of political power in the Senate. This will also address the legitimate concerns of Independents and moderate Republicans who have been won over to the cause of D.C. Statehood by the arguments over ending 'taxation without representation.' We believe that the offer of federal funding and a new fifty-one-star flag will be sufficient to win over support from the Mayor and the moderate majority of citizens within the District.

We look forward to discussing this proposal with you tomorrow morning.

"So, Jesse, what do you think? It certainly solves all of my problems. It also keeps the balance of power in the Senate, and that is important for the party. I can sell this to our Republican colleagues, and I can defend this in the Presidential campaign next year. I just need your help. Only you can deliver the legislation to give District citizens a vote in the Maryland Congressional elections. Only you can deliver the $10 billion funding package through Appropriations. But most importantly, only you can deliver the fifty-one-star flag. Who else other than the Senator for Old Glory? The Senator for the Star-Spangled Banner?"

"Well, Madam President, this is very bold. Very courageous if I may say. But I really don't think it will fly. Most of these District voters are Democrats, and many of my colleagues just can't vote for a bill that gives one million votes to the Democrats."

"Yes, Jesse, but the beauty of our Constitution is that one million more Democratic votes in a blue state like Maryland makes no difference. Those votes really don't count, but the voters feel good about voting and can't claim that they are taxed without representation."

"No, I see the point. Your political team has done a good job. The federal funding will be fine. $10 billion to land this plan. If I can't deliver that, then I shouldn't be Chair of the Appropriations Committee. Consider that done. Now about the flag. That is more difficult."

"Jesse, I know that you are very attached to the flag, but it has changed many times since the revolution. Eighty years ago, there were only forty-eight stars. A hundred and fifty years ago there were only thirty-seven stars. No one will notice the difference. When was the last time you counted all fifty stars?"

"I understand that, but it will mean replacing every single flag in America and that will cost citizens and businesses a lot of money. And the more patriotic you are, the more flags you have to replace and the more it will cost. Some in our party will call this a 'tax on patriotism.' It will be dead on arrival with Congress."

"Well, Jesse, I am sure we could provide federal funding for flag replacement. And of course, you will get to name the bill. You have such a way with naming bills. I just love the 'Stand Up for America' Act."

"Thank you, Madam President. You are very kind. But if we require everyone to replace their flags, that will just suck in imported cotton. We'll probably see Chinese factories with prison labor churning out fifty-one-star flags at knock-down prices. We'd need some protections in there to require a 'Buy America' clause on both the flags and the cotton or possibly the synthetic cotton that would be required. I'm told there's very good synthetic cotton now coming onto the market—made, would you believe, in my very own home state."

"That's very fortunate, Jesse. And I think your state has nearly fifty percent of all the flag factories in America. This would be good for me, good for you, good for the Republican Party and good for the United States of America. Can I count on your support? Let's talk it through as I show you the new crabapple trees along the colonnade, and then you can leave through the East Wing. We'll have your car brought 'round to the East Gate."

The President said her goodbyes to Senator Landry and returned to the Oval Office.

"Get me the JUPITER THING team back in here fast," she barked at her Chief of Staff. "And by the way, if Senator Landry ever congratulates you and your Amateur Hour political team on their brilliant strategy to address D.C. Statehood, just say thank you and sound gracious. He thinks it is all your work—so lucky you. But he also knows it is Top Secret, so he won't expect you to discuss it."

"Well, I don't think I can discuss it, as I have no idea what the plan is that you just agreed with the Senator."

"Damn right you don't and that's how it's going to stay. Get me the JUPITER WHATEVER gang, and fast."

Aaron, Dan, and Ruth had been waiting in the small windowless office just off the Roosevelt Room. Dan wondered if this office belonged to one of the soon-to-be-fired political team.

After a fifteen-minute wait, they were summoned back into the Oval Office.

"How did it go, Madam President?" asked Dan. "Did Senator Landry buy it?"

"Thank you for your great work," said the President turning on her southern charm. "If this CIA thing doesn't work out for you guys, I may have some vacancies soon on my political team here. You guys are the best. If you are as good at spying as you are at political strategy, then I feel a lot safer in my bed at night."

She smiled with the smile that had won over so many voters. At times like this, her charisma was captivating. Even Ruth felt herself being drawn towards the President.

"Thank you, Ma'am. That is very kind. But the Senator, did he buy it?"

"He bought it, for sure. Hook, line, and sinker..."

CHAPTER 16

FABRIC OF AMERICA FACTORY

May - the following year

"Jesse, it is so very good to see you here down in your fine home state. It's been too long since I saw you last. We had that lovely chat in the Rose Garden. It must be a year ago now. That's just too long, Jesse."

"Well, Madam President, I am truly honored that you have chosen my state, and this magnificent new manufacturing facility, to launch your 'Wallace Again' reelection campaign."

"I wanted to announce early and scare off any of our fellow Republicans with overdeveloped egos and excessive ambition. And you know, Jesse, there are all too many of our colleagues who fit into that category. It's going to be harder to beat the Democrats this time, and I don't want to waste time, money, and effort having first to beat an overcrowded Republican field."

"Very wise, Madam President. You know you have my full support."

President Wallace knew exactly how much support Jesse Landry was giving her. He had secretly been working with big Republican donors to test the potential to run a more conservative candidate against her in the primaries. The hard right felt that she had made too many concessions to the more socially liberal wing of the party on gay rights and women's health issues. Solving the D.C. Statehood issue also hurt her with the Republican base. She knew she was vulnerable to a challenge from the right, so she'd have to become more conservative on these social issues, at least until she was safely reelected. That would expose her in the general election if, this time, the Democrats put up a half-decent candidate. She knew it would be a tough race. It was important to start early.

Fayne Capital's Fabric of America giga-factory was the perfect place to launch a campaign. It was producing half of all the fabric for the new fifty-one-star flag. A second Fayne Capital giga-factory in Maryland was approaching full production and would be providing nearly all the rest. Imported cotton had been banned under Senator Landry's Buy America provisions. A few craft producers still produced some all-American natural cotton. They struggled to compete with the synthetic cotton produced by the Fayne facilities. Given Fayne Capital's huge and illegal subsidies to keep the price of Fabric of America down, the craft producers were really hurting.

Senator Landry and the President went into one of the meeting rooms for a discussion of the political strategy to complete the legislation needed to roll out the new fifty-one-star flag. The President thanked Landry for his leadership in getting the 'Stronger America Bill' passed. This gave residents of Washington D.C. the right to vote in the Maryland elections. It had required a lot of lobbying by the President to get all the Republicans lined up to vote for that Bill. Many thought she had given in too easily to the protestors and conceded too much. The Democrats wouldn't get any more Senators, but they would get one more Representative in the House. If the Democrats came back strongly in the general election, or more likely in the following mid-terms, then just one more safe Democratic seat could cost the Republicans control of the House. This prompted the beginnings of the search for a hard right candidate to challenge Wallace in the primaries.

The Democratic Senators had split. Most opposed the Bill fearing that it was just a plot to prevent full Statehood for D.C. They wanted to hold out for a Democratic President and then they could push for their preferred solution and gain two more Senate seats. They thought Wallace would probably win reelection. But having waited over two hundred and fifty years for Statehood, they were quite happy to wait another four years for a Democratic President to move into the White House. The Democrats threatened to kill the bill through a filibuster. The chance to filibuster one of Senator Landry's bills was very attractive given his record at killing Democratic bills.

In the end, the President managed to get ten Democrats on board and override the threat of a filibuster. The two Maryland Senators supported the Bill as expected. The prospect of an even more secure Democratic majority in Maryland was one attraction. They were also keen to secure the second Fayne Capital giga-factory, with its associated 'Friends and Family' investment opportunities. Getting the next eight votes was tough, but Wallace charmed the Senators and cut deals to get the final votes. The bill passed, but it only added to the growing sense that Wallace was turning blue at the edges. The search for a primary challenger gained momentum.

"Now then Jesse. You and I had a great success on the Stronger America Bill. But if we are going to keep this factory busy, and all your flag factories fully employed for the next two years, we need to land your next bill. How's that going?"

"Well, Madam President. I think this one will be easier. Next week, I will be introducing the 'Stars and Stripes Forever' Bill mandating the change in the flag to the new fifty-one-star design. We consulted the Mayor on the design and went with his basic approach, just with a slightly smaller star for the District right in the center of the 'star field.' We went with a four-pointed star to symbolize the original shape of the District as conceived by the Founding Fathers. As you requested, I have mandated a two-year transition period by the end of which flying the fifty-star flag will be illegal. We want the transition largely complete in time for your inauguration. And, just to make sure we keep all our hard-working flag workers busy, I have added provisions requiring flags to be flown every hundred yards in all residential streets and business districts around the nation. The American Civil Liberties Union are all worked up over this provision—that's just typical of those pinko leftists. They just hate America. That's the problem. It's nothing to do with civil liberties. My lawyers tell me not to worry as the ACLU will probably not be able to get the suit in front of the Supreme Court for another year or two. And if we can hold it off until your second term, you'll probably get the chance to replace one or two of those 90-year-old leftist justices and we'll have control of the Court back again. I think we'll be fine on this Bill."

"Jesse, you are a true patriot. I do so admire your altruism in making sure we honor our nation's new flag."

"Well, Madam President, I am proud to so do. I am humbled by the opportunity to serve. I have no interest in financial gain. I believe though that Sir Leslie Fayne and his local investors are doing very well out of this program. But my reward is the sure knowledge that I am doing the Lord's work in making America stronger."

The President then joined a group of hand-picked workers on the factory floor for a series of photo-ops. The political team had picked the right mix of gender, age, and ethnicity to appeal to their target voters. The group was overrepresented with Hispanics and White older men. Those were the demographics where Wallace was polling poorly. Her position on gay marriage was hurting her with these more conservative groups.

She gave a relatively dull stump speech. She'd be doing this hundreds of times over the coming months. She realized she needed a better speechwriter. More importantly, she needed to step up her game. She was fairly confident she'd get through the primaries. The general election all depended on who the Democrats put up. This time, if they were smart, they'd put up a more centrist candidate and that would hurt her.

She left the factory feeling pretty flat. It hadn't gone well. She needed to get back to campaigning match fitness. She didn't have the same fire and energy she had felt at the start of her first campaign.

Her phone rang. It was one of her political team.

"We've just heard from our source inside the Democratic campaign. Governor Ramirez is announcing his candidacy tomorrow. He's lined up a lot of endorsements from the big donors and party leaders. This looks like the real deal."

Wallace's heart sank. The Democrats had broken with their recent tradition of putting forward unelectable candidates. Ramirez was the Governor of Texas, which after over forty years had elected a Democratic governor. He was very popular and had won a second term with an increased majority. A committed Catholic, he was personally pro-life, but he accepted the Democratic party's position on allowing women the right to choose. He also personally believed in the sanctity of marriage as a union between a man and a woman, but again was willing to support his party's position in favor of gay marriage. He was pro-guns; he'd never have won in Texas if he wasn't. He was a decorated Marine Corps veteran and had pursued a successful career in business before running for Governor. If he could get through the Democratic primaries, he'd be a potent threat in the general election.

She felt a bit guilty getting this valuable intelligence from a spy in the Democratic camp. But they were probably doing the same to her.

The President thanked the staffer for the information and turned to the rest of her team.

"OK, guys. It's game on now. Ramirez is running. We're in the fight of our lives."

CHAPTER 17

ALBUQUERQUE, NEW MEXICO

October - the following year

R uth and Steve were throwing a Presidential Debate party in their beautiful 100-acre estate just outside Albuquerque. It was far removed from their small, terraced house in Cambridge.

It had been a long and bruising campaign since Wallace and Ramirez had declared sixteen months ago. Steve loved the intricacies of American politics and had followed every twist and turn in the campaign. Ruth just wanted it to be over. They couldn't vote themselves. They still hadn't decided to become US citizens. They loved their new life in America but couldn't quite make the break with Britain. Steve was much more willing to make the commitment as he had not been born a Brit. Ruth just couldn't imagine herself as an American citizen, at least not yet. The twins though had made their choices. They had their Green Cards and were on track to be citizens. They couldn't yet vote, but they had signed up to be campaign workers for the Ramirez campaign.

All Ruth and Steve's friends from the University of New Mexico and Albuquerque tech community were Democrats. The twins had invited over some of their fellow activists. The party guests were 100 percent behind the Governor Ramirez. He had come through the Democratic Primaries strongly. The more Progressive candidates had lost for a number of reasons. Some were caught up in personal scandals, a mixture of sex and money, and some were obviously unelectable. Ramirez was pressed in the later stages of the primaries by a Democratic Socialist, with enthusiastic support from students and union members. But in the end, even the Democratic base didn't back the extreme Socialist challenger, despite his ideological purity. Governor Ramirez proved an effective campaigner and swept the Democratic primaries across the Southern states. That base of Southern support would be a major asset in the general election.

The Democratic party also sensed Wallace's weakness with her own party base. She had been challenged in the primaries by a hard libertarian candidate. It had been a nerve-racking race. It was close all the way to the final state primary. By the end of the campaign, Wallace was tired and her performances became jaded. Something of the Wallace magic had been lost. Worse, her true Republican credentials had been damaged by constant attacks from her party's right wing. The Democrats thought this was their moment to retake the White House.

The first debate went well for Wallace. She was running on the back of a strong national economy, and she put in a solid if not spectacular performance. Ramirez was also strong, talking up his business experience and his record on jobs and economic growth in Texas. Most commentators called this debate as a win for Wallace by a small margin.

The second debate was on foreign policy. This is where the fireworks started. Wallace staked out a strong position on defense. She had increased national security spending year after year. She launched a strong attack on China and its increased regional expansionism. Ramirez turned the tables on her by claiming that she had allowed a dangerous gap in 'space weather defense' to emerge. Ramirez cited China's leadership in protecting its own economy and supporting its allies whereas the US, he said, had buried its head in the sand like an ostrich. Wallace defended her party's position on space weather. It was, she said, "a big hoax by Big Tech," and committed once again "not to spend a single cent of federal money on building defenses against this fake threat." The Republicans in the audience loved it and her position polled well with the Republican focus groups. But it cost her dearly with independent voters and more conservative Democrats— exactly the groups who had been so important to her landslide election four years previously.

And then came the third debate held in Tampa, Florida. This would go down as one of the most dramatic Presidential debates of all time. It would always be known as 'The Letter Debate.' This debate focused on social issues. Everyone expected it to be a tough fight. Both candidates were committed Christians—Wallace, a member of the Church of Jesus Lives Today and Ramirez a devout Catholic. Both were personally against abortion, even though Ramirez accepted that it was a matter of personal choice and it was not for the federal or state governments to interfere in a deeply personal decision.

The debate on abortion was combative. Wallace had thought Ramirez would go easy on the abortion issue, given his personal beliefs. Far from it, he attacked Wallace's record as Governor and said she had not gone far enough with her limited reforms on reproductive rights. This was a risky tactic. Wallace had inherited a total ban on abortion in her state at the beginning of her first term as Governor. She successfully introduced some exemptions for rape, incest, and the life of the mother. These small reforms were, of course, supported by most independents and some Democrats, even if they didn't go far enough. At least, many voters thought, Wallace was making some progress in a highly conservative state. However, by attacking her record on abortion as Governor, Ramirez raised more doubts about Wallace in her core Republican constituency. It was cynical, but smart.

And then the campaign took a dramatic turn. As political commentators and historians looked back on this extraordinary Presidential campaign, this was the moment they all picked as the beginning of the endgame. With less than a month to go, an already feisty and combative campaign suddenly exploded. It began with an incident that would become known simply as 'The Letter.'

In his closing comments on abortion, Ramirez suddenly switched, without explanation, to the issue of gay marriage. It was another cynical move. His party strongly supported gay marriage, as did President Wallace. Her son and his husband had recently adopted a daughter and the President had attended her christening in the Washington Episcopal Church. Gay couples – and especially gay couples with adopted children – were not welcome in the Church of Jesus Lives Today.

When Ramirez raised the issue, Wallace wondered what he was up to. She was used to attacks from her own party for her support for gay marriage, but never from Democrats. She really wasn't expecting this in the debate.

And then Ramirez produced The Letter.

"I have in my hand a letter. It is a letter from Bishop David Douglas. I believe you know Bishop Douglas, President Wallace."

"I do indeed. He is the Paternal Bishop and head of the Church of Jesus Lives Today. I have worked with him for over twenty-five years in the Church. For many years, he was my priest. I sought his support and guidance when my husband was killed."

"And you agree he is a man of faith?"

Oh my God, thought Wallace. Where is this going? But I have to answer that.

"Yes, he is. He is a man of faith."

"Bishop Douglas has written to me today. My campaign will post the letter momentarily so all Americans can see what the Bishop has said. He writes that he disagrees with my positions on many topics, but he respects me as a committed Christian. We both pray to the same God, he says, even though we pray in different churches. He goes on to say that the Church of

Jesus Lives Today has always supported the sanctity of marriage as a union between a man and woman. His Church and, President Wallace, that is your Church too, does not support the adoption of young children by homosexual couples. For this reason, he says, he can no longer support President Wallace. In his letter, he confirms that he and the governing Council of the Church of Jesus Lives Today are endorsing my campaign. Thank you, Bishop Douglas. I am proud to accept your endorsement."

Wallace was shocked. It was a huge personal betrayal by the Bishop. It was cruel to bring her family into this political debate and even crueler to make an issue of her granddaughter. But it was also a devastating political blow given the power of the Church of Jesus Lives Today. At first she said nothing,

The moderator asked her to respond. She began slowly and quietly.

"I am deeply disappointed to hear that, Governor Ramirez. Bishop Douglas is a man of faith and has been a friend of mine for many years. I am sure he only reached his decision after long and careful prayer. But I cannot accept his attack – and, Sir, I reject your attack – on my family. I have always been clear that I love my son and I love his husband, my son-in-law. I was delighted to welcome their new daughter into our family. They are a loving family. It brings me great joy to see John and Christian raise their new baby daughter, my grandchild.

"I have long wondered why God has sent me this challenge. My Church does indeed teach that marriage is a union between a man and a woman. And yes, my Church does oppose adoption by gay couples. But I cannot accept that God's love for mankind stops when a man loves another man, or a woman loves another woman. I cannot believe that God does not rejoice, as I rejoice, to see a little orphaned girl welcomed into a loving family. And I cannot accept that God wants me to choose between my love for Him and my love for my family.

"But God, through Bishop Douglas, has clearly sent me this test. It is a test of my faith. As Lincoln said, 'The Almighty has His own purposes.' I will as ever seek His guidance through prayer. Perhaps God's price is that I need to give up my political career. If that is the price that He seeks to exact, then I will willingly pay it."

The audience was silent.

When it was clear that Wallace had finished, the moderator asked Ramirez to respond. He went for the kill.

"If that is a concession, Madam President, I acknowledge it. But I would rather wait until election day to accept your concession and I look forward to that call.

"I think the American people have seen enough. I have managed to find a way to reconcile my religious beliefs with my political career. I deeply oppose abortion and gay marriage personally, but I respect the choices that other people make following their own consciences. Unlike you, I will give them the legal freedom to exercise their choices. You, on the other hand, seek to impose your religious beliefs on others when it suits you politically, as you do on abortion. But when, as on gay marriage, your Church's teachings are inconvenient to you and your family, you want an opt-out. I think the American people will see through your hypocrisy."

"Governor Ramirez, I reject your accusation of hypocrisy. I have explained to the American people the dilemma that I face in trying to reconcile my love of God and my love for my family. I trust the American people to judge me on the choice I have made. I have chosen to not reject either, but I have continued to love both."

Finally, the ordeal was over. Wallace recovered in the closing statements and ended on a stronger note. But she knew she had taken some bad body blows in the debate. Ramirez had been clever – and ruthlessly cruel – to go after her family. She would never forgive him personally, but she could see the political logic for what he had done. Politics was a brutal game.

At Ruth and Steve's party, the crowd was thrilled. It had been an unpleasant debate, but Ramirez had emerged as the clear winner. Many people felt sorry personally for Marian Wallace, but as loyal Democrats, they were pleased to see her taken down politically. Everyone was sure Ramirez was heading to the White House.

Ruth felt very uneasy. As Wallace spoke of her love for her son and his family, Ruth's eyes started to well up. After Ramirez produced 'The Letter,' Ruth could see how distressed Wallace was. As Wallace spoke of her dilemma of having to choose between loving God and loving her son, Ruth nearly broke down. Four years earlier, she had thought Governor Wallace was a neo-fascist and a threat to democracy. Now she saw a principled politician, a mother, and a widow, putting her love for her family ahead of her career. Ruth left the party and went outside to compose herself.

Back in Tampa, President Wallace debriefed with her team.

"Don't sugarcoat the message. How bad is it?" she asked.

Her campaign manager summed it up. "As you know, the second debate didn't go well. Your position on the space weather threat lost you the independent vote. And today, your position on gay marriage, lost you a big chunk of the religious vote. The Church of Jesus Lives Today endorsement was a real shocker. Bishop Douglas can deliver a lot of votes in the South. So, it's bad. It's really bad, I'm afraid."

"And if you run the live polling through our Electoral College model, what do you get?"

"Madam President, Ramirez has a strong position in the blue states and his home state of Texas. He can be pretty sure now of 250–260 votes in the College. If you lose one more traditionally Republican state in the South, he'll be well north of the two hundred and seventy he needs to be elected President."

"And how am I polling now in the South?"

"You're behind in the five biggest Southern states. Right now, Madam President, this election is not even close."

CHAPTER 18

ALBUQUERQUE, NEW MEXICO

November

Finally, it was Election Day. After the success of the debate party, Ruth and Steve invited the same crowd back for an Election Night party. This time they had put up a marquee in their garden with big screen TVs and an open bar. It was decked in 'Ramirez Now' signs. The twins were in Austin, Texas, at the Ramirez Campaign Headquarters. They were texting their parents with the latest gossip and rumors from Ramirez HQ.

The crowd was overwhelmingly Democratic. Perhaps only Ruth and Steve had reservations about a Ramirez win. But then, they had seen something about President Wallace that no voter had seen or could ever know. Secretly, both Ruth and Steve hoped Wallace would win, but they needed to be prepared for either outcome. If Ramirez won, he was promising a bold program for Space Weather Defense, but would he get it through Congress over the inevitable Republican filibusters? Could he roll it out in time, especially in the face of resistance from the more conservative states? Dan's team had war-gamed the Ramirez plan. At best, it might only protect half of America, which was not enough. The economy was so interconnected, that chaos in some states would cripple the entire nation as data centers, communications networks and the electricity grids failed. Only Wallace could provide continued support for their covert plan. Risky though it was, it remained their best option for protecting all of America in time for the approaching surge in solar activity. But for the purposes of that evening's party, they had to pretend to be die-hard Ramirez supporters.

After Ramirez's clear victory in the third debate, he seemed set for a big win. The endorsement of the Church of Jesus Lives Today was widely seen as a coup—and a debate masterstroke. It was a dramatic political moment that had been brutally effective at undermining Wallace. Pundits spoke of 'The Letter' as one of the most effective tactics in the long history of Presidential debates.

But then, just ten days before Election Day, came the shocking revelations about Ramirez. And now, all bets were off. Could Wallace pull off a surprise win from behind? Could Ramirez even hold his home state of Texas, which was now too close to call? Could he take one other big Southern state? Or would the revelations sink him? It was going to be a nail-biting evening.

At 8.30 p.m. Mountain Time, they turned on ANN's election coverage. This crowd were hard-core devotees of the very liberal America's News Network. They would never watch the conservative MTX, unless they wanted to enjoy seeing how the MTX anchors explained away Wallace's defeat later in the evening.

The pundits were having to kill time until they could report their projections once the California polls closed at 8 p.m. Pacific/ 9 p.m. Mountain Time.

"As we wait for the polls to close, let's look back over this extraordinary campaign. What a journey we have been on since May of last year, when President Wallace unexpectedly kicked off the election season early with her announcement at the Fabric of America flag factory alongside Senator Jesse Landry. She had hoped to preempt the Republican primary race and scare off challengers. Well, that didn't work. She had a bruising primary round. She succeeded, but frankly, by the end she looked like a weakened candidate.

"Democratic hopes were high with Governor Ramirez' triumph in their primaries. Here was a dream candidate—a successful, popular, conservative Democrat from the South, able to win back the Hispanic and moderate Republican votes. It was looking strong for a Democratic win, given this newfound ability to bring together a coalition across the blue and red states.

"And then the debates, and especially the now famous third debate and 'The Letter'. A brilliant political coup for Ramirez and a crushing personal blow to Wallace. It looked like it was all over at that point.

"The best the Wallace campaign could come up with was to hint at some 'October Surprise' that might turn the tide back towards their candidate. But by October 31, it was clear there would not be any October Surprise. In many blue states, the early voting and mail-in votes were already coming in. The election was strongly heading Ramirez's way.

"And just when we thought it was all over, only seven days ago – and they have been seven long days for us political reporters – we had The Invoice. After The Letter, The Invoice. Just an extraordinary sequence of events. Political junkies like us will be writing about The Letter and The Invoice for years to come."

The anchor cut in. "I should, at this point, make it clear that in line with other major networks, we will not be naming the young woman involved in this situation, out of respect for her and her family."

"Of course, we shouldn't name her. She's only eighteen now and was only seventeen at the time. What was he thinking? He was already running for President. He must have known he'd come under scrutiny. It was an all-time classic example of how not to handle a political scandal. First the denial. Then his campaign team tried to smear the source. Then a tearful and incomplete apology with his wife standing loyally by. And then he made the classic mistake of apologizing for a part of a scandal while still denying the most damaging allegation. And then, of course, The Invoice.

"No one knows how the Wallace campaign got hold of it, but it was genuine. Ramirez couldn't dismiss the invoice as a fake. It was a gift for the late-night shows: Did Ramirez think it was tax deductible? Was he planning to charge it as a campaign expense? We all had fun with that.

"Once The Invoice scandal broke, the race was back on. Ironically, it will have much more impact on voting in the critical swing states in the South, which don't allow early voting or mail-in voting. All the votes in the key Southern states will be made on Election Day, in person. We can debate whether that's good for democracy, but it certainly helps President Wallace who is benefitting from a late swing in these states. And it helps our exit polling. We can broadcast a good prediction for these key swing states as soon as the California polls close."

The timer on the screen was approaching 9 p.m. Mountain Time. The crowd in the marquee gathered closer to the big screen.

Ruth checked her phone to see whether the twins had any news from Ramirez Campaign HQ. Jo had texted that their campaign polls showed Ramirez still had a small lead in Texas and they thought he'd hold his home State. Ruth was skeptical. In-house polls were notoriously biased. It would be close.

The timer ticked over to 9 p.m. Mountain Time.

The screen flashed up with the words:

AMERICA'S NEWS NETWORK PREDICTION.

The anchor came up and announced: "Based on our exit polls in the critical swing states, and particularly our latest forecast for Texas, ANN is now ready to call the Presidential election.

"ANN is predicting . . .

PRESIDENT WALLACE RE-ELECTED.

CHAPTER 19

OVAL OFFICE, WHITE HOUSE, WASHINGTON D.C.

The following year
9 a.m. Eastern Standard Time (EST), September 1

President Wallace wrapped up her morning briefing with Director Douglass Thomson and the intelligence chiefs. Aaron stayed behind as the others filed out of the Oval Office.

"What's next up, Mr. Director?" asked the President.

"It's time to pick up on some unfinished business, Madam President. We need to brief you on developments about Operation HELIOS, as it is now called. You know, the solar flare defense program."

"OK, I was worried that might be the issue. It's been a while since you briefed me on that, but I assume the risk hasn't gone away. Let's get going."

Dan and Ruth were shown into the Oval Office.

"Well, hello there, my very good friends. It's been such a long time! How have y'all been? I've been busy getting re-elected, which wasn't all that easy, as you probably noticed. And since then, I've been doing all those second-term Presidential things, like foreign visits. I've been to see your beautiful country, Ruth. I do so like your new Prime Minister. Mike Urquhart and I go back a way. He's much nicer than the last one. I can see why his party got rid of the previous PM. I didn't care for him at all. And not just because he fired you, Ruth. But that was one very good reason for not liking him.

"But what about y'all. Ruth, how are the twins? Are they seniors at college yet? Are they happy in their new home here in the United States? I hear they are on track to become American citizens. That is so wonderful."

"Yes, thank you, Madam President. They are both very happy at the University of New Mexico and they are just starting their senior year. Congratulations on your re-election!"

"Well, it was pretty tight this time. I paid a big price for my position on gay marriage. I lost five points after that debate and that terrible incident with The Letter. There was no way I was going to denounce my son's love for his husband and my beautiful granddaughter—even if it cost me the election."

Ruth was very moved. She really had misjudged Marian Wallace.

"It was an admirable and heart-felt position, Madam President. I know many Democrats who deeply respected you for that stance."

"Well, it might have been helpful if they had voted for me and helped me out in some of the big blue states with large gay communities. Oh no! They all stayed firmly Democrat.

"I wasn't proud of my negative ads in the final stages of the campaign. But Ramirez had gone after my family. He started it. And in any case, if he wanted to take the high moral ground on marriage, he probably shouldn't have had that affair with his seventeen-year-old intern. Quite how my team found the invoice for her abortion, I don't know. I really, really don't want to know. It's a dirty business, politics. But as we say back home, 'If you want to be a prize pig, you'd better be prepared to roll in a lot of shit.' Please excuse my non-Presidential language. But I'm the Prize Pig now, and I can say what I like."

They exchanged small talk for a while. The President showed them the new artwork hanging in the Oval Office. As President, she had her pick of the paintings held in storage by the National Gallery of Art. She had chosen another Childe Hassam painting of the flags hanging down Fifth Avenue in New York. This version had been painted in the evening light and the flags glowed in the golden light of the setting sun.

"Do you like the new painting?" she asked. "I just love all those flags. The colors are so beautiful. He has brilliantly captured the way the evening sunlight turns the flags into even richer shades of red, white, and blue. It reminds me of our little project. Our extremely private, very secret little project. And we need to keep it that way. Especially after all the lies you made me tell in the campaign."

Then she introduced them to her new Chief of Staff, Jesse Baker.

"It's a great name for a Chief of Staff," she said. "Jim Baker worked out well for Ronald Reagan, so that's the standard Baker has to meet, right Baker? Jesse doesn't mind, but I've decided to call him Baker. It's simpler. Too many Jesses here in Washington. And it will help him grow into the role I want him to play.

"I've had to clear out some staff since the election. You probably read about it in the papers. Night of the long knives and all that. Well, I did pretty ruthlessly cut back my domestic political team. They weren't good enough, and I don't need to worry about getting re-elected again. I've beefed up my National Security team. With all this tension in the South China Sea, I think that's going to absorb most of my second term.

"Now tell me, what have y'all been up these last two years! We agreed that once I pressed the button on this plan and sent that old dupe Senator Landry off on his mission, I'd remain out of the loop. That helped me plausibly deny any knowledge of secret programs to protect us from space weather. You probably heard my lines during the campaign: "I can assure you that I'm receiving no intelligence briefings on any secret programs relating to space weather," and "I won't authorize a cent of taxpayers' money on this scam." I ramped up the 'big hoax by Big Tech' thing too. That always went down well at my rallies.

"But Baker here tells me things are heating up – no pun intended – and I now need to get back in the loop."

Aaron Douglass Thomson took the lead.

"Well, Madam President, we've been busy, and I am pleased to say that Operation HELIOS has run as planned. We've also decided not to keep changing the name. We hope you approve. And in any case, Operation HELIOS only has a few more weeks to go. We are entering the critical window now.

"We've prepared a short briefing note that will bring you up-to-date, and then we can discuss it. We've kept it short so you can just skim it now and we can then answer any questions you may have."

Memo to the President

From: Aaron Douglass Thomson, Director, CIA

Subject: Operation HELIOS - Progress Update

Date: September 1

Madam President,

This memo provides an update on progress in implementing the plan you authorized two years ago to complete a covert operation to protect the entire United States, and all our overseas territories and facilities. In short, the plan, now codenamed Operation HELIOS, has been successfully implemented.

Senator Landry rose enthusiastically, if unwittingly, to the challenge you set him. As you know, he introduced the 'Stronger America Act,' which gave residents of Washington D.C. the right to vote in the Maryland elections and then the 'Stars and Stripes Forever' Act mandating the change in the flag to the new fifty-one-star design. We are now at the end of the two-year process mandated in that Act for changing all flags to the new design.

Over ninety percent of the new flags are made with Fayne Capital's 'Fabric of America' material, which is the brand name used for the full-strength Solar Shield material originally developed in our New Mexico facilities. Fayne Capital built two giga-factories. One in Senator Landry's state and one in Maryland. This helped secured the votes of the Maryland delegation. Fayne Enterprises has been selling Fabric of America at a fraction of its cost of manufacturing. This was necessary to undermine any competitive threats from other products. A lawsuit for 'predatory pricing' has been brought against Fayne Capital, which they are likely to lose. The Department of Justice is helpfully going slow on the prosecution. The CIA and FBI provided the DOJ with some powerful evidence of collusion in other industries. The DOJ is now prioritizing those cases ahead of the case against Fayne Capital.

Through his operating losses and payouts to 'Friends and Family' investors, Sir Leslie has accumulated several billions of losses on our behalf. Sir Leslie is being patient, but at some point we will need to reimburse him through some new 'black program' funding.

Given the successful national rollout of nearly one billion new fifty-one-star flags, the vast majority of US households, businesses, and government installations are protected from a solar flare strike. Roadside flags, together with flags hanging on bridges and those flown by patriotic citizens on pick-ups and trailer-trucks, protect most of the Inter-state highway system.

Secrecy has been maintained and no one outside of the core Operation HELIOS team is aware of the deception. Senator Landry is completely oblivious to his role in protecting the nation from the threat of space weather. He and his family though have amassed considerable wealth through his blind trust's investment in the Fayne Capital Fabric of America factory.

We had two gaps in our plan to use land-based flags as the primary means of protection – satellites and aviation.

For Satellites, we hitched a ride on Space Force's Guardians of the Sky program. You will remember that early in your first term, Congress approved the launch of 3,000 hunter-killer satellites to protect our strategic communications and intelligence satellites. Russian and Chinese space attack drones posed a growing threat. Space Force was planning to deploy hunter-killer Guardians close to all our most important satellites where they could disable any hostile-state attack drones. When you authorized Operation HELIOS, we still had time to intervene. We required Space Force's contractors to use a new material for the Guardians' casing. We explained that this protected the guidance and control systems from electronic interference by a hostile power. To some extent, that was true. In reality, the material was a solid version of Solar Shield and was manufactured by Fayne Space Enterprises. This delayed the program by about a year for which Space Force has taken a lot of criticism. Sadly, it cost the head of Space Force her chance at becoming the Chair of the Joint Chiefs of Staff. But now, the satellites are fully deployed. The force field in space around one of the Guardian hunter-killers is large enough to protect the nearby communications and intelligence satellites.

Aviation was the other big gap in our plan. Fortunately, planes already need some level of protection as they fly at thirty-five thousand feet and are exposed directly to solar radiation, in the range of Kp3–Kp5, every day. The Federal Aviation Authority was persuaded to issue a new safety instruction to airliners that they needed protection against Kp-10 storms. A Fayne Capital subsidiary worked with aerospace companies to provide additional protection inside the hulls of airliners. To avoid creating consumer concern about the risks from exposure to radiation when flying, the airlines agreed to keep this new safety standard secret.

We have also successfully protected our European allies. This required less deception as the UK and European nations all launched government-sponsored programs to protect against space weather. The Russian disinformation campaigns proved less effective in these European nations given their stronger laws on press impartiality. We worked with our colleagues in DGSE, the French Secret Service, and friendly private sector partners in France to share the formula for our enhanced Solar Shield product. We gave them the formula for a hard panel version. We wanted something that was very different from our fabric. France rolled out a French solution, which the French people believe is based on original French science. President Giroud is privately very grateful but cannot acknowledge in public the role of the US and the UK's support in developing their solution. The rest of the EU adopted this French solution and mandated it across all 31 member states.

In the UK, MI6 used their Venture Capital fund to catalyze a new start-up in Oxford, which produced a competitor to Cambridge's original and ineffective Solar Shield product. The Oxford product was based on our technology, and they too went with a solid panel version. It provides a very high level of protection.

Unfortunately, the UK's Department of Business ran a procurement process to select between the Oxford and Cambridge products, testing their levels of protection and value for money. These Civil Servants were not briefed on Operation HELIOS and nearly blew the whole operation. We had to enhance the test results of the Cambridge Solar Shield product, just in case the UK Business Department (and the Chinese) found out that it wasn't effective. Fortunately, the UK uses the same German testing machines as the Chinese, so we were able to recalibrate them to overstate the performance of Solar Shield so that it matched that of the Oxford product. We then had to make sure the Oxford product won the procurement. So, MI6 secretly subsidized the Oxford product, and it won on value for money.

The UK and Europe have implemented the protective materials through rooftop panels, integrated within the roll-out of their wider rooftop solar panel Green Energy programs. The European approach helped strengthen US resistance to any form of solar protection. Space weather deniers and climate change deniers on the right and civil libertarians on the left strongly opposed the idea of a US Federal government program to install government-issued equipment on every American citizen's roof.

We are now positioned exactly where we had hoped to be positioned at this stage. The US is protected. However, no one in the US is aware of that, and the Chinese still believe we are unprotected. Your anti-space weather rhetoric in the campaign helped considerably. Our allies are protected. The Chinese believe that they and their allied states are protected and have not yet spotted the inadequacy of their One Shield product.

Operation HELIOS is now successfully complete.

The President put down the memo and looked at her guests with a big smile—that famous Wallace smile was back.

"Well, my friends, that's excellent progress. Other than the minor problem that we need to find a few billion dollars to pay back Sir Leslie Fayne. But I'm sure we'll find a way to lose that in the wash somewhere.

"Now Ruth, my friend, all this will be a complete waste of effort and money if the Sun stays quiet for the next few years. Any chance of that?"

"I'm afraid not, Madam President," Ruth replied. "The Sun is now entering the peak phase of its regular eleven-year solar cycle and all my observations and modelling suggest that the underlying long Carrington cycle is also coming to a peak. I currently predict a more than fifty percent chance of a direct intense solar flare hit on Earth within the next month or two."

"Madam President, Ruth's predictions are backed up by the reporting we are getting from our Beijing Station. Both SIGINT and HUMINT confirm that the Chinese scientists are predicting an imminent solar flare strike. If anything, they are more pessimistic than Ruth. As they have better data that we do, from their larger fleet of solar satellites, they may well be right. They are reporting to President Han that the flare strike could come within 1–2 weeks. President Han has put his military on enhanced stand-by to be ready to move to full mobilization within seventy-two hours."

The President looked concerned. She got up and walked over to the windows behind her desk and looked out at the White House South Lawn and then to the Washington Monument in the distance. Around the base of the monument were fifty-one flagpoles all flying the new fifty-one-star flag. She turned and leant on the desk. She reflected on the momentous challenges that lay ahead of her. The fate of her Presidency, her place in history, her standing as a world leader would all be determined in the coming days. Once again, she felt very alone.

"You're telling me that we could now be within days of the outbreak of hostilities with China. If our plan fails, the US is humiliated in the eyes of the world and Han successfully leapfrogs over us to become the most powerful nation in the world. If our plan works, Han is destroyed."

And then President Wallace looked around the room. She made eye contact with Ruth. Wallace smiled and switched into a perfect impersonation of Bette Davis in *All About Eve*.

"Fasten your seatbelts. It's going to be a bumpy night."

CHAPTER 20

USS GERALD R. FORD, SOUTH CHINA SEA

4 a.m. Beijing time,
September 4/ 4 p.m. EST September 3

Admiral Jack "Bull" Halsey addressed the crews of the joint US/UK Carrier Strike Group that was about to enter into disputed waters two hundred miles south of Taiwan and just hundred miles off the Northwest tip of the Philippines.

"Sailors and aviators of Carrier Strike Group 15 and our British allies serving in Operation UPHOLD PASSAGE, we are now sailing in waters that are recognized as international waters under international law. In a few minutes, we will cross the so-called nine-dash line and we will still be in international waters. But the Chinese dispute our right to sail in these waters. This right has been upheld in the international courts and is recognized by all the countries of this region, with the exception of China. We are upholding the freedom of navigation in these waters. We sail in peace. Our orders are clear. We will not be the first to fire, but we do have the right of self-defense if fired upon. We should expect to receive a warm welcome from the Chinese. They will test our resolve. They may well fly uncomfort-ably close to our force. But the President's orders are crystal-clear. We will not be the first to fire even if provoked. We cross the nine-dash line into disputed waters within the hour. Godspeed."

Jack Halsey was no relation to the famed World War II Admiral William "Bull" Halsey, one of the heroes of the Pacific campaign, a famously aggressive, sometimes overly aggressive, admiral with a string of famous naval victories to his name from Guadalcanal to the Leyte Gulf. But once eighteen-year-old Jack Halsey joined the Naval Academy at Annapolis as a Midshipman, it was inevitable that anyone with his surname would be nicknamed "Bull." It was also inevitable that when he was appointed as the Admiral of the Seventh Fleet, the press would have a field day with headlines such as "Bull in the China Sea." It was all quite unfair. Unlike his namesake, Jack Halsey was an extremely cautious Admiral. In addition to requiring intense training on how to fire in combat, he instituted the most rigorous programs in the Navy on how not to fire when being provoked.

Transits through the Taiwan Straits were a regular part of life in the Seventh Fleet. For the past decade, the US and its allies had maintained a frequent program of transits to uphold the principle of free and open seas, despite China's claim to these waters. That claim dated back to the mists of history. It was first set out on a map drawn by some junior official in the Chinese Ministry of the Interior in 1947. He drew eleven-dashes on a map of the South China Sea, marking out a huge expanse that stretched right up to the coastal waters of Malaysia, over one thousand miles from Mainland China. Later, the Chinese Communist Party reissued the map, this time with nine dashes encompassing over one million square miles of ocean ter-ritory. To strengthen the claim, China asserted sovereignty over disputed islands in these waters. Where necessary to extend its claim even further, it simply built new islands and claimed them as Chinese sovereign territory.

While transits were quite normal, this one was different. President Wallace had ordered the most powerful display of force ever in defense of the principle of free and open seas. In her reelection campaign, she had committed to 'get tough on China' and 'uphold the freedom of Taiwan.' China was making increasingly bellicose threats against Taiwan. Even without access to US intelligence, it was clear to the nations in the region that China was moving ever closer to an invasion. And, of course, President Wallace was reading the intelligence every day. The CIA was reporting details of Han's plans to mobilize for an invasion of Taiwan. Alarmed by these reports, President Wallace wanted to send Han a clear message that she was serious and was not going to back down from defending Taiwan and the international communities' right to passage through these waters.

Carrier Strike Group 15 was led by the USS Gerald R. Ford, the first of the Ford Class aircraft carriers, commissioned in 2013. She was powered by two nuclear reactors, with a complement of over four-and-half-thousand sailors and with twenty-five decks. At the time of her commissioning, she was the biggest, most powerful ship afloat. However, the Chinese had now launched four of its Xi class carriers, which were even bigger. This led to a carrier arms race in the South China Sea. As the oldest of the Ford-class carriers, USS Gerard R. Ford had been the first to undergo a major re-refit and was now equipped with the latest weaponry and anti-missile defense. She was once again the most powerful ship afloat, even more powerful than the Xi-class carriers. USS Ford carried over seventy aircraft including F-18s, F-35s and the brand-new US sixth generation fighter, the F-45. Despite this extraordinary firepower, the Ford was potentially vulnerable to attack from multiple hypersonic missiles coming in simultaneously from different directions. Unfortunately, China's latest sixth generation fighter, the J-36, with its six autonomous wingmen drones, had the capability to launch such a 'hypersonic swarm attack,' which almost certainly could penetrate even the Ford's defenses.

USS Ford was accompanied by nearly twenty ships in the rest of the strike force—three cruisers, five guided missile destroyers and three attack submarines plus several support and supply ships. Unusually for this passage, the strike force included three British ships, the aircraft carrier HMS Queen Elizabeth and three Type 55s, the latest British destroyer.

Shortly after 8 p.m., the Strike Force crossed the nine-dash line into disputed waters. Admiral Halsey was on the bridge of the Ford. He stood in silence. There was little for him to do now. The Ford was under the command of Captain Ron Lanzio. The Strike Force's mission was to sail in an arc through the disputed waters for the next twelve hours. It should be a relatively easy mission.

Admiral Halsey left the bridge and headed down to the Operations Room. Captain Lanzio needed to be left alone on the bridge. The Admiral would be in the Operations Room to command the entire Strike Force as they entered disputed waters.

"Admiral," said one of the communications officers, adding, "here's the latest report on Chinese air activity. As expected, we have a large welcoming party on its way from the mainland. This one is bigger than usual. Looks like they've put up six J-31s and eight J-36s."

"Excellent," replied Halsey. "We'll get a good look at these new J-36s. We can see if they are as good as they are reported to be. Are they accompanied by drones?"

"Looks that way. The J-36s each have six 'wingmen' drones."

"Should be quite a party. We'll just sit it out. No doubt they'll push their luck and try to provoke us. But orders are orders… even if they look to be preparing an attack run, we just sit it out."

"Yes, Sir. Those orders are well understood down the line. Including with the Brits."

"When will they get here?"

"Expecting first flyover in about fifteen minutes."

Silence fell in the Operations Room again. Then a communications officer called out:

"Sir, reports of communications difficulties on the Inouye."

USS Daniel Inouye was one of the most powerful and best destroyers in the Strike Group. She too had had a recent upgrade of all its weapons systems and on-board computing and communications equipment. She was captained by Josh Harwell, an old friend of Halsey's from their time at Annapolis.

"What the problem?"

"They are reporting intermittent loss of communications."

"Put Captain Harwell on now."

Halsey picked up the handset and the comms officer connected him through.

"Josh, what's the problem?"

"We keep losing comms. They just cut out. We can't find any reason. All our other systems seem fine. Our guys are on it and checking everything they can think of. They're the best comms team I've worked with—and they are at a loss as to what is going on. It's not the usual Chinese electronic interference. We've got all their usual bag of tricks well covered."

"OK, Josh. Keep at it. Get it fixed. We're expecting company soon."

Five minutes later, the Chinese J-31s and J-36s did their first fly over, at about five thousand feet. Nothing much to worry about there. Just a reminder that they were keeping a close watch on the Strike Group.

The Chinese aircraft flew on another five minutes south of Strike Group and banked. Halsey watched them on the radar. They turned 180 degrees and reduced altitude to two thousand feet and flew straight back at the strike group. The drone wingmen flew another one thousand feet below them.

"They're showing off now," Halsey said to team in the Operations Room. "Get me the Inouye."

"We've lost all contact with the Inouye, Sir. No response on any of the channels."

"Shit, this is not a good time to screw up the comms. What the hell is Harwell doing?"

The Chinese passed overhead at Mach 1.5. There were repeated sonic booms as they passed overhead.

"OK, we get it. We know you're here. Point made. Time to go home now."

"Sir, I've got the Inouye back online."

"Josh, where the hell have you been. Not a good time for your comms guys to do a total system reset!"

"Sir, we didn't do a total system reset—but someone did. Our systems shut down completely for ten minutes and have only just come back. But there's one big problem. We don't have control back yet for the RIM-88s. That entire system is down. We have no control over them. But what is worrying is that they are still physically tracking the incoming Chinese aircraft."

Halsey felt sick. The RIM-88s were the US Navy's latest surface-to-air missiles. If Inouye didn't have control over these missiles, who did?

"Shut them down fast!"

"We've tried that. They are not responding. I've sent crews onto the deck to try and disable them manually."

"Well, they better hurry up. The Chinese just turned and are heading back our way. You've got only a couple of minutes."

Halsey watched the radar. The J-31s didn't turn this time. They were heading back to the mainland. The J-36s and their drone wingmen did turn and formed into an attack formation. The J-36s dropped to five hundred feet. At that height, they would just clear the antennae on the Ford. The drone wingmen dropped to fifty feet. Halsey thought— I hope those drones can see where they are going. They are going to have to weave through this strike group at Mach 1.5. No time for an accident.

He watched the radar screen as the J-36s closed in—sixty seconds to fly past, thirty seconds, fifteen seconds…

"What the hell was that?"

On the large video screen ahead of him, he could see a huge explosion just off to the Ford's starboard side. And then another one, seconds later. Two huge fireballs exploded in the night sky. Flaming parts of the two aircraft fell into the calm waters of the Taiwan Strait.

"Get me the Inouye, now!"

"Josh, was that you?"

"Sir, I am afraid it was our missiles. We have no control over them. They just fired themselves."

"Jesus Christ, Josh. Looks like you just started World War III."

CHAPTER 21

SITUATION ROOM, WHITE HOUSE, WASHINGTON D.C.

5 p.m. EST, September 3

President Wallace sat at the head of the table and welcomed the team. "Lovely to see you again, Ruth," she said. "Thanks for coming. I'm glad you are here with me today. I need your wisdom and your support."

Ruth had flown straight back from New Mexico for this meeting, when the President asked for her. It would be good to brief the President in person. But, if Ruth was honest with herself, she just wanted to be with Wallace at this critical moment. Aaron Douglass Thomson and Dan McCraig were also in the room and a couple of the President's staff—the only ones who were cleared to know about Operation HELIOS.

"What have you got for me today, Ruth?"

"It's not good, I am afraid, Madam President. As expected, we have entered the window of highest risk. The levels of geo-magnetic activity on the Sun's surface are even more extreme than my most pessimistic models. We are already seeing large flares going out 20–30 million miles into space.

"And how far away are we?"

"We are about ninety-three million miles, so they are not strong enough to reach us. But I'm afraid there's one particularly bad aspect of these flares. We've been tracking this for some time. They all seem to be on the same axis. There must be some internal forces at work within the Sun that means that the flares are all coming out on roughly the same axis. I'm afraid it's the same axis as the Earth's orbit."

"That's bad right?"

"Very bad, I am afraid. If it weren't for this, a mega flare capable of travelling a hundred million miles could go off in any direction. But because they all seem to be coming on the same axis – pointing right into our path – the risks of a flare hitting Earth have just gone up hugely. We may get lucky as we did in 2012 when the flare missed the path of the Earth by about three million miles. But we might not. Given the intensity of activity and the number of large flares already being emitted, I'm now putting the odds of a direct strike hitting Earth at ninety percent within the next two months. And there's a 30–50 percent chance of one within the next two to three weeks, possibly sooner."

"What will the Chinese know?"

"They'll know all that. They have better data than us and their scientists are just as good as we are at interpreting that data and modelling it. They may even get a bit more advance notice than we will of an imminent strike."

"How much more?"

"A few hours. If a mega flare is emitted, it will probably take about 24–48 hours to reach us. The Chinese satellites and their models may give them a few more hours' notice than we will have. But there's nothing much we can do at that point. We just have to sit tight and hope for the best."

"Hoping is not good enough for me, Dame Ruth."

"There's always the power of prayer, Madam President."

"Ruth, my good friend. I just hope that's your famous British sense of irony at work. You and I both know full well that prayer won't save us from disaster. We need to rely on science this time. I've got the fate of the nation—and my Presidency—riding on this. I need to be 100 percent confident that the Solar Shield material is going to work. It is going to work, isn't it Dan?"

"Yes, Madam President. We're confident. The deployment has worked well, and we've continued to do more testing out in the New Mexico desert. The material works in theory, and it works in practice—to the extent we can test it without an actual live solar flare."

"And the Chinese One Shield? Are we still confident that it doesn't work?"

"Well, Madam President, that's where I have some bad news. We continued improving their test results by further miscalibrating their testing machines. Unfortunately, we think they might have noticed. As you'll remember, we turned a blind eye to the Chinese agent working at Solar Shield Ltd in Cambridge. He was a useful channel for us to pass disinformation back to Beijing. Unfortunately, he seems to have become suspicious and started some of his own testing, using new testing machines. We haven't been able to hack into those yet. A few months ago, he reported back to his superiors that he thought that there may be flaws in One Shield. And unfortunately, he's also worked out how to fix them. This has only happened recently, so they won't have had time to manufacture much new One Shield. But it's just possible they have changed the formula and manufactured enough to protect some critical military installations."

"Why wasn't I told this before?"

"Madam President, news of this leak and the potential risk that they have reformulated their product has only been confirmed in the last few days. We think their Research Director knew a few months ago. We're not seeing any evidence of a change in manufacturing strategy. But they are pretty good at hiding that from us. We just can't track all the textiles plants in China."

"So, you're telling me that our grand deception plan just went up in smoke—and the Chinese might actually be just as well protected as we are?"

"No. They can't be as fully protected as us. They haven't had time. But it is possible they have done enough to protect their military and security facilities. We can't discount it, but we think on balance that it's unlikely. Ma Jing, the Chinese Research Director, would need to be brave enough to tell Han. He'd probably be shot if he ever confessed that to Han that he and his entire team had fallen for our deception.

"That gives us some confidence that Ma Jing has just kept this to himself, and that Han will be the last person to find out that his One Shield isn't going to work.

"Han is also ramping up the Chinese campaign of disinformation – well, to be honest, it's pretty accurate information – about the imminent risk of a space weather event. We think this means he's still set on his Plan A. That adds to our confidence that he doesn't know yet that One Shield doesn't work. Over the past two days, European media have been reporting on the risk of an imminent solar flare with detailed scientific analyses. Most of it pretty accurate and none of it from us. It's so good, it's almost certainly from China. Han has clearly ordered a step up in the information war."

"I'm not seeing much of that here in the media."

"Well, Madam President, you might if you read more of the liberal press and watched more ANN. They are reporting the same stories as we are seeing in the European press. MTX is concentrating on the Big Tech hoax story. They have some evidence – all fakes, but clever fakes from the Russians – which purport to be emails between various US tech leaders on how they can use the space weather threat to sell more hardware and software upgrades."

The door into the Situation Room opened and the National Security Adviser rushed in.

"Madam President, sorry to interrupt, but we need to end this meeting now. I have the Chairman of the Joint Chiefs ready to dial in. It's urgent. Something very bad has happened."

"OK. Thank you, Ruth and Dan. We'll need to pick up another time. Keep us posted on any new developments on the Sun. Right now, looks like we have some big problems down here on Earth."

The Chairman of the Joint Chiefs came onto the large video screen on the wall opposite the President.

"OK, Mr. Chairman, how bad is it?"

"It's very bad, Madam President, I am afraid. As you know, a few hours ago, we started Operation SECURE PASSAGE. This was a regular transit through the waters of the South China Sea about two hundred miles south of Taiwan. As expected, Chinese aircraft flew low over the strike force. One of our ships reported communications difficulties and then its systems shut down completely. When the systems came back up, the captain reported that had he had lost control of their surface-to-air missile systems. It then appears that those systems shot down two Chinese J-36 aircraft."

"And the pilots?"

"Not a chance. The planes were hit at short range and immediately exploded in mid-air. No chance of the pilots ejecting in time."

"Was it our fault?"

"Madam President, it will look like that, and the Chinese will certainly accuse us of firing first. Their other planes then backed off. They never fired once on our ships."

"My orders were crystal-clear. Only to fire in self-defense. What the hell happened?"

"We are still trying to work it out. At this stage there are two possible explanations. First, we cannot discount human error or a systems error on our ship. There were problems with the Inouye's communications systems. It has a brand-new command, control and communications system on board. The central control computer initiated a complete system reset. That should not have happened while the ship was at sea, but for some reason it did. It's possible that when it was restarting, the system kicked onto automatic targeting and disabled the human override controls. USS Inouye has the latest fire control systems, which do allow for automatic firing. This was designed to combat the threat from these sixth generation J-36 fighters and their drone wingmen. They go too fast for pure human fire control."

"Well, you certainly have proved your ability to shoot down J-36s, Chairman. But that explanation is pretty terrible. What's the second explanation?"

"It is possible that the Chinese have hacked into the Inouye's operating system and taken control of the fire control system. They may have been able to circumvent our electronic countermeasures to take down all the control systems on the ship. They then may have inserted a new set of instructions into our surface-to-air systems to use our missiles to shoot down their own planes. They probably also disabled the defenses on their J-36s, rendering their own pilots defenseless. They were just human sacrifices in this operation. We won't be able to prove this until we get the Inouye back into dock and can strip down the systems to see what really happened. That will take four or five days. Meanwhile, we can't prove that the Chinese hacked our ship's systems, nor can we admit in public that they have the capability to do so. Until we can fix the vulnerability in our systems, the Chinese have the potential to take control of any of our naval vessels. Admitting that would be a humiliation and would render our entire Navy powerless until we find a fix."

"So General, under both options, you are telling me that I have to admit that we did this. I have to address the American people – and tell the world – that the United States Navy is responsible for shooting down two Chinese aircraft in an unprovoked action where we fired first. That's humiliating for me personally, but more importantly it's humiliating for the United States of America. Han is going to milk this for all he's got."

"I am very sorry, Madam President. If it would help, I would be happy to offer my resignation."

"No, that's the last thing I need. I know what Han's up to. It's clearly a false flag operation. The people to fire are your IT people, who left some gaping hole in your operating system that allowed the Chinese to take over our ship. But you're right, I can't ever admit that in public. This is just the start of Han's plan. I need you and all the Joint Chiefs in place—round-the-clock now. Han is about to launch something big.

"But I will need to ask you to relieve Admiral Halsey and the Captain of the Inouye of their commands with immediate effect. Someone needs to be seen to be carrying the can for this. And give command to the next in line—who's that?"

"That will be the British Admiral, who is leading their contribution to this joint strike force. We gave them the number two slot without thinking it would ever be taken up."

"So, on top of everything else, I've got a damned foreigner in charge of the most powerful US carrier strike force ever assembled. Jesus Christ. Anything else?"

"The British are our closest allies, and he is a very experienced Admiral, Madam President."

"You try telling that to the America First brigade in my party. They'll start accusing me of treason for putting a foreigner in charge of our brave men and women in a time of war."

A staffer entered the Situation Room and passed the National Security Adviser a note.

"Madam President," he said, adding, "in New York, the Chinese have called an emergency session of the United Nations Security Council. And President Han wants an urgent call."

"I bet he does," said the President, "I assume he called the US media first."

"Well yes, someone did. MTX and ANN are both running a story that the US has shot two Chinese planes in an unprovoked attack in the South China Sea.

"ANN is already calling for an urgent meeting of the United Nations Security Council."

"And what's MTX calling for?" asked the President.

"War."

CHAPTER 22

UNITED NATIONS SECURITY COUNCIL, NEW YORK

11 p.m., EST, September 3

The British, American, and French Permanent Representatives to the United Nations stood in a huddle in the corridor outside the Security Council Chamber. The Chinese had called this emergency meeting at 6 p.m., to meet at 9 p.m. It was now 11 p.m. and they were still waiting to get started. The UN couldn't find a Chinese-to-French interpreter. The French Permanent Representative wouldn't allow the meeting to start.

"Come on, Claude. This is getting ridiculous. We're on the edge of war in the South China Sea and you are holding this back because there's no simultaneous Chinese-to-French translation? You're all totally fluent in English. The whole Council is totally fluent in English. The Chinese are going to speak in English. Let's just get started."

"No way. Sorry guys," said the French PR in his perfect accent, which betrayed a slight hint of Boston vowels from his time at Harvard. "Paris just won't let me do that."

"I've heard rumors about this happening before, but I never believed that you actually did this."

"I'm afraid so. *Pour la gloire de la France et la Francophonie,* and all that…"

Another half-hour passed, and finally the UN Secretariat confirmed that they had found the missing interpreter who had been out at dinner and his cellphone had run out of battery power. At least that was his excuse. When they had called his home, his wife had thought he was still at the UN. They reassured her that he probably was, and he had just been uncontactable, given the poor reception inside the UN HQ.

The fifteen Permanent Representatives took their places around the famous horseshoe-shaped table. The rows of seats in the auditorium looking down on the Council were unusually full. This promised to be an historic meeting.

By a quirk of timing, Russia held the rotating Presidency this month. That didn't give them any additional voting rights, but it gave them control over process and made it harder for the Western allies to pull any procedural tricks to avoid a vote. They knew that a vote would not go well for the US. If there were any way to avoid a vote, the US Permanent Representative would try to. But that didn't look hopeful. There was no alternative but to take it all on the chin.

The Chinese Permanent Representative led off. Although entitled to speak in Chinese, one of the UN's official languages, he spoke in perfect English. In his case, he had a slight Texan drawl; he had read international studies at the University of Texas in Austin. The University of Texas (UT) had a large concentration of Chinese students—possibly because of the very strong links between UT and the US military and security agencies. The Chinese PR was addressing the world, and he delivered a fluent condemnation of US aggression.

"I speak to you tonight at a grave moment in world history. My nation has been attacked by the United States. This is a heinous crime. This attack was completely unprovoked. Two brave Chinese airmen are dead. Chinese sovereignty has been violated. Our aircraft were simply patrolling Chinese territorial waters. There is no doubt over our sovereignty over these waters. They have been part of our nation's birthright for thousands of years. The American and British warships illegally entered Chinese waters at approximately 4 a.m. local time. This was no routine so-called transit. This was the most powerful carrier strike force assembled in the Pacific since World War II. Never before have two aircraft carriers entered these waters as part of the same naval force. They were accompanied by over a dozen powerful warships. There can be no peaceful interpretation of the intentions of this strike force. It was set on attacking the sovereign interests of the People's Republic of China. Naturally, as would any sovereign nation, we sent out aircraft to track this hostile invading force. They flew peacefully over the strike force. President Han had issued orders—you can see them on the screen above, with English, Arabic, Russian and French translations. His orders made clear that the planes were not only not to fire on the strike force first, even though they had illegally entered our sovereign waters. He also made clear that, even if fired upon, they should not respond. They should withdraw and avoid escalating the situation. President Han was concerned about the risk of further loss of life, particularly among the innocent sailors on board the American and British ships. Those American and British sailors do not deserve to die because of the aggressive actions of their political leaders. Sadly, though two innocent Chinese pilots were cruelly killed by surface-to-air missiles fired from one of the US destroyers. There can be no justification for this hostile act. The Chinese people call on the United Nations to join them in condemning this brutal aggression by the imperialist American and British forces. We urge the members of the Security Council to support Resolution 3572, which condemns these actions and calls on the US and British to respect the integrity of Chinese sovereign waters in the South China Sea."

The Russian President of the Security Council then asked other members to speak. It didn't look good for the Americans and British. Of the fifteen members, the ten non-permanent members were an unusually anti-Western collection of nations. The African members typically voted with China these days, reflecting their high level of indebtedness to Chinese banks; offering up their UN votes to support China was one of the least costly ways to service these debts. The South American member came from a country whose populist President was rabidly anti-American. The Gulf state was strongly aligned to Russia and China, dependent on them for arms sales since Congress had imposed a ban on sales of US weapons. Even the Europeans, normally reliable supporters of the Americans in the Security Council, were divided. In two of the European states, the political elites were heavily influenced by Russian and Chinese money and could not be relied upon to support the Americans and British.

The French Permanent Representative came in strongly, in French of course, to express regret at the loss of life but to support the American and British right to sail in international waters. He called for calm, and for time to allow the Americans to conduct a full inquiry into what had led to this tragic accident. The British PR similarly expressed regret, called for calm and the need to wait for the results of the inquiry.

It was then the American Permanent Representative's turn. There was little she could say to turn the tide of the Council. "The United States deeply regrets the unfortunate incident earlier today in the South China Sea. US forces, operating with our British allies, were upholding their rights – indeed the rights of the entire international community – to sail in these international waters. We cannot accept any one nation unilaterally exerting claims over waters that belong to all nations. This is a fundamental principle of international relations. China has repeatedly asserted illegal claims to islands in the South China Sea, built new islands and installed military equipment to extend its aggressive intentions against the peace-loving countries in that region.

"Nevertheless, we deeply regret the events that transpired earlier today. The United States accepts full responsibility. The President has authorized me to extend our most sincere apologies for the human error that led to this unfortunate incident. She has commissioned an independent inquiry. We will share the results of that inquiry with this Council as soon as it is finished. We have offered substantial financial compensation to the families of the Chinese airmen who lost their lives. We call for calm at this difficult time. The resolution would only serve to inflame an already difficult situation. We urge the Council to reject it."

It was then the Russian Permanent Representative's chance to speak. Thick-set, bull-chested, heavily bearded, and prone to rhetorical flights of fancy at the Council table, he was a memorable figure. His style clearly played well back in Moscow. He was said to be a particular favorite of President Bortsov, who found his rants against the West amusing. He had kept his job when many others in the senior ranks of the Russian diplomatic service had unexpectedly 'died of natural causes' or 'committed suicide' in strange circumstances.

"I will now speak in my capacity as the Russian Representative, putting aside momentarily my duties as President of the Council. I join my Chinese colleagues and indeed the majority of this Council in condemning this heinous crime by the United States. We are not surprised by these actions. The US and its lapdog ally, the British, were clearly spoiling for a fight. President Wallace has repeatedly promised to get tough on our Chinese friends and on the Russian people. Now she must live with the consequences. President Wallace tells us that she is a Christian. This was not the act of a Christian. I urge her to read her Bible more closely. Hosea Chapter 8 Verse 7 says: "For they have sown the wind and they shall reap the whirlwind." The Americans and the British shall indeed reap the whirlwind. Now our American colleague has promised to share the results of their 'independent inquiry.' I call on her to accept Russian and Chinese participation in that inquiry. Then it will truly be independent. If it is just the Americans, marking your own homework, as you say in America, then we know the results. It will be a whitewash by the White House. We stand with our Chinese friends, whose sovereignty has been violated. They are victims of unforgiveable Western aggression. We support Resolution 3572."

The Council then voted. Supporting China were Russian, the African, Latin American, and Gulf states, and two European nations. The resolution had the nine votes necessary to carry. The US, British and French had no option but to exercise their vetoes. The Americans could have done on it their own, but the show of unity by the three Western permanent members was important. Even so, the damage was done. The weight of international opinion was now against the West. The Chinese could claim a victory, just as the West had repeatedly claimed moral victories when the Chinese and Russians vetoed resolutions condemning them in the past.

The Chinese Representative asked for the floor to make a concluding statement. The Russian President of the Council agreed.

"The Chinese people thank the members of the Security Council for their strong support against this unjustified aggression by American and British military forces in Chinese sovereign waters. My nation asserts its rights to defend its territory both in its sovereign waters and in respect of a rebellious island controlled by an illegitimate government. We can no longer accept these Western imperialist threats against our sovereignty. The integrity of the Chinese nation must be restored. Today's vote by the Council, though vetoed by the aggressors, shows that the international community supports China's right to self-determination and the preservation of its territorial integrity. The Chinese people can wait for justice no longer."

The US Representative tried to intervene to counter the Chinese closing statement, but the Russian President was not going to let the US have the last word. It was going to be his.

"That concludes the 12,155th meeting of the Security Council," he said. "Given the perilous situation created by this egregious Western aggression, let us hope it is not the last."

CHAPTER 23

OVAL OFFICE, WHITE HOUSE, WASHINGTON D.C.

8 p.m. EST, September 4

The President sat alone at the Resolute Desk. She had cleared her diary for the evening. The light was fading fast after a glorious Washington September day. Following the extreme heat and humidity of July and August, September brought slightly less humid weather, but the temperature was still up in the high 80s. She got up and walked out onto the colonnade, pacing up and down. The sky was a beautiful dark blue as the Sun set over to the West, behind the Lincoln Memorial. She looked at the lengthening shadows on the South Lawn. The late evening sunlight on the grass made the scene look so calm and peaceful. It was hard to believe that the Sun was about to jettison a massive geo-magnetic flare that could change the course of human history.

She needed time to think. She needed someone to talk to. Someone she trusted. Someone she knew was only out to help her and not out for themselves. But he wasn't there. He had gone off on that mission, which he should never have been on. She missed him, but she was also so angry at him. Once again, she was alone and would have to work this all through by herself.

How would the history books record her leadership in this crisis? Would this be her Cuban Missile Crisis, that would set her place in the history books? Or would it be a fiasco that undermined US leadership in the world? Would the next few days go down as the end of the American century and the beginning of the Chinese century? Until yesterday, she had been confident that Han's gamble wouldn't pay off. But then Han outplayed her brilliantly with his false flag attack. That had put her completely on the defensive. Did he know everything? Perhaps the Research Director had confessed. Han was smart enough not to kill him straightaway. That would reveal to the Americans that the Chinese had spotted the deception. Han might just be running a double bluff. Was he luring her into a trap? Were his forces now protected from a solar flare strike?

Han had humiliated the US in front of the entire world, making it harder for her to respond if he did launch an attack on Taiwan. And if there wasn't a solar flare strike on Earth, he now had a clear run at Taiwan. The US Navy's ability to protect Taiwan was compromised until they fixed the hack. That could take weeks. All of a sudden, Han looked like the smart one. Perhaps he really was the champion chess player, who had had a plan all along. He had always been several moves ahead of her. Her only chance now was to hope that there was a solar flare strike and that Han remained ignorant about the failure of One Shield. She ran the odds in her head. It didn't look good. If both were 50/50 bets, the chances of both of them going her way were no more than twenty-five percent. Any betting person would now be backing Han to win this tussle with her—and that would mean the end of her political career. Worse, it would mean the emergence of China as the world's superpower.

Her call with Han earlier that evening had not gone well. She had apologized for the unfortunate error that led to the loss of the two pilots and extended the offer of compensation. It made her feel sick in the stomach to have to apologize to Han who she knew had knowingly sent those two pilots to their death. But the deception plan required her to keep up the pretense. Han had berated her, as expected, for the hostile incursion by the USS Gerard R. Ford Strike Force. He at least had had the courtesy to give her some advance notice of the ultimatum he was about to announce to the world.

Thirty minutes later, at 8 a.m. Beijing time, 8 p.m. Washington, Han issued his ultimatum. He timed it to catch primetime TV in the US. The Europeans would learn about it when they woke up in a few hours' time.

Han's message was all too clear.

"The United States and United Kingdom naval forces have violated the territorial integrity of the People's Republic of China. They have opened fire, without provocation, on two Chinese airplanes which were peacefully asserting China's right to patrol its own airspace. Two Chinese pilots have been killed by the American forces. The Chinese people are peace-loving and patient. We have repeatedly sought to resolve this dispute through negotiation. But rather than allow these negotiations to continue, the Americans and British have launched an aggressive military strike against China. This cannot be allowed to stand. I hereby give notice to the Americans, British and any other hostile nations that, as from 8 a.m. Beijing time tomorrow, all foreign warships within Chinese territorial waters will be treated as enemy combatants. The Chinese naval forces have been authorized to use all necessary means to neutralize the threat posed to China by these warships."

It was a credible threat. Chinese hypersonic missiles and the new J-36s could take out even the most advanced warships that the Americans and British had. Some of the older ships were extremely vulnerable to 3rd generation hypersonic missiles—and the Chinese would definitely target them. Even the USS Ford and the British Type 55s would have trouble seeing off multiple hypersonic missiles in a simultaneous swarm formation. The President knew that if she sent the strike force back into disputed waters, it wasn't a strike force any more. It was a flotilla of sitting ducks. Han had a clear run to invade Taiwan. He could launch his invasion fleet secure in the knowledge that the US and British fleets could not get close enough to stop him. And if he thought the US would be disabled by the impending solar flare strike and that he was protected, then he'd certainly give the invasion order. It was all falling into place for Han's grand plan.

She pressed the screen on her desk. "Send in the Operation HELIOS team in now. I need an update before I give my address to the Nation."

Dan came into the Oval Office, together with Baker, the Chief of Staff. They remained standing. The President wasn't in the mood for an extended meeting. She just wanted the latest news.

"Where's Ruth? I need Ruth here now."

"Ruth left a couple of hours ago, Madam President. She's on her way back to her lab. We need her there with all her kit and her analytical team to guide us through the next few days. It looks like we are right near the critical moment. Solar activity has increased sharply in the last twenty-four hours. Ruth's team are now seeing flares of 50–75 million mile range each hour. Ruth expects that we will have at least one mega flare with the range to reach Earth within the next 36-48 hours."

"And Dan, what will the Chinese be seeing?"

"Madam President, they'll have exactly the same information as Ruth, possibly a few hours ahead of us. We are getting some reports that Han has moved his military forces up to their equivalent of DEFCON 2. They have moved to that state of readiness so that he can launch an invasion fleet within twenty-four hours of giving the order."

"And on the political front. What are we seeing?"

"We are seeing a lot of media speculation now about an imminent solar flare strike. European Governments have reassured their citizens that protective measures are in place. Chinese client states are also putting out reassuring messages. Here, it's the usual story. You're being attacked by the

Democrats and liberal media for having left the nation unprotected, but your party and your friends in the right-wing media are holding the line that this is all a hoax and nothing to worry about. Businesses assume it will be fine. Large businesses have typically bought the European product and protected their data centers. Small and mid-sized businesses are assuming this is all a hoax and, if it isn't, then they'll come begging for a massive federal government bail-out—just as they got in the Covid pandemics.

"We're seeing some protests now forming outside the White House, but nothing exceptional. The largest crowd is a peaceful group with 'End of the world is nigh' signs. It's their moment in the sun—if that's not an unfortunate phrase at this time."

"OK. Pretty much as I expected. I'll need to say something about this solar flare issue in my address to the nation at 9 p.m. Baker, can you get Peggy and Co. to put something in my remarks—it's all fine, nothing to worry, God loves America, and He will protect the US of A. Just pray and he will answer your prayers… that type of thing. OK, get the TV crew in here and get it all set up.

"In a few minutes, I'm going to address my fellow Americans. I'll scare the living daylights out of them when I explain what Han is up to, and then I'll comprehensively lie to them about the threat from solar flares. In fact, I think I'll be telling them more lies in a single broadcast than any other President ever told them in an entire term of office—and that's quite a high bar to meet."

"It's all in the national interest, Madam President."

"I know. But it still stinks. I had hoped to leave this Office with some principles intact."

CHAPTER 24

OVAL OFFICE, WHITE HOUSE, WASHINGTON D.C.

9 p.m. EST, September 4

"**M**y fellow Americans, I am addressing you tonight from the Oval Office at a time of great tension in the world. I know many of you are concerned about the situation in the South China Sea.

"There is no hiding from the fact that President Han is set on a very dangerous course that threatens peace in the region and threatens our essential national interests.

"I will be straight with you tonight. I know that the American people want the truth, however, uncomfortable it might be.

"I spoke earlier today with President Han. It was a difficult conversation. I apologized for the regrettable human error that led to the tragic loss of two Chinese airmen. I explained to President Han the initial findings of the investigations that have already taken place on the USS Daniel Inouye. A combination of human error and computer system failings led to the tragic accident. I repeated our offer of generous financial compensation to the families of the two airmen. President Han refused to accept my apologies and rejected the offer of compensation.

"Earlier this evening, President Han made a statement in which he said that any US or British ships in disputed waters would be treated as enemy combatants. America and its allies cannot accept this ultimatum. We will continue to assert our right – recognized in international law and upheld by the international courts – to sail in these international waters. Over thirty percent of the world's trade is transported through these waters. China cannot just assert control over the entire South China Sea, its vital trade routes and all its rich resources in flagrant breach of international law. I told President Han that the US would not accept his illegal ultimatum and we would continue to assert our right to sail through international waters.

"President Han is also threatening the people of Taiwan. Our position has been clear for many years. We stand shoulder to shoulder with the people of Taiwan. The future of their island – and whether it should be independent or unified with the People's Republic – is a matter for the people of Taiwan. It cannot and must not be determined by force. I warned President Han not to threaten the island of Taiwan and I reminded him that the full might of US and allied forces stood ready to defend the people of Taiwan if they were attacked.

"I urged President Han to withdraw his ultimatum and return to the negotiating table. I offered to send a high-level US delegation to Beijing to restart those negotiations without preconditions. He rejected this offer.

"And so, my fellow Americans, we stand at a historic crossroads. Do we climb down in the face of aggression, or do we stand up for freedom?

"I know you will all join me in concluding that this is not a choice. America never climbs down in the face of aggression. America will always choose the path of freedom.

"Let President Han be in no doubt of our resolve.

"Before I leave you tonight, I wanted to address one other subject that is getting a lot of attention in the media and may be of concern to some of you. You may have seen alarmist reports in certain news media and on some TV channels suggesting that the Earth is about to be hit by a giant solar flare that will disable all our electronic communications. It sounds like something out of science fiction.

"Let me tell you tonight that there is nothing to be worried about. Americans can sleep easy. There is no threat to America. The risks have been hugely exaggerated, not least by our enemies abroad and by some unscrupulous businesses trying to sell their products on the back of these false claims.

"I can assure you that America is safe.

"The Good Lord is watching over us and will protect us.

"I will be praying to Him tonight for guidance and wisdom to help guide us through these troubled times and to wrap us all in his loving and protective arms.

"God is with us. God loves America. I know that He will protect us from danger. Remember with me the words of Psalm 23.

"*Though I walk through the valley of the shadow of death, I will fear no evil, for thou art with me.*

"I urge you all to join me in prayer tonight for the good Lord's protection."

The picture switched from President Wallace behind the Resolute Desk in the Oval Office to images of the Stars and Stripes flying over American homes. The National Anthem played, swelling to its rousing chorus.

The camera cut back to the President.

"God bless America. God bless our troops. And God bless our flag that flies o'er the land of the free and the home of the brave. Good night."

The image of the President faded and then the networks cut back to their news shows. The talking heads would now go over her every word and criticize, or support, her.

"Off air now, Madam President."

"Thank God that's over. I feel sick to my stomach having to mislead the people like that. Did I sound sincere?"

"Absolutely, Madam President, you came across as very sincere and authentic."

"Well Baker, as I always say, the key to success in politics is authenticity. And if you can fake that, you've got it made."

CHAPTER 25

FAYNE LABS, UNIVERSITY OF NEW MEXICO

8 p.m. Mountain Time, September 4

Ruth made it back to Albuquerque New Mexico in just five hours door to door. With a two-hour time difference, it was only 8 p.m. Mountain Time when she got back home. The Operation HELIOS team had access to one of the CIA's Gulfstream H10s, which made domestic travel within the US just about tolerable. The team couldn't afford the risk of the delays and cancellations on commercial flights. It was just as well, as when Ruth landed in Albuquerque, the United Airlines flight was still sitting on the tarmac at Dulles, grounded by thunderstorms in the Washington area.

She just had time to say hi briefly to Steve and the twins, who were at home for the evening. A few months ago, Steve had finished his work at the facility in the desert and taken up a new academic post at University of New Mexico. He'd negotiated a delayed start and was now on sabbatical. He was enjoying working out how to spend his newfound wealth. He and Ruth had made nearly $100 million in windfall profits from the sale of his Cambridge business to Fayne Capital. With all this time on his hands now, he had taken up some hobbies. He had just finished a master chef course at the Culinary Institute of America. He had enjoyed working at the other CIA.

Ruth only had half an hour to enjoy Steve's latest creation—a rather fine Timbale de ris de veau. Steve was proud of his creation and had hoped Ruth could stay long enough to enjoy it.

Over dinner, they discussed the President's Address to the Nation. The twins were outraged that the President was still in denial. Ruth agreed with them and put on a good show of criticizing President Wallace, but she found it hard misleading her own children. She didn't want to alarm the twins, so she told them that, while a flare was highly likely, she didn't think it would be strong enough to reach Earth. But if it was, she said, then the President would look very foolish indeed for having ignored the science. Steve kept quiet and talked about his cooking lessons. Ruth was cross with him. He could have helped out. As it was, she was having to do all the deception within the family.

"Sorry, Darlings. I just have to get back to the lab tonight. I have some urgent work I need to complete."

Steve knew what she meant. He felt a sense of panic growing inside him. Would the new improved Solar Shield really work in real life as it had in the lab tests? Did they have enough coverage of all the vulnerable installations in the US? If it didn't work, would the CIA and MI6 really protect him from the inevitable lawsuits that would follow?

The twins though had no idea what Ruth really meant. She often worked late. They were still completely unaware of their parent's double lives. They had enjoyed the move to New Mexico and settled in well to university life in the States. Many of their British friends had also gone to American universities. They thought it was pretty cool that their father had finally made it as an entrepreneur, and they had never really understood what their mother did all day as a scientist. But whatever it was, that seemed pretty cool, too.

Ruth drove her electric SUV to the Fayne facility on the UNM campus. Her team greeted her with hugs and immediately took her to their most secure meeting room. They projected the latest readings on the Sun's surface activity and the projections from the quantum computer modelling.

"The headline, Ruth, is that the Sun's about to blow. Surface activity is more intense now than we have ever recorded. The solar flares are continuing to be ejected on the same horizontal plane. We still don't understand why, it must be some currents with the Sun driving this pattern. But it has been consistent for days—and still pointing right into our line of orbit.

"The flares now have a range of 50–75 million miles up from 30–50 million miles two days ago. On the Kp scale we're now seeing flares at intensity six to seven. Nine is when we start to get nervous. These Kp sixes and sevens are being emitted at regular intervals of 3–4 hours. If this pattern continues, and the rate of increase in intensity remains the same, we think we will get our first 100-million-mile flare within the next 12–24 hours. And when it comes, we have about 24–48 hours to impact."

"We've been preparing for this moment for years," said Ruth. "And now, there's nothing more we can do, right?"

"We're all ready. Nothing more to do. We just have to sit and wait. Ruth, you may as well go home. We'll text you on your secure phone with hourly updates."

Ruth didn't want to leave the facility. But she knew that once a flare was on course for Earth, she'd get no sleep for forty-eight hours or more, so any sleep she could get now was worth it.

She texted Dan, who was on overnight duty in the Situation Room in the White House.

Ruth - 9.30 p.m. Concert due to start soon. I'll text you as soon as I know that HELIOS are coming on stage. We'll have to endure some warm-up bands first before the Main Event.

She didn't need to text in fake code. The phones were completely secure. But it provided some light relief for Dan and Ruth.

She drove home and checked her phone as soon as she pulled into her driveway.

Lab - 10.05 p.m. No activity in last hour

She went straight to bed but couldn't get to sleep. She checked her phone.

Lab - 10.45 p.m. Large flare. Estimated range 75 million miles. Direction 30 degrees ahead of Earth's position on orbital path. No risk of strike.

Ruth was only sleeping fitfully. Waking up every hour or so to check the phone.

Lab - 12.00 a.m. No activity since 10.45.

Lab - 1.30 a.m. First mega flare. Estimated range 100 million miles. Direction 45 degrees behind Earth's position on orbital path. No risk of strike.

Lab - 3 a.m. No activity since 1.30.

Lab - 3.30 a.m. No activity to report.

Lab - 3.51 a.m. Get in here fast. Huge eruption. Kp-10+ scale flare. Estimated range 110 million miles. Direction—directly on Earth's path. Time to Earth strike 40 hours.

Ruth leapt out of bed and ran down the car. She had been sleeping in her clothes so she could make a quick exit.

At the first set of lights, she texted Dan in the Situation Room.

Ruth - 4.01 a.m. Operation HELIOS is go. Strike due in 40 hours. Duration of strike could be up to 24 hours.

The lights changed and Ruth drove on. She ran into another red light and checked her phone.

She read Dan's reply

Dan - 4.03 a.m. Got it. Any more details?

Ruth - 4.04 a.m. Likely to hit Earth late tomorrow - at 10pm EST, 7pm Pacific time so Continental US will be away from the Sun and protected initially. It will be late afternoon in Hawaii.

The lights changed. Ruth drove for another few miles until she hit the next set of lights and checked her phone.

Dan - 4.05 a.m. Shit. That's a disaster. Chinese will smell a big stinking rat when Hawaii escapes unscathed. That screws up whole plan.

Then after a pause.

Dan - 4.06 a.m. WTF are we going to do?

CHAPTER 26

SITUATION ROOM, WHITE HOUSE, WASHINGTON D.C.

615 a.m. EST, September 5

D an turned to the staffer sitting in the corner of the Situation Room behind the control panel for all the communications systems that supported meetings in this room.

"Get me the Director, National Intelligence—ASAP."

Fifteen minutes later the Director came on the screen. She was just back from her early morning exercise and was still in her running gear.

"Cindy, sorry to bother you at this early hour. We have a big problem on Operation HELIOS. I need access to your best cyber guy—urgently."

"What sort of cyber guy—offense, defense, technical expert? We've got the lot, but they come in very different flavors."

"Offensive cyber…"

"OK, got lots of them. But against what target as we have different guys for different targets?"

"The target is the State of Hawaii."

"What! Dan, have you lost your mind? We can't do that without direct POTUS authorization."

"I know. We'll go over all of this with the President at the morning intelligence briefing. But before then I need to talk to a real expert to see what we could do and what the risks are. I need that conversation in the next hour before the POTUS Intelligence Briefing meeting."

"OK. I'll see what I can do."

"Whoever it is will need to be cleared to the highest level. This is as tight a compartment as we have."

"They'll be cleared. But it's always a bit academic trying to put restrictions on these guys. They can hack their way to find any classified intelligence in our system if they really want to find it. They're not allowed this access, but the best ones seem to be able to get in without leaving a trace. Chances are this guy will know all about Operation HELIOS already."

"Now you tell us! No wonder this stuff leaks out. We're lucky none of your guys have defected to Moscow recently."

The connection ended and Dan took a short break. He swung by the White House mess to pick up coffee and a bagel for breakfast. He might not eat again for a while.

At 7.15 a.m., the screen lit up and someone called David from US Cyber Force logged in. He didn't look like a hacker. Dan was expecting some teenager with greasy hair and a scruffy tee shirt. David looked like a Mormon missionary. Dark suit. White shirt. Black tie. Buzz-cut hair.

"I'm David. Director Short said you needed some help. She said I could talk to you about possibilities, but you could not give me any instructions."

"I know, David. I just need to talk through options with someone who is a real pro at this offensive cyber stuff. Are you the offensive cyber expert or are you from the legal team to go through all the protocols before I get to the expert?"

"No, Sir. I am the offensive cyber expert. I know I don't look like one. I'm seconded to the NSA from the Marine Cyber Corps, and I have a PhD in cyber security from Brigham Young. In Utah, even the computer geeks look like this. Don't worry, though. We're really good at this work."

"OK. Here's the situation. I need a plan to take down the communications of the entire State of Hawaii at around 4 p.m. tomorrow evening. And a few Pacific islands like Guam and American Samoa. But I need to do it in a way that doesn't actually cause any lasting damage or threat to human life.

"Sure, we can do that. Just need to run through a few questions."

"Hang on. How come it's so easy? You guys aren't meant to be able to attack the US."

"We practice attacking the US all the time, Sir. I lead the Red team on most of our cyber war-games. I've taken down more US cities in more simulations that anyone else on the Red team. That's why the Director put me forward for this exercise."

"It's not an exercise, David. This one is for real."

"I know that Sir, but the Director told me it was an exercise, and I didn't want to upset her by revealing that I knew she was lying. I assume this is all part of the Operation HELIOS thing. By the way, great plan. But it has one big flaw."

"You're not meant to know about Operation HELIOS. What's the flaw by the way?"

"Well, what we're about to talk about I assume. At least I hope there's only one flaw in the plan. You didn't allow for the scenario where Han realizes that the US is unaffected by the solar strike."

"Correct. That's the problem. It's a remote risk. The problem arises if Han has found out about the ineffectiveness of One Shield and has had enough time to implement additional protections on his command-and-control systems. If he hasn't done that, then it doesn't matter.

Han will lose all his communications when the flare strikes, and he won't know what's going on in the US. But if he has had time to build in extra protection, he'll become suspicious when he learns that Hawaii has been unaffected. It's a remote scenario, but we just missed it. The plan still works, but not just as well. We have to convince Han that Hawaii has lost all its communications.

"I should have planned for this scenario. I didn't want to risk a 'Red team' exercise as that would have brought a new set of people into the compartment. The security risk was too high. Bad call. But anyway, how the hell did you find out about it?"

"I found the files while conducting a penetration test on the CIA systems. They'd put the Operation HELIOS files in the most secure part of their system. Obviously, that's the bit that any hacker really wants to get to. It's actually the worst place to hide the really secret stuff. It's a honeypot for cyber intruders like me. In the NSA's penetration test on the CIA last week, I got into the inner sanctum and planted a flag in the HELIOS compartment. The CIA cyber defense team were so embarrassed they haven't worked out how to tell their bosses yet."

"Apparently so … but it won't matter in a day or two, as this thing could be all over by then. For better. Or as it looks at the moment, for worse. What do you need to know?"

"What exactly do you mean by 'take down the State of Hawaii'? Do you want it to stop operating for a day—nothing works? Or do you want to selectively take down bits like the internet but not the water supply? Public transportation but not the Emergency Services? We can basically turn off anything you want us to turn off and then turn it back on again. But that gets dangerous if we start turning off essential services."

"I just need every person and every business in the State of Hawaii to lose all contact with the outside world for twenty-four hours."

"That's easy. We'll just disable all the undersea cables running into Hawaii and block any satellite communications over the islands. That's pretty simple. The communications companies have terrible cyber security."

"You need to cut off the military communications out of the island as well."

"That's fine. That's the first thing we do in the war game—so we know how to do that against all the armed services. I assume you want aircraft to land but not take off."

"Correct."

"And we'll protect hospitals."

"Of course. The President has made clear no fatalities. Fine, now get on with it." Dan was getting impatient.

"And when?" asked David.

"Late afternoon, from about 4 p.m. Hawaii time and simultaneously for the Pacific Islands," replied Dan. "The window for the strike is between 5 p.m. and 7 p.m. local, but we need to go early in case the flare accelerates as it approaches Earth's magnetic field."

"OK. I'll work up the plan and await the presidential authorization."

Dan didn't know whether to be impressed or terrified. This clean-cut young marine from Utah seemed trustworthy and loyal. But what would happen if he decided to defect to the other side? Or if the Russians or Chinese had their own version of David—able to turn off entire US states at a click of mouse? That was something to worry about another day.

At 7.45 a.m., Dan walked up from the Situation Room to the Oval Office to join the President's Daily Intelligence briefing. He picked up his copy of the top-secret President's Daily Intelligence Briefing from the CIA Officer waiting in the Roosevelt Room.

Dan started to read . . .

POTUS DAILY INTELLIGENCE BRIEFING. SEPTEMBER 5

China mobilization order given ahead of Taiwan invasion

Yesterday, at 10 p.m. Beijing time, President Han ordered his military to move to full invasion readiness. The fleet is now ready to depart from mainland harbors within twenty-four hours. The cover story is that this is a large-scale exercise and show of strength in retaliation for the downing of the two Chinese jets. Bombers, fighter jets and troop carriers are being readied at four airbases in Fujian Province. Invasion force is estimated at twenty-five thousand troops in first wave of sea landings and five thousand troops by air. Subsequent waves will increase occupation force in Taiwan to over one hundred thousand troops by day five, with an additional two hundred thousand to follow within two weeks.

Heightened anti-American protests throughout China

Crowds have gathered every day this week outside US Embassy in Beijing and in all US Consulates in China. Police have waived restrictions on protests. Crowds are well organized and clearly coordinated. The protestors are calling for reintegration of Taiwan into China and attacks on US vessels in the South China Sea.

Solar Weather propaganda

Chinese media are carrying extensive reports of heightened activity on the Sun and the potential for extreme space weather over the coming days. Media reports celebrate President Han's leadership in ensuring that China is protected through their One Shield product. International reports from China's allied states report enthusiastic support for China's philanthropy in providing cheap access to One Shield as part of the One Belt, One Road, One Shield program.

Dan skimmed through the other reports from trouble spots around the world, and then came to final section. A series of punch points with other snippets of information for the President's quick informa-tion. The final point caught his eye.

Missing scientist

Ma Jing, Director of Chinese Solar Research Institute, has gone miss-ing. His social media sites have been taken down. Director has not been seen for forty-eight hours.

Oh my God, thought Dan.

Han knows.

CHAPTER 27

OVAL OFFICE, WHITE HOUSE, WASHINGTON D.C.

8 a.m. EST, September 5

The President strode in for the first meeting of what promised to be a very long day. She had hardly slept. The address to the nation had been well received, but she felt deeply guilty about the level of deception. Even if this plan worked, one day she might have to explain to the American people why she had lied through her teeth in her address. Would they ever trust her again? She was worried that the Operation HELIOS plan just wouldn't work. She had rather fallen in love with the strategy as it was so clever, and it solved all her problems. But she was worried that the team hadn't tested it sufficiently. Had they missed a fatal flaw?

If the plan failed, her career was over. China would leapfrog the US as the dominant global super- power. There were so many potential points of failure. What if Solar Shield didn't work? What if there just weren't enough US flags flying in the right places? What if the Chinese One Shield turned out to be more effective than we thought? And worst of all, what if Han had found out about Operation HELIOS? He'd been one step ahead of her all through this crisis. Was he about to play his trump card?

The senior intelligence briefers came in, led by the Director of National Intelligence. Aaron Douglass Thomson from the CIA entered next accompanied by Dan, followed by the Chairman of the Joint Chiefs.

"OK everyone," said the President. "Let's start with the Sun … Over to you, Dan."

"Madam President, in the early hours of this morning the Sun emitted an unusually large solar flare. It's bigger than anything we have measured before—over ten on the Kp scale. It is directly on target to reach Earth at around 10 p.m. Eastern tomorrow evening.

"OK. I'm hoping the timing of that is good news," interrupted the President. "It's dark here so I assume we'll largely shaded from the impact."

"Yes and no, Madam President. The flare is so large that it will take over twenty-four hours to pass over the Earth. We will get the full force in the Continental US during the day of September 7th. That's OK, as we are confident in our protection. The problem is Hawaii. It will get hit before us at about the same time as Beijing."

"Isn't Hawaii protected?"

"That is the problem. It *is* protected. And if Han finds out that it is unscathed, then he'll realize that the US isn't as exposed as he thinks. He's currently planning to give the invasion order later today. We think his scientists will be giving him exactly the same estimates as we are giving you. Our Beijing Station has reported that Han called a meeting of his National Security Council for 9 a.m. Beijing time tomorrow morning their time (that's 9 p.m. our time this evening), and we think that meeting will endorse the invasion order. His plan is to have his fleet leaving the harbor twenty-four hours later just as the flare strikes and the US gets shut down. He's assuming our 7th Fleet will be disabled immediately and that chaos will unfold in the US as dawn breaks on September 7th. He thinks that our listening stations and communications systems in the Pacific will be shut down as soon as the flare strikes. He believes that we won't find out about the invasion until we restore our communications systems in a few weeks' time. The danger is that, if he spots that Hawaii's fine, he'll realize that the US is protected. At that point, he will probably call back the invasion fleet or turn it into a genuine exercise."

"OK. Got it. Sounds bad," Wallace remained calm. "What do you recommend?"

"With your permission, Madam President, we'll just take Hawaii off the grid tomorrow afternoon. We will shut down all communications into and out of the island from 4 p.m. onwards Hawaii time for about six hours. We'll do the same in our Pacific territories. We'll issue some public statement about a massive failure in the Pacific undersea cabling network, which unfortunately occurred at the same time as a software upgrade in the key communications satellite. With your approval, we'll brief off the record that the Chinese launched a cyber-attack on the undersea cables and interfered with our communications satellites. That would probably play well on the Hill."

"Will Han fall for that cover story?"

"Probably not, but we just need to buy enough time for the flare to take down all of his systems before he recalls his invasion fleet. Then it doesn't matter what he thinks, as he can't do anything about it. We want maximum humiliation for Han so it's best if he has given the invasion order and his fleet is still steaming towards Taiwan. Then it will be disabled at sea. The plan still works if he calls it off but not as well. Han would not be completely humiliated and might survive the fallout from the failure of One Shield. He could blame corruption in the Research Centre and have some plant managers executed. As long as he can find a scapegoat, which he will, he can survive a manufacturing flaw in One Shield. But a humiliating failure of the invasion, with the fleet drifting helplessly in the South China Sea, would be a historic defeat for China. Han would lose so much 'face' he'd be disgraced and quickly overthrown."

"OK, so now you need my authorization to shut down all communications in the State of Hawaii? Fine. You're good to go. Hawaii voted Democrat in the Presidential elections, so I don't owe them anything. No, just kidding. Not for the record. As I was saying, as a matter of the highest national importance, I am prepared to authorize a three-hour (that's all you get) blackout of communications systems in the State of Hawaii and all the US Pacific islands, excluding any systems essential for protecting human lives, American or any other national. Got it? After three hours, you restore everything. Can you assure me that there will be no fatalities?"

"Yes, Ma'am. No one will be at risk if the shut-down is just three hours. They'll survive even in the most hostile environments on Hawaii like the top of Mauna Kea. Thank you."

"Is that it?" asked Wallace. "That wasn't too hard."

"Unfortunately, not" replied Dan. "We have a much bigger problem. We now think Han has worked out that his Research Director has been lying to him about the One Shield product. You'll have seen the last bullet point in the Daily Brief—the Research Director has gone missing, presumably terminated. Now there are lots of reasons why Han might have terminated him. Perhaps he was pilfering money from the research funds. Happens all the time in their system. But the one thing we need to worry about is that Han got tipped off about the mole in Cambridge and his realization that One Shield doesn't work."

"Oh my God!" Wallace was less calm now. "That's exactly what we feared ... And what's our contingency plan?"

"We don't have one. We are pretty confident that the Chinese can't have manufactured enough new product with the enhancements in the time available to protect the whole country. We would have noticed them rolling that out. We are confident that most of China will go down. What we don't know is whether they have managed to do an upgrade on the invasion force and all the military communications systems they need to run the invasion. They might have been able to accomplish this with new enhanced One Shield, or they might just be doubling or trebling up the layers of the old weaker One Shield product. That could provide some additional protection. In the time available, all they have probably been able to do is to add extra layers of protection on their key systems,"

"Will that work?"

"It might buy them a few more hours. The only good news here is that this is such a strong flare, it would probably penetrate several layers of the original One Shield. The invasion fleet might get a few hours out of port before losing all their communications and power."

"So, we just have to wait and hope that the flare burns through whatever additional Han has managed to rig up—is that what you are telling me?"

"Yes, Ma'am. We just need to wait and see what happens when the flare hits Beijing."

"How long do we have to wait?"

"About thirty-eight hours, Madam President."

"Dan, that's going to be excruciating. Is there anything we can do?"

"No, Ma'am. We just have to sit it out now."

"And pray, Dan, pray. I'm beginning to revise my views on whether prayer is going to help. It might be our only hope."

CHAPTER 28

USS GERALD R. FORD, SOUTH CHINA SEA

10 a.m. Beijing Time,
September 7 / 10 p.m. EST, September 6

Admiral Jack Halsey had been relieved of command following the shooting down of the Chinese jets, but he had not been confined to his quarters. The Chief of Naval Operations (CNO) had been remarkably courteous when telling Halsey that he was being replaced by the British Admiral, Sir Rupert Lyttleton. Halsey was pleased that he'd been spared being confined to his cabin. It didn't make any sense, but he wasn't going to argue.

The Strike Force was sailing just outside the nine-dash line. It had orders to stay 2–5 miles outside disputed waters and sail a long oval loop so that the ships could cross the line within minutes once the order came.

It was an overcast day. Low, grey clouds hung over the sea. Halsey stood on deck and looked at the F-18s, F-35s and F-45s lined up and ready to go at a few minutes notice. In line with the new orders, the Stars and Stripes flew every fifty yards along the side of the carrier's deck. Halsey thought this was a concession too far to the right-wingers in Congress. It would be fine for when the Ford sailed back into port. But they were now on action stations, and these flags would just get in the way. But the order had come from the CNO himself. All the other ships were decked out with flags. What's the point, Halsey thought. No one can see us out here.

He looked up at the clouds overhead. They seemed to flicker with a strange color every so often. Patterns of blue, pink and orange flashed on the grey clouds. They reminded him of those incredible Northern Lights displays that he had seen when on Artic patrol duties. But here it was day-time, and they were at only twenty-four degrees north so they couldn't be the normal aurora, unless something very strange was happening in the upper atmosphere.

One of the crew asked, "Ever seen anything like that, sir?"

"No, never," replied Halsey. "We'll be getting reports of UFOs before long!"

An ensign ran up to Halsey. "Admiral, your presence is requested in the Operations room. Admiral Lyttleton has requested that you join him there immediately."

Halsey walked briskly to the stairs and slid down the three flights to the Operations room. This was the nerve center of the entire Strike Group. Admiral Rupert Lyttleton sat at the head of a table. All four walls of the room were covered in high-definition screens. But old naval habits die hard. They also had a large old-fashioned paper navigational map on the table with small markers for the strike force. Halsey could see the island of Taiwan just to the north of the Strike Group and three feet away on the map, about four inches off the coast of China, there were dozens of small markers. Something was up.

"Admiral Lyttleton, you wanted to see me. Am I allowed in here?"

"You are now, Admiral. Just got this in from the CNO. You have been restored to duty. You're now back in charge. Commander Jones will brief you on what you've missed over the last few days."

Halsey sat in the chair that Lyttleton had been occupying. Lyttleton moved one the right, and the other offices shuffled down. Jones began his briefing:

"For the last forty-eight hours, we have been monitoring the buildup of Chinese naval forces along the coast of Fujian province. President Han has ordered a large-scale exercise to simulate an invasion of Taiwan. He has announced that this is a show of Chinese resolve in the face of Western aggression. Our intelligence, with a high degree of confidence, says that this is not an exercise but is the real thing. Yesterday morning at around 9 a.m. Beijing time, Han gave the order for the invasion fleet to set sail at 9 a.m. this morning. Two Chinese carrier strike groups are accompanying the invasion fleet which comprises over fifty amphibious assault ships, carrying we think around twenty-five thousand troops for this first landing."

Halsey interrupted. "But that makes no sense. That's not nearly enough to establish a secure beachhead on Taiwan. They'll get cut to pieces by the Taiwanese army. Are the spooks really confident in this intelligence?"

"They absolutely are, Sir. They say that President Han has assured his National Security Council that the landing force will meet with no resistance. In fact, he thinks they will be welcomed as liberators."

"Han's completely mad. The Taiwanese defense forces are going to wipe this 'liberating force' out the minute it tries to land. So where is this force now?"

They set sail at 9 a.m. The lead ships are about five miles out to sea now. The crossing will take these ships about 3–3.5 hours.

Admiral Lyttleton cut in. "Our orders are to stay this side of the nine-dash line but be ready as soon as POTUS gives the order to cross the line and intercept this fleet. With two Chinese carrier strike groups protecting the convoy, it could get quite hot in there. But those are our orders. The Chinese have their AWACS keeping a close watch on us, so they know exactly what we are up to. They have a couple of J-36s patrolling their side of the line."

"Well, I hope the top brass know what they're doing. When we cross that line, we're sitting ducks for the hypersonic missiles and the suicide drones."

"We've been through that with them, Sir. The order comes from POTUS herself. CNO told us that they have war-gamed through every scenario. POTUS assured the Chairman of the Joint Chiefs and CNO that she'd only give the order if the risk to US life was acceptable."

They sat in silence for the next fifteen minutes. The Chinese invasion fleet edged out further from the coastline on their electronic screens and on the physical map.

The silence was broken when the CNO came on the secure video conferencing system.

"Gentlemen, I suggest you turn on your TV channels out there in the South China Sea. There are some pretty amazing scenes in Beijing being reported by our Embassy staff who are filming the situation and streaming these images live to all news outlets. They are now just breaking on our news channels. scenes

One of the video walls now projected MTX, ANN, BBC World News, Al Jazeera and MSNBC. All were showing similar pictures.

Across the bottom of the screen, the news tickers were scrolling….

SPACE WEATHER STRIKE BRINGS BEIJING TO STANDSTILL

ALL ELECTRONIC COMMUNICATIONS IN MAINLAND CHINA DOWN

US EMBASSY STILL ONLINE AND CONNECTED TO INTERNET

HONG KONG FINANCIAL MARKETS SHUT DOWN

PANIC ERUPTS IN ALL MAJOR CHINESE CITIES

The images filmed by the US Embassy were striking. The Embassy walls were topped with flagpoles every 100 yards. The Stars and Stripes flew proudly. All around the perimeter were crowds of Chinese using their phones to pick up the Wi-Fi system that the Embassy had opened up. The Wi-Fi zone reached about hundred yards beyond the Embassy perimeter. The only websites that were working were Western sites. All Chinese internet sites had crashed. The only news channels working were Western news channels.

ANN cut to some expert talking head. "Well now we know for sure that space weather is no hoax. All the talk of a solar flare strike turns out to have been completely accurate. The mystery is why the Chinese – who appear to have predicted it with impressive precision – have now been devastated by its impact. They seem to have lost all their electronic communications across the entire country. One Shield must have failed completely. And yet, the US Embassy, and we think some other Western Embassies, have maintained their systems. This is very puzzling."

MTX also had experts, but they reached a different conclusion. "This is absolutely not a solar flare strike. And proof of that is that the US Embassy is still working. There's no credible explanation for how it could have survived one of these mythical solar flare strikes. It is quite clear what this is. All credit to President Wallace for finally delivering a message that President Han will never forget. He has been saber rattling all week. He issued an ultimatum threatening to fire on our warships if they crossed into the waters that China illegally claims. And a few hours ago, one of his underwater drones took out all of our underwater communications cables to Hawaii. No, this is nothing to do with space weather. This is a brilliant, rapid response, cyber-attack by the US to take down President Han. I'm backing President Wallace all the way on this."

ANN cut to the Fayne Solar Research Facility. "We are joined now by Professor Dame Ruth Wright, the world expert on solar weather. Dame Ruth, you have been predicting that a massive solar flare would strike Earth for some time. Is this what you expected to happen?"

"Well, this is a significant solar flare, but it is likely to be quite short lived. It is highly concentrated and seems to have hit mainland China particularly hard. I expect its impact will continue to be felt through Central Asia and the African continent, weakening as it goes. Europe is well protected. Of course, the US has chosen not to protect itself, which I have always argued was a very foolish policy. But the President has lucked out this time. The flare will have burned itself out by sunrise on the East Coast tomorrow morning. This will be a lucky escape for the US. I hope the President and her colleagues in the Republican party will take this risk more seriously in the future."

"Professor Wright, how do you explain the failure of the Chinese One Shield protections? President Han staked a lot of his personal credibility on that product."

"It's hard to say. It is a very difficult product to manufacture, and it's possible that they had some serious problems as they moved from small scale lab tests to large scale industrial production. Some of the European producers experienced those problems but they found a way around them. The US of course never got that far. The President and Congress never authorized a program of space weather defense. If this strike had happened twelve hours earlier or later, we'd be seeing these devastating scenes in US cities."

Back in the USS Ford Operations Room, the junior officer interrupted. "Admiral, you need to see what's on the other screen."

Halsey turned to the maps. The Chinese invasion fleet was still moving. There was no loss of speed, still making thirty knots and right on course for Taiwan. They were now thirty miles off the Chinese shore and about two and a half hours from the coast of Taiwan. The J-36s were still patrolling the nine-dash line. The drone wing men were flying in tight formations alongside each J-36. Beijing may have lost all its electronic communications, but this fleet and the Chinese Air Force seemed to be much better protected. The invasion of Taiwan was still on.

What the hell was happening?

CHAPTER 29

SITUATION ROOM, WHITE HOUSE, WASHINGTON D.C.

11p.m. EST, September 6

The President sat at the head of the table. With her were the Chairman of the Joint Chiefs, the Chief of Naval Operations, her National Security Adviser, Director Douglass Thomson from the CIA and Cindy Ross the Director of National Intelligence. The Vice President also joined the meeting. He had complained to the President recently about having been cut out of national security issues, and President Wallace conceded that he could now join more meetings, especially if there was an opportunity to be in a photo that would help his profile for the next election. The Situation Room in a crisis was always a good photo-op. The VP had only recently been briefed on Operation HELIOS. Dan sat in the back row ready to answer any questions.

"What the hell is going on?" asked the President. She was using her most threatening, low soft voice.

CNO spoke up first and gave a situation report on the invasion force. It had sailed from the Chinese port two hours ago and was still making good progress across the Taiwan straits. The Chinese naval force had covered nearly half of the distance and would reach the western shores of Taiwan in about two to two and a half hours. The Chinese Air Force was continuing to operate and was providing air cover to the fleet with a mix of J-31s and J-36s. The airborne landing troops were still on their air bases on the Chinese mainland, and not due to take off for another hour or so. All signs were that these airbases were still operational.

"And what about the impact of the strike on Taiwan?" asked the President. "Dan, what's the situation there. Has your plan worked?"

"So far, yes, Madam President. It looks as though the Taiwanese Government, military bases and security installations are all protected. The civilian population has lost all electronic communications. But the Government is rolling out emergency mobile Wi-Fi stations that are enabling civilians to get back online and link into Western media and websites."

"Excuse me," the Vice President chipped in, "why are the Taiwanese protected? They don't have access to One Shield, and the Europeans wouldn't export their product to Taiwan for fear of provoking the Chinese. And I don't see them flying a lot of US flags at their government offices or military bases."

"Dan, can you explain to the Vice President? But please, keep it short."

"Mr. Vice President, you will remember that six months ago the President authorized the admission of Taiwan to the Community of Pacific States (CPS). This caused outrage in Beijing. It took a lot of work with our Pacific allies to get them to agree—and with the French, who view themselves as a power broker within the Pacific. But Han's aggressive rhetoric and threats against Taiwan helped us to persuade our allies to support Taiwan's admission into the CPS. The Taiwanese Government were delighted and agreed immediately to our request that they fly the

Community of Pacific States flag at all government and military sites as a symbol of their commitment to the CPS's values. The US was also able to provide them with a gift of 100,000 CPS flags that the Fayne Fabric of America plant had helpfully produced. As you'll remember, Han then banned the CPS flag from all Chinese media. For the Taiwanese, flying this flag became a symbol of resistance to Han. Taiwanese civilians also bought their own flags—provided this time at a full price by Fayne Capital. Taiwan is not completely protected from the solar flare strike, but it seems to have suffered far less than the mainland. Most importantly, their military are fully operational and ready to attack the Chinese invasion fleet the minute it enters Taiwanese coastal waters."

The President looked impatient as Dan updated the VP. This was exactly the reason why she didn't want the VP in these meetings. It just slowed things down, particularly with this VP. He wasn't the sharpest knife in the Republican Party drawer. She'd only picked him to bolster her position with the mid-Western states who didn't like her brand of Southern Republicanism. Even so, she had lost a couple of these States, including the VP's home state. He really wasn't worth the baggage that he now brought to the Administration.

"Thanks for that update, Dan. Now perhaps the Director of National Intelligence can fill us in on what we know about the solar flare protections on the Chinese fleet."

"Madam President, here's what we are learning from our sources close to the Chinese Politburo. One of our best agents has managed to get close to the Embassy and is communicating with us on an open line. For the moment, there's no chance of the Chinese security agency listening in. We now have pretty good intel on the state of play. Han has already been put under house arrest by the People's Liberation Army High Command. Han's credibility collapsed the minute it became clear that One Shield had failed. Han found out about the flaws in One Shield about a week ago. That is indeed why the Director 'disappeared.' His replacement as Director only had twenty-four hours to come up with a contingency plan to save the invasion fleet. The best they could do – as we expected – was to double up and in some cases triple layer the One Shield protections on the key communications equipment."

"OK. Dan, how long will double or triple layer protections last?"

"Can we patch in Ruth who is the expert on this and has been modelling the likely level of protection?"

Ruth came up on the video screen on the wall opposite the President.

"Welcome, Ruth," said the President, "Nice job on live TV earlier today. You were masterful. I particularly liked your attacks on me for not preparing the nation for this threat. When we first met, we talked about integrity. I'm real impressed at the progress you've made. You were so good at lying on national TV that perhaps you have a future in politics!"

"It was very uncomfortable, Madam President. I put my scientific reputation on the line for you. We can't ever let the real results get out about the strength of this flare."

"We can worry about that later, Ruth. I need to know how long this invasion fleet can keep going with the additional protection levels we think they have added".

"I estimate somewhere between two and four hours after the initial strike. Fortunately for us, the flare is far stronger than we had expected, running at over Kp-10 in strength. The Chinese will, reasonably enough, have assumed a flare in the range 8–9 and so a triple layer would have protected them enough to make the crossing. Now, it is touch and go. There are signs that the flare is already weakening in intensity. My latest reading is 10.5. If the flare's power continues to fall, the fleet's protection might last the full four hours and the invasion force could make it into Taiwanese Coastal waters, possibly even ashore."

"And then what happens?"

"It depends on the strength of the flare by 1 a.m. our time. If it continues to decay as fast as it now is decaying, the invasion force might have some residual communications capability."

"You're saying we just have to sit this out and wait for another couple of hours."

"I'm afraid so."

The President got up and walked around the table. She ordered another round of coffees for the group. It was going to be a long night.

"Put Halsey up on the screen. I want to hear from the front line."

Ruth disappeared and the screen cut to the Operations Room on the USS Gerald R Ford.

"Look, Admiral, I am very sorry about having had to relieve you from command. Glad you're now back in control. I can't explain all the details, but rest assured we know that it was not your or your crew's fault. We just had to maintain cover on a bigger intelligence operation."

"Thank you, Madam President. I completely understand. I appreciated not being confined to my quarters. My good friend, Admiral Lyttleton, did just fine in command of the Strike Force. He is here with me in the Operations Room."

"What are you seeing at the moment?"

"No change, Madam President. We are continuing to sail just outside the nine-dash line. The Chinese J-36s are patrolling along the other side. We think they are armed with hypersonic missiles, so if we cross the line we'll come up against pretty heavy fire straight away. We don't yet have the defenses we need against hypersonic missiles."

The VP chipped in. "But you took down two J-36s last time without a lot of trouble."

"Up to point, Mr. Vice President," Admiral Halsey explained. "The Chinese disabled their own defenses on the J-36s. If those defenses had been operational, the drone wingmen would have sacrificed themselves by drawing our missiles away from the J-36. In about ninety seconds, we can wipe out all six drone wingmen on one J-36, but that gives the pilot just enough time to fire the hypersonic anti-ship missile swarm. Madam President, what do you want us to do now?

"I won't give the order to cross the line until we are sure the Chinese defenses are down. But unfortunately, that is still a few hours away. Keep on your current course. What can you tell us about the Chinese invasion fleet right now?"

"We've got good satellite coverage despite the low cloud cover. We see right through that. The fleet is still moving at about thirty knots and holding formation. We've got stealth mini-submarine drones up close. We can bring them to the surface at any point if we want close-in video of the fleet. At the moment, we don't need that and it's risky to raise the periscope on these mini-sub drones. We haven't found a way to make the periscopes invisible to the naked eye. The Chinese train their sailors well for spotting periscopes."

"OK, Admiral, we'll just sit tight. We're not expecting any change for an hour or two, maybe longer. We'll all be right here if you have anything to report."

The President stood up.

"Time for a break," she said. "But first, what's the situation on Hawaii? Are they back online?"

Dan responded.

"Yes, we brought them back up as soon as we knew Beijing's communications were down. They were only offline for ninety minutes. No reports of trouble. Some pretty angry tourists stranded up on the top of Mauna Kea, but other than that no serious problems."

"Good. Let's just stick to the story of a Chinese cyber-attack. Fifteen-minute break now everyone."

When they reassembled, it was midnight. The tension was painful for everyone in the room. What if the flare weakened faster than Ruth had estimated? What if the invasion fleet made it to Taiwanese Coastal Waters? The Taiwanese would attack, and we'd have a live war in the South China Seas? Would it spiral quickly out of control? The US defense commitments to Taiwan would mean that America had to intervene. Within a few hours, the US and China could be at war. There was nothing they could do. They just had to wait and hope that the flare burned through the layers of One Shield protection.

They passed the time watching TV channels reporting the situation in China and across Europe. The CIA added further details from their sources. Ruth was back online to provide updates on the strength of the solar flare.

Mainland China was experiencing mass civil unrest. The solar flare had destroyed most of the electricity grid across the country. All mass transit had been stopped. People were trapped in subway cars and buses. All communications systems were off-line. The financial markets had shut down without warning, unable to process any trades or post prices. Panicked investors couldn't check their investment accounts. Digital wallets were frozen. Payment systems were out of action. All of sudden, old fashioned paper money was the only secure store of value. Long lines began to form outside the few remaining bank branches in the major cities. Banks ran out of paper cash within the hour. Hospitals were running on back-up batteries, but for how long could they last? So much for President Han's great One Shield. It had completely failed to protect the Chinese people from this massive flare.

Unable to communicate electronically, people went onto the streets. Rumor spread fast. Crowds were forming in all major cities. They were no longer calling for death to Western imperialists but instead chanting that Han must go.

The only connection to the outside world and to each other came through the open Wi-Fi zones outside the US Embassy in Beijing and US consulates in other major cities. The US had installed additional back-up batteries and bio-diesel generators at all their facilities throughout China. Word spread that there was some Wi-Fi access. Chinese citizens gathered outside the US sites and their phones could pick up a signal. They could connect and communicate again.

The only truth they could get was from Western media, although even there they had a choice of alternative truths. The Western media couldn't agree on the cause of the Chinese power and communications crashes, only that they had happened in China and its allied countries and hadn't happened in Europe. That realization stoked anger across China.

As dawn had broken in Europe, there was little disruption to European communications systems. Life went on as normal. The French President addressed the nation and saluted the leadership of French scientists in developing the successful Shield of Charlemagne that had protected all of Europe. Dan had to suck that one up. He'd give his friends at DGSE a hard time for that. The UK likewise emerged unscathed, with the Oxford product proving its worth.

Dawn would be breaking soon in the Eastern Provinces of Canada. They should be fine, thought Dan. Canada's Anglophone provinces had bought the Oxford Product. Naturally, Quebec had chosen the Shield of Charlemagne. The Canadian media were already crowing about their superior level of protection compared to the US. Wallace was going to have some explaining to do when America escaped unscathed.

Dan and Ruth had come up with the cover story that Ruth had used in the TV interviews. So far that narrative seemed to be holding up OK. But the explanation had vulnerabilities.

Just after 1 a.m., the President wanted to go over the press lines for the morning, and especially the explanation for how the US had escaped unscathed from the solar flare strike. Ruth was back on the screen. The

President had dismissed the military chiefs for this part of the conversation. It was just the intelligence team and her political advisers, plus Dan and Ruth.

"Ruth," said the President, "Do you think we can maintain the line that the flare weakened before reaching our shores?"

"Well, it is weakening now."

"Not too much I hope," interrupted the President. "We need it on full force for another couple of hours."

"It's down just below Kp-10 now. It's falling half a point every hour. It's going to be touch and go on the invasion force. It just depends how much protection on the ships was burned off in the first couple of hours of the solar strike."

"But back to our cover story, Madam President. I can fake my own readings in the Fayne Solar Research facility. We are the only major lab in the US that is tracking the solar strike so our figures will have credibility. Any independent or amateur readings may in fact be quite accurate, but Dan assures me that your political team can discredit them quite effectively."

"What about Europe?" asked the President.

Dan cut in. "The Europeans have pretty good labs, as do the Brits. Our friends at MI6 will deal with the British labs at Oxford, Cambridge, and Manchester. Our only option for the European labs is to hack into them and alter their readings. Fortunately, these labs all use the same German testing equipment as the Chinese did, so we have the hacks ready to go. We will need your permission Madam President to launch this sort of invasive cyber-attack on our allies. But it's the only option we have."

"Fine, do it. Just don't get caught. I couldn't face having to apologize to the French and Germans again. I really didn't appreciate doing that last time when your snooping into their personal emails became public. That was not an easy discussion. I really don't want to be calling them up again to apologize for your espionage activities against our allies, especially as we saved their butts on this one. Of course, we won't get a word of thanks."

The door opened and the Chairman of the Joint Chiefs came back in.

"Madam President, we need to get Admiral Halsey online straight away."

Halsey came up on the screen. The other screen also started showing shots of the invasion fleet up close, presumably taken by the mini-sub drones.

"Madam President, we are seeing the disintegration of the Chinese invasion force's communications. A few minutes ago, the J-36 wingmen drones started to behave erratically and veered off course, crashing into the sea. The J-36 pilots then seem to have lost the ability to control their aircraft which just flew in a straight line for a few minutes before the pilots ejected and the planes self-destructed. We brought the mini-sub drones to the surface, and we now have a live video feed from right alongside the invasion fleet. As you can see, several ships in the fleet have their bridges on fire. We think their comms equipment probably burst into flames. Some of the ships are drifting. They have lost aircover as most of the planes have either downed into the sea or exploded in mid-air. Radio contact between all the ships has been lost."

"OK, then," said the President, "You are authorized now to cross the nine-dash line. Your mission is to provide humanitarian support to the Chinese navy whose 'large scale peaceful naval exercise' seems unfortunately to have run into 'operational difficulties' caused by this freak solar flare. I'll call the Taiwanese President and you can expect the Taiwanese Navy to help out as well. Now get to it, Admiral Halsey."

The President leaned back in her chair. She felt a huge wave of relief run over her body. Her adrenaline had been pumped up for days and now she could feel the stress levels ebbing away. She closed her eyes and enjoyed a sense of complete calm.

She sat in silence for a couple of minutes. No one wanted to break the quiet. Finally, Dan spoke up.

"I think we can declare Operation HELIOS to be complete."

"Yes," said the President. "It's complete now, and it was a total, unqualified success. Well done everyone. It's amazing what you have all achieved.

"Let's just hope no-one ever finds out about it."

CHAPTER 30

THE BRITISH AMBASSADOR'S RESIDENCE, WASHINGTON D.C.

December

The Presidential motorcade drove up Massachusetts Avenue and pulled into the driveway leading up to the British Ambassador's Residence. Unquestionably the finest Residence in Washington, the mansion had been designed by Sir Edwin Lutyens and built in the late 1920s. It had now finally reopened after a seven-year refurbishment.

The British Prime Minister was in Washington D.C. for an official working visit. The President had hosted a formal dinner at the White House the evening before. Tonight's dinner was being billed as a personal event, a private dinner between two political friends and fellow conservatives. They had first met over a decade ago at various libertarian economic conferences. Back then, Governor Marian Wallace was the rising star of the US Republican Party and Mike Urquhart was an ambitious but as yet unknown junior Minister in a short-lived Conservative Administration. As this was a private event, the Embassy declined to issue a guest list or in fact give any details about the evening's event.

The Presidential Limousine, now an EV – the so-called E-Beast – drove itself through the gateway between the Lion and Unicorn statues and pulled up under the archway outside the main entrance to the Residence. President Wallace got out and greeted the Prime Minister and the British Ambassador who were on the steps to meet her.

"It's great to be back at your lovely Residence, Madam Ambassador. I've not been here since the renovation. You'll have to explain all the changes to me."

They walked into the entrance hall and then up the grand, red-carpeted double staircase. The entrance was intended to impress—and it did. Lutyens designed the Residence at the height of his powers and in his most imperial and imposing style.

The President, Prime Minister and Ambassador walked up the stairs.

"I see you've kept the portrait of King George III," said the President.

"Indeed," replied the Ambassador "We feel it is important to have the last King of America represented in this Residence. It reminds us of our common history."

"Not exactly the high point of our common history, Madam Ambassador," replied the President. "And who is this portrait of? I don't recognize her."

"That's Queen Anne, Madam President. Until your election, she was the last female head of state of America."

"I'm detecting a pattern here, and I'm not sure I like it. But I see my favorite of all your portraits is still here. The great Warhol portrait of Queen Elizabeth the Second. What a great person she was! She is still very much revered in America. And what a wonderful portrait! It's strange that it took an American pop artist to create the most iconic, most definitive image of your longest serving sovereign."

The party proceeded down the shining black and white marble corridor, and out onto the portico. Even in early December, the evening was still mild enough to enjoy drinks outside. The Ambassador thought she'd hold off any comments on global warming. The Prime Minister was a noted climate sceptic, and Wallace pretended to be one when she was with her right-wing political friends.

Gathered together on the portico were the team that had made Operation HELIOS happen. Steve and Ruth had flown in from New Mexico. Aaron and Dan only had to drive in from Langley, which they did in separate, unmarked cars. Sir Leslie Fayne had flown to Washington by private jet for the official dinner at the White House the night before. He was also receiving an award from the Kennedy Center the next day for his generous $100 million donation to its new capital campaign. The Prime Minister was joined by C, the head of MI6, and Steve's old friend Mike Withers, now the CEO of Venture Exports.

On the terrace under Lutyens' soaring portico, a string quartet from Howard University played arrangements of Mozart arias. The President stopped to listen. As the musicians finished, she thanked the students. "You played so beautifully, thank you. I have one request. Could you play my favorite aria, *Porgi, Amor?* I feel so deeply for the Countess. The music perfectly captures the pain of her loneliness and her enduring love for her unfaithful husband. It moves me so much."

As Ruth listened to the melodies of *Porgi, Amor,* she closed her eyes and tears began to form. She felt for the President's loneliness. Wallace had clearly never recovered from the loss of her husband. Whatever their political differences, she had grown to admire Marian Wallace as a leader and respect her as a woman. She had enjoyed working with Wallace and would miss her now that Operation HELIOS was over. Ruth remembered that evening over four years ago at the Santa Fe Opera when she and Steve were happily reconciled. This too was a perfect moment.

The President was chatting with the Ambassador when she saw Aaron. "Excuse me, Madam Ambassador. I just need a private word with my Director. Something came up when I was in the car on the way over and I need to let the Director know. I won't be long."

President Wallace asked Aaron to walk with her into the magnificent rose garden. The roses were still out in early December. The floodlights illuminated the red, orange and yellow blooms. Wallace took Aaron by the arm and led him into the garden. They went about fifty yards from the Residence. She wanted to be well out of earshot of the main party.

"Aaron, we meet almost every day, but I never get a moment with you alone and away from my officials and all those recording devices in the Oval Office. I want to say something, and we must never discuss this again.

"Aaron, I am sure you and your team had something to do with The Invoice. There's no need to comment. I just wanted to say 'Thank you'. Thank you from the bottom of my heart."

"Madam President, you are mistaken. Let me be clear. We did not steal that invoice from the abortion clinic. That would be illegal. The CIA can't operate on US soil, as you know."

"So, what happened?" asked Wallace.

"The Russians stole it. President Bortsov had launched a campaign to get 'Kompromat' on all the Presidential candidates, including you. They found nothing on you, Madam President. But Ramirez walked right into their trap. They were following his movements closely. They knew about the affair. They followed the girl to the clinic. It was easy for them to hack the clinic's billing system."

"Did the Russians leak it?"

"Absolutely not, Madam President. Bortsov was very pleased with his agents for getting this 'Kompromat'. He ordered them to keep it and use it to blackmail Ramirez once he became President. We were alerted to Bortsov's plan by one of our agents inside the Russian Federal Security Bureau. We could not stand by and let Ramirez become President. He would have been a pawn of the Russians.

"Your predecessor left us a standing instruction authorizing action by the CIA should there be a risk of Russia compromising a future President. We acted under that authorization. We instructed our agent in the FSB to pass it to another foreign intelligence service and they sent it to your campaign. As you can see, the CIA wasn't involved. Well not directly, anyway. We didn't do it to help your campaign, Madam President. We did it in the national interest."

"Indeed. In the national interest, Aaron. In the national interest, of course. But I still like to think that you were watching over me. No-one else does. I'm grateful that you do. Thank you." She took his hands in hers, leaned forward and gave him an affectionate kiss on the cheek.

"Now, Aaron, let's rejoin the party. It should be a fun evening."

This group had never all met before and would never meet again. A condition of attendance at this private celebration had been to sign additional non-disclosure agreements with strict criminal liability provisions. There would be no personal memoirs of 'My Role in Operation HELIOS'. Both the UK and US Governments had agreed to seal the Operation HELIOS files for a hundred years. This evening would be the only time that they could all talk openly about it and enjoy their success.

After drinks, the party moved into the dining room. In celebration of the joint UK / US collaboration the PM and President had arranged to give (secret) honors to each of the protagonists.

The PM led off with honorary knighthoods for Dan McCraig and Aaron Douglass Thomson for their role in conceiving the plan and creating the US facilities needed to produce Solar Shield at scale. The President responded with Presidential Medals of Freedom for Professor Ruth Wright and István 'Steve' Szabó-Nagy for the pioneering science that created Solar Shield in the first place and for their leadership throughout the program. The President turned to Sir Leslie and said that, as he already had a Presidential Medal of Freedom for his philanthropic activities, she could not give him a second one. However, she had ensured that Fayne Capital businesses would be successful in several forthcoming Department of Defense procurement competitions which should ensure that he recovered his full investment in the Fabric of America plants.

The President then proposed a toast to absent friends.

"Let us start," she said, "with my good friend Senator Jesse Landry without whose patriotism – and gullibility – none of this would have been possible."

"Senator Jesse Landry," the group replied.

"Now I am very grateful to Senator Landry for another reason," the President continued. "Given some extremely successful investments by his blind trust, the details of which he claims to be unaware, he has generously agreed to be the founder donor on my Presidential Library."

"Now I am not going to propose a toast to President Han, although without his foolhardy aggressiveness none of this would have been possible—or necessary. But as we have the Director of the CIA and C from MI6 here, perhaps you can give us an update on the leadership race in China."

Aaron Douglass Thomson led off.

"In the chaos following the solar flare strike, the army immediately imprisoned Han. The last we heard he was still alive but it's probably only a matter of time before he is terminated. Factions within the Politburo quickly aligned behind two candidates, both positioning themselves as economic and social modernizers. Both though remain strongly hawkish on defense and keep up a very high level of anti-Western rhetoric. The Standing Committee of the Politburo will meet in two weeks' time to choose between Zhou Kei and Liu Khiang. We're hoping they pick Zhou Kei. He was a student here at MIT. He had some … well, how can I put it delicately in this company? Let me just say he had some idiosyncratic sexual habits, several of which are still illegal in China. We have video recordings of some of his more extreme activities. A few years ago, through a trusted intermediary, we let him know about our video collection. If Zhou Kei gets the top job, we have all the compromising material we need to keep him in line."

"Well, Aaron, that's what I pay you guys at the CIA for. It's reassuring to know that it's not just the Russians who have mastered the art of 'Kompromat' against foreign politicians."

C caught the Prime Minister's eye and, without saying a word, seemed to be asking for his permission to speak. The Prime Minister nodded. C spoke up.

"Aaron, that's great work by you and your team. It sounds like we are in good shape if Zhou Kei wins. But we've got our hopes riding on Liu Khiang. While your Zhou Kei was at MIT indulging his more exotic interests, young Liu Khiang was at Cambridge writing a thesis on "The Suppression of the Proletariat in 18th Century Enlightenment Philosophy." Rather than becoming outraged at how the 18th Century elite treated the poor peasants, Liu became passionate about the ideas of the Enlightenment: freedom, tolerance, respect for scientific inquiry, skepticism of ideologies and even a belief in democracy. He also fell in love with a fellow student at Cambridge. Little did he know that she was one of ours. She recruited him for MI6. After graduation, he returned to his career in China's Ministry of State Security. While he was a junior officer for the MSS in Hong Kong, he provided some useful intelligence for us, and we paid him well. We then let him go quiet and we haven't used him once in the last ten years. But we continue to pay a stipend into his account in Switzerland, and we know he checks it once a year when he is on overseas trips."

The President laughed out loud. "We've got Zhou and you've got Liu. The Special Relationship is alive and well. Either way, we've got the next President of China exactly where we want him, and we don't need to worry about the outcome of their leadership contest. Heads I win, tails I win. Best odds I've had in a long time."

At the end of the evening, the party withdrew into the drawing room. The President had lined up a final gift. She presented a 51-star American flag to each participant in Operation HELIOS. The flag was folded into a triangle and mounted in a wooden display box, with a brass plate stating simply 'For your service.'

As the President left and walked down the grand double staircase of the Residence, a band of Royal Marines struck up *The Star-Spangled Banner*.

The President paused, put her hand to her heart and sang along silently with the anthem.

O say can you see, by the dawn's early light . . .

THE END

ACKNOWLEDGEMENTS

Many friends and members of my family kindly agreed to read the first draft of this novel. They provided helpful feedback on characterisation, plot structure and technical detail. I am very grateful indeed for their suggestions and their encouragement. As many of them currently hold or have held senior positions in their fields, I have chosen not to name them in order to preserve their confidences. You know who you are. Thank you!

I would like to thank my editor, Kieran Devaney at Reedsy.com who gave sympathetic and detailed suggestions to improve the pace and flow of the story and patiently corrected the final manuscript.

The excellent team at Bookbaby.com designed the cover and interior formatting and guided me through the process of self-publishing. They created a very high-quality product, both in printed and electronic form.

Finally, I would like to thank my readers for buying the book and reading this far. I hope you enjoyed it.